CW00383180

# THE HAPPY WAR

A NOVEL

EVE GAAL

Published 2021 by Next Chapter

Edited by First Van.

## "I COULDN'T PUT IT DOWN"

### REVIEWERS OF EVE GAAL'S PENNILESS HEARTS SAID:

A thoroughly enjoyable entertaining read that I found hard to put down. Looking forward to reading more of this talented author's work. -Julia Sutton, author of **The School of Dreams**

I know this story will stick with me for a long time and I certainly hope this author plans on writing more books. I look forward to reading her next story. -Donna Yates, author of **Always**

Couldn't put it down!!-**Murder Mystery Queen**

Penniless Hearts is one of the best novels I've read in a very long time-Norma Beishir, author of **Chasing the Wind**

If you like high-flying (excuse the pun) adventures with quirky heroines set in exotic locales then you're really going to like Eve

Gaal's "Penniless Hearts."- Mike Billington, author of **Corpus Delectable**.

**Reviewers of Eve Gaal's Penniless Souls said:**

I'm a fan of Eve Gaal's writing style and wish she would write more books. I've read all 3 of her publications to date and I enjoyed them all. -C. Brownson

Skillful writing easily lured me into the plot. -Arch Font, author of **The Last Voyage**

Gaal tackles serious issues - the sex slave trade, and the seamy side of Vegas - with honesty and well-researched facts and details. At the heart of her story is the desire to bring to light the nefarious exploitation of women who are vulnerable and have nowhere to turn and no one to save them. -B. Roman, author of **Whatever Became of Sin**

As usual, the author packs a lot more into her novel. Find out how Penny manages to save a plane load of young girls destined for the sex industry and plans a rip-roaring escape from her employer and gang members. -Mari Collier, author of **Gather the Children**

Suspense and action in Penniless Souls never stops as Penny, the main character, unknowingly crosses paths with the hidden world of human trafficking. -Suzanne Saunders-author of **Vines-A Gripping Tale**

**Praises for The Fifth Commandment:**

Under the sweetness there's a cynical edge I found delightful; I must confess! An interesting read. -Lynne Spreen, author of **California Blues**

I found this novella a delightful read. Ms Gaal keeps the reader intrigued right up to the very end. Charming and easy to read. -Eileen Thornton-author of **The Trojan Project.**

Gaal writes well, creating a short piece that covers a lot of ground. Well done. George Gurney, author of **The Water Jar**

This is a deeply moving story of morals and expectations, beautifully told & perfectly executed. -A.J. Griffth Jones, author of **The Circus**

Eve Gaal writes with great empathy, and drafts her characters in layers, making them fully-rounded and easily relatable. -Craig A. Hart, author of **Serenity**

*This book is dedicated to my loving husband.*
*He was a child, during real, unhappy and tragic war.*

# ACKNOWLEDGMENTS

Thank you to the peacemakers. We can dream of world peace or we can take tiny steps and do something. One tissue wipes away a single tear. One joke creates several smiles. One kindness can have a domino effect. My novel is strictly imaginary. However, there are genuine steps and resolutions in the real world we need to look at, regarding violence, war and injustice.

Meanwhile, I want to thank those who risk their lives for peace. To those who fight for fairness and freedom in a peaceful manner by learning to communicate. To teachers who help us understand the why. To those who argue without raising voices, but by researching and establishing truth. To those who assist anyone trying to make the world a better place. To first responders, nurses and doctors who stop the bleeding by offering aid and comfort. To the artists and poets who give us hope. To friends who help when called. To those who pray.

You make a difference.
And you. The person holding my book. I appreciate you.
May peace be with you.

"Whenever you sit in front of water and send out messages of love and gratitude, somewhere in the world, someone is being filled with love and gratitude. You don't need to go anywhere. The water right in front of you is linked to all the water in the world."

**—From The Hidden Messages in Water by Dr. Masaru Emoto**

* * *

"He will lead them to springs of living water, and God will wipe away every tear from their eyes."

**-Revelation 7:17**

# PROLOGUE

She pushed the elevator button and stared at the ominous text. "Hurry, there's something wrong." Tom Rainer had sent it an hour ago. During that time, she had been bogged down, listening to a tedious analytical report ordered for a real estate transfer in North Virginia. Under the white lab coat, Dr. Jackie Bloomfield wore a gray pantsuit and fashionable red pumps. The stylish new shoes squeezed her toes. The lined, designer outfit started out comfortable, but now, bordered on sweltering hot. Maybe the message made her nervous.

Inside, the sleek, modern building of the New England Municipal Water Testing headquarters, everything appeared normal. Men and women in lab coats tested water for hardness, lead, copper and contaminants. Under bright florescent lights, scientists poured water into beakers, checking for unusual particulates under a microscope. Small plastic containers with tiny glass vials cluttered the countertops. Stainless laboratory freezers lined the pale blue walls.

"There you are," said an agitated Tom. A few people turned, briefly greeting the respected doctor, but they turned back to the immediate chores they were working on. Pointing towards the back of the lab, Tom indicated she should follow. As the Environmental Operations specialist, he oversaw the wastewater treatment for over thirty-five water testing plants in several states. Always serious, Jackie didn't like the look on his face. She especially didn't care for his quick, long steps.

"What? Whatever it is, you should lighten up. It's 2019, way past Y2K and certainly not, the end of the world." She wanted to smile at him, but the pointy-toed pumps were bringing tears to her eyes. Once they reached the back, he presented his microscope with open palms, the way a host would seat someone at a luxurious restaurant; quietly, and with an air of superiority.

"When titrating and checking for scaling, this showed up. It doesn't seem that bad, except this is from the water that goes through D.C. All the samples look like this."

Dr. Bloomfield put her eyes on the microscope and tilted her head to get a better view. "Hmm," she responded, staying bent over the instrument while trying to hide a smile. "This is the water going toward the White House?"

"Yes, Doctor. It's not normal. We've tested it over and over, several times."

She stood to face him. "Not much we can do about those enzymes. Rest assured it's not lethal. I say we keep quiet, and hope it dissipates naturally." A tear caused by her tight-fitting shoes rolled down a cheek. Tom turned around for a box of tissues, and while he did, he surveyed the room to make sure no one had listened to their conversation.

"Here, how about a tissue? I didn't mean to upset you."

"Oh, it's not that," she replied, tugging two sheets of the soft paper from the box. "I'm sure the President doesn't drink tap water. Everything will be fine."

"But...."

"Tom don't worry about it. I'd say the marina needs some major testing. Have your team concentrate on that for now, and leave this to me." Nature will take its course. Imagining the public turmoil something like this would bring upon the water district made her want to forget she ever saw those samples. Right now, the shoes were killing her, and she expected a call from the Bagram Air Base. "I have to go; my boy is going to call tonight."

# CHAPTER ONE

Desperate. Why else would she, Linda Simpson, a fairly attractive, young, and successful businesswoman, be sitting across from an unusual looking pharmaceutical salesman, on a blind date? In all probability, this would be the last time she listened to her sister. Becca had rambled on like an annoying drone, about the features and benefits of Eric. "He's unlike anyone else you've ever met," she had said. "He's smart, cute and funny. You'll love him," she repeated over and over. "Give him a whirl. I promise you'll like him."

Linda looked at Eric's thick, tortoise-shell glasses, his messy hair, his tattoos, and his pierced nose. What in hell? Despite her uneasy feelings, they had gone to the movies and were sitting across from each other at a diner. She ordered a slice of chocolate cake and a cup of coffee. He opted for fries and a soda.

"I think this movie escaped me somehow," she said, wondering how a guy like this could sell anything. *Didn't they have to look and appear professional? Was she becoming her mother? Are cool looking, strange people, the new 'normal'. Are gothic millennials the fresh faces of technology?* While she pondered all that, she tried to avoid the glint reflecting off his substantial proboscis. *He probably doesn't even own a suit.*

"What do you mean?" He repeatedly jabbed a french-fry into a small container of ketchup. With his faraway gaze, she figured he couldn't imagine she didn't understand the film. "It wasn't that confusing, was it?" He took a bite of french-fry, and dipped again. Jab, jab, jab, until small pieces of potato floated to the top of the sauce.

*The scene in front of her looked bad. Bad, as in the horror show she wanted to walk out of hours ago. At least he didn't hold her hand or try moving his arm, up around to the top of her shoulders, at the cinema. With his weird taste in movies, it was easy to think, they'd have nothing in common.*

She shrugged. "I didn't get it. How did all those people die?"

He bit his lip and smiled. "Don't you remember the vials in that General's drawer? In the very beginning of the movie...."

Pursing her lips, she squinted, and thought back to the movie. "Vials, yeah, I guess, but that didn't seem important at the time. There were so many things going on. I thought they died from some type of poisonous gas."

"But the baby running the tap...the mom washing dishes, the guy fly-fishing; those were all clues."

With every clue, another french-fry dived into the blood red sauce. The ketchup made the innocent fries look slaughtered. Defenseless spuds--sliced and fried were heading for Eric's mouth. None of it made sense. This date, the movie, all of it made her feel separated from reality. Stumped, she took a big bite of cake. Perfect frosting, like her mother used to make, with a trace of espresso. "I don't get it. How are those clues?" Trying to figure out the apocalyptic movie left her hungry, even mentally depleted.

"Linda, your sister's a nurse."

"Yeah, so?" She didn't see a connection between nursing and warfare. Once he wiped his fingers in a white napkin however, red grease smeared all over, it reminded her of a scene from a different movie, where wounded soldiers were treated with torn bandages, during the Civil War.

"She would have loved it."

What a strange thing to say. Sure, her sister knew many things about administering medicine, but that didn't necessarily mean she'd like this film. Eric Anderson didn't rack up any extra points with his small jab. Only instead of fries and ketchup, this one seemed personal. "What does that mean?"

"The film talks about chemicals that alter brain function. It's all about chemical warfare. Don't you see? The world gets wiped out from a mad scientist and his crazy experiment that goes wrong. He puts chemicals in the world's drinking supply and boom, everyone begins to die. Even that cute baby. As they travel the world, people in the farthest reaches of Asia are dead. There was nothing they could do." To drive home the point, Eric banged his fist on the laminate table. "It was a great movie." Smiling smugly, he looked satisfied with his monologue, picked up another french-fry and began assaulting potatoes again.

Now on top of everything else, he made her feel stupid. *Nurses, doctors, lawyers and priests received all the respect. Maybe, if he knew something about advertising and marketing, he'd understand. If, he realized how much work, that she, and her co-workers, put into product placement, demographics, behavioral studies, logo designs, complex target marketing, social media blasts, keywords, layouts, ad copy, web content, and press releases, he'd have some clue about branding. Perhaps, if he'd see how her department took raw data, mixed it with technology, swirled in human interaction, responses and reactions to create the hardware and software--of her job—maybe --he'd have insight into her world. But he didn't ask, and seemed to assume she sat at a desk answering phone calls. Or, even worse, he didn't care.*

"Guess I'd rather see a movie about the opposite." She picked up her coffee and took a long swig of the cooled, bitter brew. *Besides, she wondered how a 'sensitive guy' as her sister had called him, could love a movie with so much violence. Linda thought about the word sensitive and Becca's interpretation. Whether he wore his hair in a man-bun or kept his flannel shirt untucked like an astronomer at a rock concert, his insides were still ego-filled, self-absorbed man. The guy must be some sort of passive-aggressive, that doesn't ask about her career, and pounds tables like a caveman. As if, nothing mattered. Maybe, at this stage of the game, it didn't.*

"The opposite?" He leaned back and had a strange expression on his face. *Wheels were turning but she* wondered where he had drifted. His unfocused eyes had momentarily disappeared to a far-off place, maybe miles from the diner. A pale tone brought out the contrast of stubble, and the five o'clock shadow glittered under the diner's florescent lights. She didn't mean to throw him for a proverbial loop, and he seemed to ponder her words for several seconds. Listening, before making a quick, hasty reply made her feel better, and gave him brownie points.

That moment made a difference. It had to do with much more than long hair contrasting wildly and horribly, with cowboy-like silver snaps on a plaid shirt. While he appeared to be a paradox in many ways, and a myriad of mysterious disparities, she felt herself opening up to him. Meanwhile, her mind's eye saw a fortune wheel, flashing neon letters that spelled out 'proceed with caution'. Imagining her foot on thin ice, she stood blindfolded on the edge of destiny. Though apprehensive and risky, she moved forward. Her mouth didn't want to stop. She began to explain what she thought about everything.

"Yes!" Under the table her feet danced across the frozen pond. He's listening. *Don't be shy, she said to herself. I have to tell him how I feel about movies that glamorize violence.* "Doesn't all the hate bother you?" Every night she heard the senseless killings on the evening news; the shootings, the road rage, the incredible pain of survivors. "Well, why not? Why not create chemical warfare that destroys depression, irritability, bad moods and aggressive behavior?"

"For real?" Eric began to laugh, and she noticed he had attractive dimples. He laughed so hard he grabbed his napkin and had the decency to hold it in front of his mouth before pieces of potato shot across the table. She wondered what he found so funny. "Oh, my God, that is hilarious." The boisterous outburst almost made him choke. Tears rolled down his cheeks.

"What?" *She rolled her eyes, thinking he might be short a fuse or two.* "What did I say?"

"I sell those things. You described the symptoms. Ketamides, anesthetics, and antidepressants like Paraxethines, Zolough. I'm sure you've heard of Woezap."

*What the heck was he laughing about?* "Okay, yes. I've heard of some of those." She stabbed her fork into a piece of cake and brought it to her lips. Before she could enjoy the delicious morsel, he touched another nerve.

He pointed at her plate. "Some people order cake because they have low serotonin levels."

Linda placed her fork down. "Are you telling me I'm depressed?"

"I don't know, are you?" He chuckled again and even snorted. "Hey, I'm just kidding."

"Rest assured, I'm fine," she mumbled in a soft tone. Scanning the diner, she lowered her voice. "But that movie gave me a spectacular idea. Wouldn't it be great to put Woezap in the world's water supply?" Thoughts zigzagged like lightening in her mind. *Why would I tell this stranger my innermost thoughts? Must be those sincere looking, amber eyes, or maybe the big nose makes him appear trustworthy.* Embarrassed, she looked into her coffee cup. She felt red circles burning on her cheeks. *I hope he didn't drug me. And though it was way too early to tell, by some strange turn of cosmic events, Becca may have been right.*

"That would be awesome," he replied with a big grin. "It would also be a huge crime."

*No, it has to be the dimples.* She took a bite of cake and swallowed. "It might be worth it."

# CHAPTER TWO

Three days had passed, and she decided to give the guy another chance. Outside of interesting looks, he had what appeared to be a gentle soul. Plus, he listened, and that alone made a huge difference. Though he didn't seem too interested in her job, his intense, piercing eyes focused on her lips, as if everything she said was somehow important. Normally insecure, filled with trust issues, relating to old boyfriends, like Wayne, most of her doubt vanished around Eric.

When she saw his car however, she began to think she should walk, and rather quickly, towards a galaxy faraway. "It's a nice ride but what's all the stuff on the seats?" The gleaming sportscar seemed to shout 'single and loving it' to curious passersby.

"Oh those, sorry, I'll move them. Samples—you know the type of samples I give doctors."

"They look like notebooks."

Eric tossed some of the boxes into the back seat. "Right? Each sample comes with some information from the manufacturer. It also includes a list of side effects, legal mumbo-jumbo and descriptions of current advertising campaigns." A few of the cardboard folders had slipped onto the passenger side floor. Out of breath and embarrassed, he scooped them up and threw them behind his seat. "We also provide each doctor with emergency phone numbers in case something goes wrong. These are all FDA approved medications, but you never know."

"Can you see out the back window?"

"I hope so." He slipped in behind the wheel and patted the passenger seat with his hand. "I think it's safe to enter now."

Still hesitating, she moved away, slowly. Something felt different. The feeling rubbed her the wrong way. "Maybe we'll do this some other time," she said, leaning down to catch his eyes. But he stared right back into her blue ones. They seemed to plead along with his words.

"Oh, come on. I have something to show you."

They had spoken briefly on the phone. She told him she had enjoyed the cake at the diner. He wanted to make up for the bad movie by taking her to a brewery where they had computer games, billiards, darts, and dancing. But what had sounded fun on the phone, didn't appeal to her at the moment. "I don't know."

"Come on, please. I've been thinking about what you said, and I have to show you something." He started the engine.

*What? What had she said? Eric made her crazy and she couldn't figure out whether he made her crazy in a good way or a bad way. It felt palpable and electric. Perhaps this was what they meant by chemistry.* "Oh, okay. Since you put it like that." She got in, nestled into the bucket seat, closed the car door, but kept wondering what he meant. Wearing jeans and cowboy boots, she thought she'd fit right in at the country bar. "I've never done any line dancing," she stated, locking in the seatbelt.

They moved towards downtown and he stopped at a light.

"I've never line danced, two-stepped or dosey-doed either. I guess there's a first time for everything."

Silence filled the car for at least five minutes. No computer disc or radio and they didn't talk. When it looked like he passed the turn for the bar, she spoke up. "Isn't that place on Main Street?"

"It is, but don't forget, I want to show you something before the sun goes down."

"That's cool. As long as you don't kidnap me; it's not like I know you that well."

A dimpled grin lit up his face. "Are you kidding? I'd love to kidnap you. You're the prettiest girl I know."

"Well that's only because you hang out in all the wrong places."

"You'd be shocked at the places I used to hang out." He laughed at his comment and turned onto a steep, dirt road.

"Shocked in a good way or shocked and saddened?"

"Probably both—I did two tours, Fallujah in Iraq and Syria. They sent me right into combat, back in '04."

Now things began to make sense. "I'm impressed. Thank you for your service, Eric." She tried to imagine him wearing camouflaged clothes and a helmet. "Marines?"

"Semper Fi, baby!"

That explained the small scars on his hand. Her eyes focused on his knuckles gripping the steering wheel. "Are those scars from Iraq?"

"Shrapnel, I have small scars all over. And yes, Iraq."

Well, she wasn't interested in seeing them. *Not in the least. Keep them hidden soldier boy.* The twisting road grew narrow, and the incline increased along with her heart rate. This had to be one of the stupidest things she had ever done. Why would she allow herself to fall into such a vulnerable position?

Gradually, trying not to be obvious, she inhaled, filling her lungs with air, hoping to calm errant nerves with breathing exercises. Exhaling slowly, she asked an obvious question. "Now, you're scaring me. Where are you taking me Eric?" Not wanting to scream, and knowing it wouldn't help anyway, she forced her cheeks into a smile.

"Don't worry. The view is lovely up here." The car bounced along the rocks and dust, finally reaching a ledge next to a behemoth water tower. Pointing ahead, he said, "Look at that sunset."

"Reminds me of a song about California sunsets," she began to hum the song until he stopped the engine. "Unless you're delusional, we're not at the make-out stage yet," she intoned, gazing down at the city below. "But you're right, it's breathtaking."

"I know, I know," his voice excited, he smiled, and held up the palm of his hand to indicate he wanted silence. "Look around, there's no one within five miles. No city sounds at all, just peace and quiet."

"So, I noticed," she replied, wondering whether he'd kill her now, or later. *She began a mental inventory of her purse, and the items she could use as possible weapons: a pen, lipstick, a compact with a small mirror, a wallet with five dollars and some coins. If I thrust the pen into his jugular, I might have a chance. If he ties me up, I might be able to use part of the mirror to cut the rope. Fortunately, I have a cell phone, but this area doesn't look like it gets any reception.*

*Maybe, I could use the mirror to flicker a distress signal and tie his hands behind his back with the shoulder straps? The more she thought about it, the worse it looked. All the contents in her purse might be heavy enough to slam on his head. I don't have a flaming chance in a bonfire. He had been a soldier trained to kill. He outweighs me by at least twenty-five pounds. Her eyes were drawn to the rough ink drawing of barbed wire around his biceps. On top of everything else, he could drug me with his sample stash, in the back seat. This is crazy, but I can't show fear.* "You have so many pills. What kind are they?" She managed to squeak.

"Linda, the reason we're here is because I want to help you. You know, that idea you had about changing the world?" Pivoting his body, he turned to face her.

"Huh?" *He's not a killer. He's not a killer. He's not a killer, kept reverberating in her mind.* Fear coursed through her veins. She had to convince herself he had good intentions, or she couldn't breathe. She slipped her left hand into her purse and grasped the pen while watching his eyes. They looked soulful and gentle, like the police sketches at the post office.

"You talked about...". He sighed, paused and started over. "You had this incredible idea about putting Woezap in the world's water supply. And, I'm willing to help you do it."

Trapped by an apparent madman, her eyes scanned the horizon but returned to her captor. *He's insane.* She tilted her head, like a dog trying not to fail obedience school. *What did he just say? Did she hear him correctly?*

"Are you crazy?"

"Good question, we'll get back to that later. Seriously, everything you said at the diner made sense. The despicable acts that humans are committing, need to be eliminated. Violence and hate are at an all time high. It's like an epidemic and maybe we can "cure" it.

"Right, the world does need a kick in the ass, but why would I, or we, be the ones to do it?" Nervous laughter made her turn back to the gorgeous view. She relaxed her grip on the pen. *They'll never find my body anyway.*

"Listen Linda, I'm serious. In addition to my experience

with WMD's, I feel the two of us are strong enough, both mentally and physically, to carry it off. That's one reason I brought you here. See this water tower? It's easy to access. They are built without too many locks. The reservoirs and the underground aquifers are easy to manipulate."

The small hairs on the back of her neck stood at attention. This geeky guy, though obviously not a murderer, and perhaps seriously demented, had characteristics that made her listen. There were unexplainable, unusual things she liked about him. Especially, when he described her as strong. "No one drinks tap water anymore."

"But they do. And it doesn't matter. Where do you think they get bottled water? It's pumped from clearly accessible mountain springs."

"What about the Prozzak or Woezap, or whatever? We can't afford enough of the stuff, and I doubt you're willing to lose your job by pilfering it."

"You see Linda, that's the thing. I have worldwide contacts that work with similar drugs. We would form a team. Plus, I also work in research and development, where they let me experiment. Phloxetine is only one type of serotonin enhancer. There's also sitalopram, certraline, paraxethine...."

Waving her hand, she cut him off. "Okay, I get it. There's more than Woezap. Are we going to steal it?"

He inhaled and began a litany of staccato answers. "Not really. See all these samples? They have five to ten pills in each folder. Some have more. The companies are desperate to get these into the hands of doctors. I have other friends who sell pharmaceuticals. In fact, I've been with this company for five years. They treat me pretty good," he said with an audible sigh. "They pay me well and yup, they trust me." Eric squinted and bit his lower lip. "That goes back to the military. I served with my boss and many of the other employees. Lucky for me, I outranked almost everyone. They talk to me with respect. Our entire staff wants the world to know the truth about chemicals."

Words escaped her. She nodded. *My kind of insane,* she thought, forgetting her fear.

"I realize doing this will be a risk. But come on, it's a risk I'm willing to take, especially, if I can save children, and all the innocents being victimized." His impassioned speech didn't end there. Tears rimmed his eyes. "I want you to know that whatever I do, it's all the way. All or nothing."

"But..." she tried to interrupt.

"No 'buts' Linda. Every inch of my heart wants to do this. Ever since our first date when you mentioned this, I haven't been able to sleep. Plus, I have loyal friends everywhere; Paris, Rome, Vienna, Ottawa, Cape Town and a slew of other places. I speak Spanish, and a little French. Some of my best contacts are in Mexico and South America. Those guys are thrilled to have U.S. doctors asking for their products. I can get my hands on enough Woezap and Zolough to make your head spin."

Shaking her head in disbelief, she didn't want to argue. All of it made her head spin. "I doubt that you can get enough for the entire world's water supply." Her mind raced as she thought of recent news reports about a man who intentionally ran over children. There were the disgusting pedophiles, the hit and run drivers, mothers who abandoned their children, and those who aborted babies before they were born. The list included wicked perpetrators who held up mini marts, street gangs, arsonists, evil human traffickers, and copious amounts of anger, rage and hate. It had to go. All of it. She'd be willing to go to war for it. "The Earth is big," she said, with a tremulous sigh.

"You think I'm kidding, but I can get enough supply." He reached over to clasp his fingers around her hand. "Linda, I really like you. Besides, you inspired me with this idea. I think we can make a difference. Are you with me?"

"I still think you're crazy." Looking out over the town, she hesitated briefly. "Okay, so tell me about this team. Can you trust them?"

## CHAPTER THREE

"Yes, you can trust them with your life. Seriously, I've known them for years. Let's see, I'll start with Garcia. Mi amigo, he grew up in my neighborhood. Like brothers, we joined the Marines together. Right now, he lives in Italy with Giulia." He rolled his eyes when mentioning Giulia. "Some of the others served under different flags, from other countries. We accidentally met fighting insurgents, during mortar fire. For example, Etienne is French, but he saved my life. Jack was our Chaplain. Man, I met those two at the worst time. Jack's the reason I have this tattoo. Reminds me of Jesus."

He held up three fingers. "There's more. Let's see. Oh Milo, of course. He joined the Army because he wanted to be a U.S. citizen. As a kid, he had a thing for ham radios and distant frequencies that brought Western rock and roll into his room. Even now, he's an IT guy. But, don't try outshining Milo at karaoke. He knows all the best songs. Anyway, back then, he kept us connected to base. Oh, and Sparky was our electrician who kept the lights dimmed during enemy attacks. I hope he'll want to be part of the team."

"Sparky?"

Eric waved a hand in a dismissive manner, "Oh, he has some other boring name. I think its Paul. To us, he'll always be Sparky."

Linda exhaled. She could hear a rapid pulse thumping in her ears. "Well, I've had about all I can for one night. Either we go dancing...or it's time to go. You've stressed me out."

"But...."

She repeated his earlier rebuke. "No 'buts'. Eric, I have to work tomorrow. Give me a rundown of your peeps, tomorrow at six. We'll meet at that same diner. Try and get a booth way in the back, so no one can hear our conversation." Since her career centered on customer service and time management, she realized she sounded exceedingly business-like. Still, he hadn't asked about her work yet, and this stunt at the water tower had scared her to death. He deserved much worse than her office voice, but it would have to do for now. Punishment wasn't her style.

Nodding, his tone deferential, he asked, "Can I have one dance? You promised."

"Sure. Only because I want to see this hyped-up, sports-bar-meets-the-Wild West, with my very own eyes. I've heard hearts go haywire in that place. My internet friends call it the meat market of the century," she stated, with the judgmental air of some old-fashioned grandmother. "The place sounds like a vortex, where good intentions intertwine with chaos."

Clearing his throat, as if she had landed on the truth, made him blush. "I've heard those rumors too." The car bumbled down the dusty drive, back to the highway. "Aren't you excited?"

Eric acted like a guy who knew a little too much about all the fun places. She worried he had tried all the fun girls too. Maybe even the loose young women who visited bars next to military bases. The tawdry stories she had heard about cheap girls who waited for soldiers to disembark military ships were distracting her, making her think horrible thoughts about Eric. And yet, the dimples, the nose, and gooey caramel eyes made him seem vulnerable, almost pathetic. "About going to the dance place?"

"No, I mean about our plan. We're going to change the dark to light. We'll abolish wars. The world will live in peace. Can you imagine it? Linda, your idea is phenomenal."

God, she was either tired, annoyed or both. Why did he have to be so enthusiastic? Blah, blah, blah. She didn't want to talk about it. Some fantasies should remain hidden, perhaps buried along with kinky fetishes in a tight-fitting box, secure and unopened for eternity. This far-fetched idea belonged inside Pandora's Box. Nailed shut and bound with chains. Her eyes were closed. She rubbed her temples. It seemed too late in the day to portray excitement, and yet she found herself responding to Eric's eager plea. "It's a crazy dream but I doubt it would last. It's not like we can keep resupplying high doses, on every continent, in perpetuity. This is a one-shot thing. It has to have lasting, positive consequences."

"Actually, some of the medication, I'm not sure which one, has lasting qualities. Some medicine is for treating patients on a long-term basis. We need to find the pills that can cure, not just treat depression, schizophrenia and borderline symptoms. It has to be something that can alter serotonin receptors forever. There are natural protein inhibitors that can relax human DNA. What we need exists, and I plan on doing some...stealth research. Once I find what we need, we'll use those capsules to make everyone happy."

"You're quite the idealist," she replied, curtly. Maybe he'd notice she wanted to talk about something different, something less hopeless. *Fact is, she knew in her heart, that not everyone wanted to be happy. Certain people are simply impervious to joy. Doesn't Eric know there are people who regale in sad songs and intense poetry? There are societies of mourners paid to cry at funerals. There are members of religious sects who whip themselves for thinking bad thoughts. There's even a German word for those who enjoy the pain of others: schadenfreude. Depression is at an all-time high. Truckloads of medicine couldn't help the hardened cases. What made Eric think it was even possible?* When the car turned into a gravel parking lot, she opened her eyes and straightened up. "I guess we're here. Let's go check it out."

Loud music blared from the stage. A country band of bearded men played above a crowded dance floor. The lead singer wore a leather cowboy hat and sang an upbeat tune accompanied by various musicians, even a banjo. When they walked in, Eric reached into his pocket to pay the cover charge. "Howdy," the young man at the door greeted them, and stamped the top of their hands with glow-in-the dark ink. The familiar way he slapped Eric on the back, made her think they were friends.

Near the door, couples played darts, shot some pool or played arcade games. Everyone looked like they were having fun. If only the entire world could hold hands in a giant line dance, she thought, almost laughing out loud. Glad to have worn boots, Linda kicked aside sawdust and peanut shells on the messy floor.

They sat by the stage watching the hoofing and clapping, until the lights were turned down, and the band mellowed into a romantic ballad. "Come on Miss Linda, you owe me this dance."

"I don't owe you, or anyone else, a thing," she snapped, wanting to make sure he knew his boundaries. Surprised at her comeback, his eyebrows arched above the rims of his glasses.

He looked impressed with what he probably thought of as strength. To Linda, it went beyond strength. Eric gave her confidence because he listened. And, since he frightened her earlier, she thought of it as gentle sparring. *Yes, I am a warrior and he better watch out.*

She looked down at his black and white sneakers and, for a fleeting moment, forgot about everything. This guy didn't need boots or a cowboy hat to have a good time. His wry smile, brown wavy hair and dreamy, bedroom eyes pulled her from the wooden bench. "Hold on, I'm coming," she added, when he reached for her waist. The singer crooned the mushiest words she had ever heard about someone being separated from his sweetheart. Eric didn't appear to be a fantastic dancer, but he held her tight and whispered into her ear. Two simple actions she forgot how much she enjoyed. Maybe he was a sensitive guy after all. Maybe, she needed to loosen up and smile too.

"Still stressed out?"

"No," she replied, inhaling the smell of soap on his neck. "This is better than I expected."

He smiled again, flashing mesmerizing and enchanting dimples. "If I was an arrogant bastard, and I hope I'm not, I'd say, 'it's because you're with me."

"Be arrogant. It ***is*** because of you." The song ended. By that time, she had surrendered. They stood in the middle of the dance floor kissing. She thought, the way his glasses were getting fogged up was the cutest thing, ever.

# CHAPTER FOUR

Becca squealed through the phone-line like a farm animal being sheared. Linda loved making her little sister laugh uncontrollably. "Yes, I can't believe I'm admitting you were right, but this time you absolutely nailed it."

"Really?" her sister asked, as she caught her breath and attempted to pull herself together. "Spill it, I want all the details."

"No saucy details yet, and even if I did, that doesn't mean I'd tell you everything. But you were right about how he's smart and different. I like the way we contrast. I look like a normal person and he looks like a guy from a 90's garage band."

Giggling like a little girl at Christmas, her sister wanted to hear every romantic detail. "Come on, tell me more. Don't be a prude. What's wrong with a little grunge?"

"What? What's with the sudden desire for voyeurism? Isn't your darling hubby living up to your wildest fantasies?" Linda liked joking around and making fun of Gary. She thought Becca's husband put the ass in asinine. Though Gary worked hard in pest control and he adored her smart, redheaded sister, he never kept up with the latest news, hated politics, didn't read books, and lived for sports. Any team, as long as they showed it on television. They could be showing football, soccer, golf, tennis, horse-racing, boat regattas even gymnastic trials. The loudest weekends revolved around pro-wrestling, baseball, fast cars or monster trucks. He'd shout and feel involved in every moment, until one of his favorite teams, or players lost. After which, he'd pout for days like a lost child. The playoffs, bowls and Olympics were the absolute worst. Family get-togethers felt like funerals, unless his players won.

"Linda, that's not very nice. Gary is a busy guy. Corporate is flying him back East tomorrow for some roach convention. Maybe I should talk to you after he's gone. Sheesh. Why would you hit me below the belt? I thought I'm your favorite sister?"

"Very funny, you're my ***only*** sister and I'm sorry."

"All right. Well then tell me more."

There didn't seem to be too much to tell. While she enjoyed her date with Eric, most of the time had been spent debating the cerebral items related to her mischievous plan, which, he took much more seriously than she did. While there wasn't much romance, she wanted to give Becca at least a morsel of information. "Let's see--now don't go posting this on the internet--but we kissed. He's a fantastic kisser and I liked it."

Becca inhaled a bit too fast. Words came out in spurts, along with small pockets of air that sounded like spit, or maybe bubbles hitting the phone. "Exactly-the type-of information-I wanted to hear."

"For what? You sound like that news anchor. What's her name? Oh yeah, Sandra Beck. It's not like we're ready to plan a wedding or anything. We kissed and I kept my clothes on. All of them."

"Well, you know Mom and Dad want grandchildren, and it doesn't look like I'll be able to make them happy."

Thank God she climbed off the subject of Eric. Becca always had a deep desire to please. As a nurse, she had to be caring and had to listen. On top of everything, Becca had what might be called an entertaining personality. She spread kindness and hope to countless sad, depressed patients entering hospice. When she ran out of material to make people smile, she'd reach into her pocket and pull out a book filled with knock-knock jokes. She'd make the best mom, Linda thought. "Keep trying and don't give up. You can't put this huge onus on my shoulders. Our parents are tough. They can handle the wait."

"Trust me, we are trying. In fact, I'm exhausted and glad Gary's leaving. Nothing makes the heart grow fonder...."

"Yeah, a little time apart might be good." With her sister's biological clock ticking, Linda asked the same question every week. "What did the doctor say?"

"Same thing you're telling me right now. Guess when I'm in the stirrups, the ole doc forgets I'm an R.N. I've heard this stuff until my ears turn blue. He also gave us a link to an article about how tight underwear kills sperm count. Hot tubs kill sperm count. Certain foods kill sperm count. It went on and on. Gary didn't want to hear it. He likes his tightie-whities and he loves relaxing in the outdoor sauna every night."

Glad she didn't work in the medical industry, Linda tried not to laugh. "For heaven's sake, you mean there's a cure? All he has to do is stop the sparkling spa-treatment for a few weeks and loosen his pants?"

"I think so, but Gary won't budge. He's happy the way things are. I went and bought him three kinds of loose-fitting boxers and he hated them. One pair had a pattern of red hearts."

"Awe, Becca. Did you tell him there's too much at stake?"

"I should have. My gentle giant made me return all the loose ones. He had a weird bi-polar-type hissy fit. Even drove me to the store to make sure I'd take them back. We stood in line for a half an hour at the return desk. Finally, the customer service lady came to inspect each pair of underwear. She kept asking repeatedly, whether he had worn them or not, while she stared at the crotch and checked the seams. The worst part was when she put on a pair of reading glasses, as if she needed to zoom in on something. I almost died of embarrassment. Gary worried if we didn't go to the store together, I'd stay home and plot out some crazy scheme where I'd dump all his regular undies in the garbage or something."

Linda couldn't help bursting into laughter. "You crack me up, but he's a dope."

" Linda, he's a love muffin. I hope someday you'll know what it's like to share your life with someone good and peaceful."

"Peaceful? Didn't you just tell me he threw a fit about the boxers?" Linda recalled the Sunday dinners that ended up with Gary shouting at the television. *Peaceful? Like a monkey at an all you can eat banana buffet. More like Fred Astaire dancing on hot coals. Did love make people delusional?*

"Come on Sis. You're supposed to be telling me about Eric. Stop changing the subject."

*So smart--no attention deficit—she couldn't get anything past her sister. Linda could weave a complicated story about a wild trip around the world in a helium balloon and Becca would always remember every last detail of how it took place, and where the balloon finally crashed to Earth.*

"Eric is unlike anyone I've ever met. He might be too cool for me."

"Now you're being stupid. Why would he be too cool for you?"

"I don't know. I'm not used to his style."

"How can my gorgeous, intelligent sister say something so ridiculous? You're not even a blond. Is it the tats and the piercing?"

"No—maybe--and I can be a blond if I want to be. So, you were right, he's a sensitive person and listens to everything I say."

"Isn't that a good thing?"

She glanced at her watch. "It is a good thing. I'm just not sure I can handle it." Tonight, she'd be meeting Eric at the diner to formulate their nebulous plan. Though her heart wanted to save the world, she wasn't sure she could save herself.

# CHAPTER FIVE

The road into town had washed out from heavy rain. The storm pounded on the sidewalks, knocking gently on the windows. It created a pleasant and ominous sound akin to soft, distant drumbeats that warned of imminent danger. Big, kerplunks fell onto Linda's umbrella while she waited for Eric in front of the diner. By the time he arrived, she had become lost in thought, envisioning an entire percussion section tinkering with the heavenly, waterlogged music.

A familiar voice broke into the flow of her imagery. "Hey pretty lady with the light brown hair," Eric called out from under a saturated, olive-green hoodie.

She knew the voice, but at first didn't recognize him. "Mystery man, huh?"

He stuck his head under the umbrella and gave her a quick kiss.

That clean soap smell had become alluring. "Wow. A bit presumptuous, but it sheds some light on your disguise." Surprised at his forward manner, she smiled.

"If I remember correctly, you told me to be arrogant. I'm aiming to please."

"Can we go inside before we drown?"

"This is nothing. You should see the torrential floods they have in the desert." He opened the door and she followed him inside. They went to the far side of the building, past the counter and slid into a booth near the rest rooms.

"You are soaked."

He removed his jacket and placed it on a chair. "At least it's warm in here."

A waitress came with menus. "Can I have a coffee?" Eric asked the teenage server, her cheeks ablaze with acne. He turned to Linda, "how about you? Coffee, tea or me?"

Embarrassed, she looked at the young woman who seemed to wear a telling smile. "I'll have coffee too," Linda answered, shaking off his comment. "Thanks."

"No problem. I'll bring coffee, and you can order later. I don't want to rush you". The server put her pad into her apron pocket and retrieved two mugs from the drying rack.

After she stepped away, Eric glanced at his watch. "Hope you're not in a hurry because I asked my friend to join us. He's staying about fifty miles away, attending some medical conference. Based on the flooding, he might not make it."

Using a businesslike tone, she answered, "We have to plan for storms, fires and anything unexpected that could hinder our plans. I guess this is like a drill. If he doesn't show up, then you might want to reconsider his place on the team and find a replacement. This is a matter of life and death. I'm sorry, but I hope your friend has a boat."

Eric's face lit up, he laughed, bumped his chest with a fist and made a peace sign. "You sound like a sergeant. Bravo. I'm super pumped." Though the wafting aroma of soap made it obvious he had taken a shower, his damp hair hung loose, giving him an unkempt, sloppy look. He pulled a folded map from his breast pocket. "First, we'll have a little history lesson. All stuff you may, or may not, already know, but we have to be on the same page regarding everything. Is that cool?" The wrinkled map looked like it had seen better days. He unfolded it in front of them and anchored the top corners with salt and pepper shakers.

Why did he laugh when she wanted to be serious? "Yeah, sure—shoot."

"Wait. Let's order some fries, or something to snack on, while I go through everything. Our server is a doll, but I'd feel more comfortable making sure she doesn't see anything." Eric placed a few napkins over the map and ordered two sandwiches. When she brought the food, he told her they were going to eat slowly. He also reminded her; they were waiting for a friend. He told her to check back when his friend arrived. As soon as she walked away, Eric uncovered the map of the Middle East.

"We have to start here." He pointed to the center of the map. "The birthplace of civilization, and because of wars and unrest, it seems to have the most hate. This right here is what's called the Fertile Crescent. It stretches from Egypt, goes up towards Israel, Jordan, Palestine, Iraq, Syria, Kuwait, Lebanon and Turkey. It's like a moon-shaped basin of negative thought. Over six thousand years ago this was called Mesopotamia, home to the Sumerians."

Linda yawned, and wondered why he had to go so far back in history.

"This is modern day Mosul right here, surrounding Nineveh, which is one of the oldest cities in the world. The earliest architecture, original forms of writing, all go back to this area." His fingers swept the region and he lowered his voice. "This right here is the Tigris and the Euphrates Rivers and here," he paused, as a cloud settled on his features. "This is where I was stationed." He pointed to a small red spot on the map. "Look at the tributaries around the Tigris. All this, drains into the Persian Gulf. The river basin is currently home to over twenty-three million people. Then, over here is the Jordan River and the Nile. All of it connects."

Linda stared at the map. "Wouldn't all the surrounding bodies of water dilute what we're trying to do?" The Black Sea and the Caspian Sea were up at the top, the Mediterranean filled the west part of the map, and the Red Sea came around in the south. On the southeast side she noticed the Persian Gulf. Though she had heard stories on the evening news about wars, most of her thoughts of the area related to the Bible.

"Yes and no. By the way, that's a great question. Back in the nineties, some of the farmland dried up because of dams that diverted and drained the water. Even though the area became desert, most of the water returned through torrential downpours and flooding. I remember the Tigris river flooding at least a month before the Euphrates, because it's shorter. There's water everywhere, and most of it flows southeast. But, as you may know, not all rivers flow south. The Nile for example, flows north, which, for our purposes, is great."

Both elbows on the table, her hands cradled her face. "Eric, this is only one part of our gigantic world."

"Right, and?"

"I don't know, take Nebraska for example. Don't they have more miles of rivers than all the other U.S. states?"

He rolled his eyes and forced a sidelong smile, "Probably, but we're not talking about the states yet. Linda, give me some credit. You're right, the world is big, and that's exactly why we need to zero in on the hotspots. It'll be crucial to reach as many of the negative areas that we can. Everything, and everyone on our team, has to be in sync." Cupping his hands, they formed a ball when he said, 'in sync'.

"And as far as Nebraska goes, most of the state is a farming community. I'd say it's pretty calm over there. Can we focus on one continent at a time?"

Confused, and unhappy about being scolded, she felt like a vegan at a slaughterhouse. The last chicken roaming the butcher's yard. A lamb heading for danger. Eric couldn't know she had goosebumps sprouting along her arms.

"That being said, this section of our planet, since the dawn of time, has had most of the problems." He moved the saltshaker off the map. "Since I'm familiar with this region, I plan on being the man for this area. We'll call it section A, for top priority." He reached into his pocket for a pen, and drew a big A with a flourish on top of the map.

"What about me. What's my area?"

He avoided her question. "Remember Juan, the guy I told you about? Juan grew up in my neighborhood. Anyway, he has what it takes to handle the entire West half of the United States. The man is a walking hydrological map. He knows the Colorado River and the Rio Grande, like I know the back of my hand. I'm sure he's familiar with Nebraska too. Only problem is, he's living the dolce vita with his sexy girlfriend Giulia, in Italy."

"Eric," she was determined to find out her role in this growing fiasco. "What about me?" The goosebumps spread to her back where they made her shiver.

"I'm getting to that, my dear," he replied, moving the pepper aside. When he looked up, he asked, "Did you like your sandwich?"

"I did thanks." She watched him fold the map and put it away, but her expression didn't change. His speech had zoomed right over her head. Like a stolen stealth bomber smuggling boxes of contraband, Eric had overloaded her database with too much information.

"We'll have different maps for each member of our team. I'm sure you know there are children dying in Sudan and Somalia. "Sparky might be our guy for that area, or maybe my friend Jack. Then, there's Pakistan, North Korea, the Congo and other places that haven't known serenity for a long time. Look at Afghanistan. Wouldn't it be great to let those people live in peace?"

Peace. She understood the goal. "Of course, that's the idea," Linda looked up and heard the server asking whether she wanted more coffee. "Yes, please," she replied, rubbing a hand up and down her arm. "Must be chilly in here, maybe it will warm me up."

Eric put his hand over his cup. "That'll do me. Only so much caffeine I can handle."

The three of them noticed a man approaching. With the glistening, bright window directly behind him, the dark silhouette looked hard to identify.

The server poured Linda's coffee. "I guess your friend finally made it." Stacking the sandwich plates and clattering the silverware, she gave them a weather forecast before turning towards the kitchen. "It's still pouring outside."

Each heavy step sounded like a sloshing, wet, mess. Water dripped from his hair, down his nose, all over his saturated polo and khaki pants. Though an hour late, Eric's friend had finally made it. Earlier, Eric had explained, that this guy would do anything for him. Through thick and thin, this man had saved Eric's life. According to Eric, this extraordinary man would go the extra mile, talk the talk, walk the walk, even leap from tall buildings if necessary. Eric would do anything for this man, and this man would do anything for Eric.

To Linda, the unimpressive little guy looked like he just

swam the English Channel. When he reached over to shake hands, Eric moved out of the booth to envelope him in a bear hug. "Man, it's been a long time. So glad you came, Bud. Let me introduce you to Linda."

The older gentleman looked embarrassed after noticing the puddles he brought into the diner. Seconds later, after noticing his embrace had left splotches all over Eric's shirt, he developed a heartwarming, toothy grin. A dripping wet arm reached over to shake her hand. "Bonjour, beautiful lady, my name is Etienne."

# CHAPTER SIX

Linda yawned and whispered, "Eric, I'm tired and have to wake up early."

Eric looked at his watch. "It's not even eight o'clock. We have a lot to go over, and now, Etienne can add to the discussion. I already gave him a brief summary of our plans. He's excited too. Please hang with us a little while longer."

Etienne kept pulling napkins from the dispenser to dry his forehead, cheeks and nose. Like a recirculating fountain, after a few seconds, water dripped down again making him blink faster. A tear shaped drop hung from the end of his nose. His hair looked plastered to his forehead. When Eric mentioned Etienne's excitement, he nodded, "Oui, oui, it is time to do this. Magnifique."

Linda's mind had zoned out during much of Eric's historical lecture about the Tigris and Euphrates. Much of her fatigue and inattentiveness had to do with unusual developments happening at her work, including an upcoming media merger. This, in most cases wouldn't be that bad, had her boss shared even a microscopic piece of something about the future of the company. By omitting things, they had caused stress and complacency among the employees.

The morning began with meetings and the afternoon ended in meetings. Now, here she sat in the middle of another meeting. Here, a Frenchman sat in his own personal pond. "Etienne, aren't you uncomfortable? Maybe we should regroup tomorrow?" She looked him up and down and didn't feel impressed. The fact that he wasn't wearing a jacket, made her think he couldn't be too bright. Added to that, graying temples, delicate features, and a soft voice, made the fellow appear weak. She saw him as a fragile, worn out rag doll, thrown into the gutter and dragged into a café.

Etienne probably noticed her observations and smirked. "I came today, like I promised Eric. Yes, most of the road is washed out. I am tired because I had to walk the last three miles. Please excuse my shabby appearance."

Eric grasped Etienne's arm before he said another word. "Let me get you a cup of coffee and a sandwich. You'll have to stay at my place until they fix the road. Is that all right?"

Etienne nodded. Linda tried to imagine what he might look like in dry clothes without wet hair. High cheekbones, a thin aquiline nose and pale gray-blue eyes were distinguishing features, but even with the sophisticated French accent, he wasn't looking like the hero Eric had described.

"Great, then we'll reconvene tomorrow night at my condo." Eric flagged down the server and asked for a menu for his friend.

"Eric told me you saved his life," Linda interjected. Eric chewed quietly on his bottom lip.

Etienne nodded again and put his right hand on his chest. "My job with the Troupes de la Marine...." Memories of combat seemed to flood his face. Where water dripped, anxiety and painful emotions continued to fill his eyes, wrinkles, and the crevices on his forehead. "Eric is my brother; now and forever."

Great, she thought to herself. *I'm stuck with two guys suffering from PTSD.* "So sorry you both had to suffer through combat together. Did either of you ever see a doctor regarding post-traumatic stress disorder?"

"But of course," Etienne replied.

"That's the first place they send you when you come back," Eric added, "Even winners of the Croix de Guerre, like my buddy here."

Though nothing at this moment seemed funny, both Etienne and Eric snickered like two boys with a secret. "Linda," Etienne began--in what later—when she looked back--would sound like a defensive argument for absurdity. His tone became serious, his face somber. "We are sharp, educated and trained for this mission. No one else can succeed at this, unless they have been through what we have been through and have seen what we have seen. We cannot forget who we are, and we have learned from every experience. Good or bad, these are the things that have forged us into Eric and Etienne." He turned his head towards the ceiling and closed his eyes. "Mon Dieu, our unique sensitivities, our hearts and our souls make us fighters who want to bring the world smiles, instead of bullets. We are the select few; enthusiastic...warriors for peace."

Taken aback at his heartfelt speech, she took a deep breath and felt like saluting. The smell of coffee filled the diner. She now realized that her once silly comment had morphed from a mustard seed into a fully thawed-out mammoth. There would be no turning back. Not with these two. They were those maniacal, stubborn but honest types—men who followed through on every promise. They were examples of the true-blue loyal friend, the impassioned sculptor searching for an angel in the marble, or the determined, tenacious dreamer, searching for windmills of gold. These two were now part of her life and her future, whether she understood all the ramifications or not. Like the three musketeers, it was all for one, or one for all. Though tired at the moment, something deep inside made her feel ready for the challenge. "Okay, I need your address and phone number, Eric."

He pulled the last napkin from the dispenser in order to jot his address and phone number down. "Stay dry, lovely lady." He handed her the paper. She buried it deep in a pocket so it would stay dry.

The two of them moved towards the door. Eric paid the cashier, while Etienne stayed seated, waiting for his meal.

"Nice to meet you Etienne," Linda called back, before opening the door into the cold rain.

"See you tomorrow night around seven," Eric said, with a wave.

And, as the door to the diner closed, the faint voice of Etienne said, "au revoir."

# CHAPTER SEVEN

The rain seemed lovely at first. In the fall, raindrops are greeted, like old friends after a long hot summer. This early spring rain however, had overstepped all the boundaries and was overstaying any welcome. The rivers had flooded, some of the older bridges had washed out and several roads were closed. Gray skies had blocked the sun for what seemed like endless weeks. Potholes had developed all along the main highway through town, and even sinkholes big enough to swallow cars had opened up on urban streets. Many small homes on the outskirts of town had flooded. Animal rescue teams were busy hauling away livestock and horses. Linda didn't like it one bit.

As she drove her small car slowly through town, she saw helicopters airlifting elderly patients from the hospital, and people kayaking with dogs to the shelter. The minute she got home, she needed to call her sister to find out how they were. Darkness surrounded her creating limited visibility. Even with the windshield wipers set on high, driving was difficult. The car in front of her turned left. Gripping the steering wheel, she attempted to follow. Accelerating through a giant puddle, she felt her vehicle move in a strange, sideways direction. In the rear-view mirror, she noticed the car behind her looked stuck at the light. As she turned the steering wheel towards home, she lost control of her car. It began to float. Fear coursed through her veins as water seeped through the doors and floorboards. Flowing down what looked like a rushing river, the brakes stopped working. Her automobile sailed through intersections as if on a skiff. Ice-cold water crept above her ankles and knees. The water swirled around her, pulling everything down into a gigantic, swirling sink hole.

Since Californian's never took these things too seriously, television news programs had warned everyone about this type of calamity several times. Especially during the rainy season. There were logical steps to take, as long as Linda could remember not to panic. At least she knew it didn't take long for the worst to happen, and she needed to escape the car immediately. First, she rolled down the power windows. The glass panels stopped and didn't go down all the way. Then, she put the vehicle into park and struggled to undo her seatbelt. After all the yanking and kicking in cold water, she began to feel overheated. Her bulky, coat made things difficult. Grabbing her purse, she looped the straps over head to keep her hands free. A voice yelled something from the side of the road but she continued to focus. The water kept pouring in and reached the steering wheel. With immense difficulty, she pushed her body out the narrow window, splashing into the moving current. The wet sidewalk seemed far away, but she half-swam, half-groped along, clamoring and squealing like a walrus, to where a man in a uniform waited with a blanket.

"Come on young lady, I'm here to help." A fireman in

yellow waders and a red helmet stepped off the curb. "Let me get you somewhere warm." Trying to stand amid rushing water proved difficult, but the fireman grasped her arm, pulling her to safety. Once she stood on firmer ground, he pulled off her water-logged coat.

The words 'young lady' sounded funny coming from a guy in his early twenties. Teeth chattering, she didn't want to be colder than she felt. "Can I keep my coat on?"

He raised his bushy eyebrows as if she couldn't possibly be serious. "It has to dry first. I'll come back with another blanket. Stay here. Try folding some of that blanket over your head," Knowing she had water in her ears, he gesticulated with his arms and pointed to his helmet. With the heavy rain coming down, even listening to someone a foot away became difficult. The fireman ran off with her coat, towards a fire truck, parked several blocks away, and came back ten minutes later with a wheelchair and two blankets. "Sorry, I took so long. Get in." He unfolded the seat and directed her to sit in the chair, which he wheeled around giant puddles in torrential rain to his truck. By the time they got there, the blankets were soaked. When she sneezed, she felt like a snorkeling cat and thought she probably looked like one too. A cat ready to hurl a hairball.

"Where do you live?" the fireman asked.

"I live five miles down the road on the right, in the Williamson Manor Apartments," she replied through chattering teeth. Alive, but frozen to the bone, she felt humbled by the irony. Perhaps her plot to change the world's water supply had come to haunt her in the wildest of ways. Though not superstitious, she thought it could be a bad omen. She reached into her wet purse hoping to call her sister, but her cellphone didn't work. "I need to make a call. Do you have a phone I can use?"

"Of course," the fireman answered, handing her a dry blanket. "Use mine." He gave her a phone and went to attend to someone else. Good thing he had a large supply of blankets; soaked and shivering people were hovering all around the fire truck.

Becca picked up on the first ring. "Where are you sister of mine? "She sang in the sweetest voice.

"Oh Becca, I'm in trouble up to my eardrums. My car got flooded. I'm standing somewhere on Grand Ave near the shopping center. The roads are washed out. I almost made it home, but the fire department had to rescue me."

"Oh no! I can hear your teeth chattering."

"Oh yes, it's like a bad movie. I will probably be on the eleven o'clock news tonight."

"Well, too bad I won't have time to watch. I'm still at work."

"This is crazy." She pulled the blanket tighter, leaning under a ladder protruding from the truck.

"Tell me about it. The hospital's flooded too. They made me work extra hours to help patients move to other facilities. This is a nightmare. I'll be here for a long time tonight. Like until tomorrow. Sis, I'm sorry, I don't think I should go outside to find you on Grand. Especially after hearing how bad it is around there. Do you know if your apartment is safe?"

"Hold on and let me find out." Linda walked over to the fireman who had helped her. He stood next to another firefighter, who held an infant. The one holding the baby spoke in Spanish to the distraught mother.

"She'll be fine," the fireman repeated several times in English and Spanish. Wrapped into a blanket, like a cheese enchilada, the crying baby seemed to enjoy the way the fireman rocked him back and forth. "We will transport you, and your child, to the school auditorium. Maybe your husband is already there." The other fireman translated, but the woman kept sobbing. Swirling tears mixed into the water drops falling from the sky. The baby fell asleep.

A news chopper hovered above. "Hold on Becca," Linda shouted into the phone. "I know you're busy. Please hold on for one second." She moved closer to the firemen. "Excuse me, but is there a way I can get home?"

The one who had rescued her, tilted his head and leaned closer, making sure he heard her question. Sparkling drops of water dripped from his helmet. "Not any time soon, Miss. Didn't you say you live in Williamson Manor?"

"Yes," she yelled, to make sure he'd hear her voice above the helicopter noise, the pounding rain, and the fire truck engines.

"Williamson Manor has had a mandatory evacuation in place all evening."

"But I live on the top floor, in a third-floor penthouse." You know, she wanted to add, the expensive units facing the park.

Not wanting to deliver bad news, he closed his eyes for a second. Empathy radiated from his hardworking face. "Sorry, every floor in that building is a total loss. Part of the roof caved in due to the storm. On the bright side, you survived that giant sinkhole. Bear with us. We'll be taking a large group of folks over to the high school gym, in a few minutes."

Did he say total loss? "Becca!" She screamed into a silent phone. Most likely, her sister had to put her on hold to handle an emergency at the hospital. "Becca," she shouted again, as tears began to flow. "Becca," she repeated, before she hung up. Her sister couldn't even call her back. "Thanks for the phone," she said to the fireman. A large gray glove reached for the phone, but Linda decided to call Eric. "Wait, sorry. I have to make another call."

He nodded and tipped his helmet. Rivulets of water poured onto his nose. "No worries."

At least an hour had passed since she left the diner.

Etienne and Eric were either in a similar predicament, or, they were sitting in a warm condo having hot chocolate and planning world domination. But Eric's number had been in the recently called panel of her nonfunctioning, sodden cellphone. His number had not even made it to the contacts section yet. Curse words flooded her mind before she remembered the napkin at the bottom of her saturated coat.

Linda, sounding exasperated, interrupted the firemen who were still trying to communicate with the mother of the child. "Excuse me, I'm sorry to bother you again, but I have a piece of paper in my coat pocket. Do you think I could....?"

"No problem, Miss." The fireman slogged over to the truck and reached into the cab for her tweed coat. "Here you go," he said, handing her the heavy article of clothing. "Looks like the rain might be moving west," he added, with a kindhearted smile.

"Thanks, I'll return your cell in a minute."

"Okay," he replied with a wave. She watched him jog back to his partner and the woman with the baby.

When Linda reached into her front pocket for the napkin, it dissolved, becoming a glob of white mush in her hands. Eric's phone number had become illegible. Frustrated, Linda walked back to the fireman and handed him the phone. The first responders had saved her life and yet she felt anger churning in her gut. "Thanks," she said, holding back a sob and not wanting to sound ungrateful. Sadly, the tone of her voice didn't sound appreciative, but she hoped that experienced firemen were used to what had to be shock-induced behavior.

No one would notice if she began to weep gallons of tears. The tears would roll down her cheeks onto the road, mingle with the rain, perhaps meeting up with her car. From there, they might turn the corner where they would float down the street and come across her designer suits, her elegant shoes, framed photos of her parents, her computer, her books and even her bed. Possessions didn't matter anymore. Her sister mattered, and she found herself thinking, Eric mattered. If only she could figure out how to reach him. Saving the dog-gone world from hate mattered more now, than ever. And, as fate would have it, she had a fire burning within. If ever there was a good time to cry, this was it.

# CHAPTER EIGHT

Linda sat on a cot at the high school gym. The Fighting Tides logo was emblazoned on an entire wall. Each cobalt wave had giant incisors that crested onto a round circle made up of basketballs, soccer balls, tennis balls and footballs. It made her reflect on months of cold morning practice sessions with the marching band. The team spirit, the camaraderie, the discipline had made playing the flute worth every minute. The entire experience more than music, but about life, and getting along with other humans.

"Excuse me, Miss. Is anyone sitting here?" A stranger with wild, graying hair and worn clothes pointed at another cot. Black and white bangs were plastered to her forehead.

Linda shook her head to indicate the woman should sit down. "Please, have a seat." Disheveled and frumpy, the homeless looking senior citizen sloshed around in wet, pink sneakers.

Gently, as if carrying something breakable, the middle-aged matron placed a soaked plastic bag on the floor. "Wild weather, huh?"

Linda sighed and nodded. "This is the worst I've seen around here."

The woman smiled. "That's 'because you're a young'un. The town had to be rebuilt after a storm in 1963. They called it Tropical Storm Jennifer-Katherine. Hard to forget when your mother's name is Katherine and your daughter is Jennifer."

"Sounds horrible."

"It was, but this might be worse. We were evacuated a few hours ago and told we can't go back. Good thing I had sense enough to run back and grab my husband."

Dog-tired, but glad to have someone to talk to, Linda looked around wondering where the woman's husband might be waiting. "Is he here?"

The woman nodded and began her dramatic story. "The firemen yelled at all of us to leave before the roof caved down on top of us. I didn't have time to get anything but this musty coat." She fooled with her messy hair. "A hat would have helped. Anyway, the lights went out and I don't see very well. They came in and yanked me right off my couch. I know they were trying to rescue me and, of course I'm thankful, but the sudden blast of cold air, the grip on my arm that will probably bruise, and the way they yelled like obnoxious referees, seemed rude to me. Maybe someday I'll complain about it."

The words, 'I'm thankful, but', made Linda cringe. "Well, they saved your life."

"They sure did. The roof fell in about a minute after we left."

The woman's harrowing account made Linda's hand move to her chest. She remembered the fireman telling her the roof on her apartment had collapsed. The sprawling complex covered over two city blocks. It had a pool, tennis courts and a gate on all sides. It didn't surprise Linda that she never saw this woman before. "Do you live in Williamson Manor?"

"Well, I did."

"Oh my God, it's a miracle you're alive. Does your daughter live with you?"

"Nah, she's a fancy lady living the high life in Connecticut. They have two kids; cutest grandbabies ever." The woman fussed with her purse and pulled out a photo. "Tell me the truth; have you ever seen cuter kids?"

Linda looked at the photo and shook her head. "They are adorable. Do you see them often?"

"Never had the chance, because she's still mad at her momma about something stupid I said about her maniac husband. Funny thing is, he's been cheating on her all along and now they're getting a divorce. Her momma ain't an idiot. That man looked and acted like the devil."

"I'm sorry."

"Don't be sorry. I'm glad my Jennifer is getting away from that dark character who practically ruined her life. That man had serious drinking problems. He hit her and believe it or not, he even hit the kids. That man, if you can call him that, even kicked the dog. Now she can start again. Those little ones deserve a good dad."

"Maybe now they'll come visit you, and your husband."

The woman reached down, gingerly picking up the white plastic bag, removing a large brass urn. When she sat back up, she appeared out of breath. "This is Rick, my husband. My best friend and the love of my life. That nasty fireman almost didn't let me run back and get him."

# CHAPTER NINE

Beyond exhausted, Linda pretended to sleep, while her mind mulled over ways to reach Eric. Every imaginary road made her feel like a hamster in a maze; one where she cowered hopelessly at several dead ends. Finally, around three in the morning, after tossing and turning and listening to whispered sob stories of other flood victims, she had a kernel of an idea. The guy at the door of the Bootstrap Bar and Grill, acted like a friend of Eric's, maybe he would have a phone number. At daybreak she fell asleep thinking about the rustic place where the two of them had danced, and shared memorable kisses.

Rays of sunlight pierced through tiny windows at the top of the gymnasium. A new day promised a fresh start. Perhaps the beginning of a new life. Her car, her home, clothes, and everything were gone. The Red Cross volunteers offered her soap and a toothbrush. They allowed her to use a phone so she could call her employer, but something made work feel unimportant. *Did it matter anymore?* Everything needed to change.

She thought about the old woman with her urn and her daughter, Jennifer. People like Jennifer's husband were going to have an involuntary attitude adjustment. Hitting children and kicking dogs was beyond unacceptable. It might take karma decades to catch up with his sinister and vile ways. The woman's story had cleared any doubt with crystal lucidity, making the enemy real, almost personal. "No, I don't need to call my work. Thanks." The mission had begun.

Later, that afternoon, she planned on getting a taxi ride to the far side of town, to the Bootstrap. First, she needed an ATM machine to withdraw enough money for a new coat, clean pants and dry shoes. "It's been ages since I've been to my high school," she told the lady at the door. "I'm all turned around. Can you point me towards Main Street?"

During those few seconds, while discussing the way to the bank, listening to the kind volunteer ramble on about the directions, Linda's mind wandered onto yet another radical idea. The thought of it made her heart beat faster. She couldn't wait to share her epiphany with Eric. Foolproof! An act of God had flooded everything, but it might have opened a celestial door of opportunity regarding the plan. A plan she began to think of as the Happy War. A gentle war against every form of hate, that she, along with Eric's team, could nip in the bud before the evil could germinate into something big and devastating. *This will be great,* she thought, nodding as if she understood all the complex directions.

"Thank you," Linda sang to the volunteer. The woman wore a Fighting Tides sweatshirt and deserved a hug. Linda didn't want to make eye contact, because the previous evening, when the first responders brought her to the gymnasium, this same volunteer had asked her to fill out several forms. At the time, she was mentally and physically drained, so she left the papers blank. Every single one. She didn't sign any releases or legal waivers. With everything going on, maybe she thought it would be easier to fill them out later.

Throngs of people had swarmed around the front tables asking for assistance. There had been so much commotion. Children cried for their mothers in a constant stream of panic. Babies tested their lungs by screaming, and also the endless patience of those looking for dry diapers. Radios blared with the news, telephones with strange ringtones rang continuously, doors slammed, teens ran around with squeaky tennis shoes and small alarms such as the ones on a coffee maker or a dryer, buzzed. Meanwhile, the jarring sounds of emergency sirens entered from outside. Of course, in the ensuing melee, they never noticed, she didn't fill out the forms. And, unless this woman remembered her face, nothing could get in the way of her fresh new ploy.

Turning to leave, she mumbled another, "Thank you." *This will be fun!*

Like sparkplugs, her mind ignited the fire under her bizarre new strategy. *All of it could work, but only if Becca and Gary are willing to go along with the colossal, somewhat morbid charade entailing my demise.* Linda smiled to herself, thinking about faking her death. Since she didn't have a home to go to and they wouldn't find a body, the authorities would presume she had succumbed to the ravages of the giant flood. She envisioned the cemetery, bouquets of flowers and the preacher saying kind things. Her boss, the graphic designers, and a collection of salespeople from her office sullenly crowding into a non-denominational church. *I need to speak to my sister, now,* she thought, stepping out of the gym into the cool, damp air.

Outside, she realized that using her ATM card would give her away faster than a Ferrari on the Autobahn. Accessing even a dollar of her savings account would tip off the authorities and they'd know she didn't drown.

Linda walked along the sidewalk and looked up at the cloud-filled sky. *This has to work*, she thought, feeling free and untethered. The minor frustration involving money, paled in comparison to the logjam of things she wanted to tell Eric. In her hand, she carried her smelly coat and purse. She wore a Red Cross tee-shirt and wrapped a dry blanket over her shoulders like a shawl. Her pants were damp, but at this point, she didn't really care.

Unbeknownst to anyone, she had survived. Ahead, a vast unfamiliar dark abyss, beckoned quietly at the crossroads of her life. To be or not to be, wrote Shakespeare. In the big scope of things, not too many people have a chance to take steps into a mysterious new life. When the light changed, she giggled, feeling free of old responsibilities, burdens, bills and lease payments. The universe had brought her a new set of tasks. It was time to be incognito; an unrecognizable cog in the planetary wheel of fortune, an invisible wizard or perhaps an angel of mercy. Either way, she was ready for her assignment and whatever new duties the world threw in front of her. Facing the unknown felt strange, and liberating at the same time.

When Linda looked down at the gutters, she noticed they were filled with personal items. Necessary things like shoes, pacifiers and baseball hats were tangled into branches, leaves and trash. There were books, magazines and socks. She scanned the street, wondering if she'd see her car or anything familiar. The water had receded, leaving behind broken pallets, sodden boxes and a plethora of junk. Lost dogs wandered around sniffing candy wrappers and Styrofoam containers. A naked doll with matted hair and one missing arm, peered out from under a truck. Though sad for the little girl who lost the doll, Linda, being of sound mind and body felt comfortable in her own skin. Pulling the blanket tightly around her shoulders, she took her first steps without remorse, fully confident, and ready to do what needed to be done.

# CHAPTER TEN

Her shoes squeaked throughout the entire, chilly, two-mile walk. The noise created a backbeat rhythm she hummed along with until she stood in front of the hospital's double doors and realized there would be no sneaking up on her sister. Becca worked in the ICU. It wouldn't be easy to get to her floor without being seen, especially heard. Maybe the blanket she squeezed with icy fingers could help pass her off as a patient.

"Hello," Linda said when she reached the Nurse's Station. "I'm looking for Becca Wood."

"You just missed her," a young nurse replied with a generous smile. "In fact, she's out for a couple of weeks on a well-deserved vacation."

*What? How did she avoid telling her sister?* "I see," Linda replied brightly, though she felt disappointed.

"Can anyone else help you?"

"Nope, I'm good." She turned to leave, but heard the nurse mention Hawaii.

Linda spun around, "Did I hear you say she's going to Hawaii?"

The young woman smiled from ear to ear. "Yes. Isn't that exciting? Her husband got tickets at the last minute. Something about a famous PGA golf tournament. They were supposed to have a staycation at home, and then he showed up wearing a coconut bra over his parka yesterday. Her husband is a riot."

"Thanks," Linda said, thinking about her sister's fool of a husband. A riot, if it meant an insurrection, then, maybe. And, while Gary probably didn't have a bad bone in his entire lug of a body, he certainly wasn't funny. She waved at the woman at the counter while her shoes made funny little shrieks all the way back to the elevators. *Sorry Becca, but I might have to ruin your trip to paradise.*

Once outside, in front of the hospital, she took a deep breath. Without her sister, she was screwed. No money, no new clothes, no transportation and no way to get to the Bootstrap to interrogate that bouncer at the door. How would she go about finding a needle in a haystack without attracting too much attention? Going back to the high school and sleeping on one of those uncomfortable cots again wasn't a desirable option. Dreams of saving the world were washing down the drain, heading for the sewer, when she heard what sounded like her name.

"Lin—Daaa,"

Blinking several times, she squinted across the wide boulevard seeing someone flailing his arms and jumping up and down like a goofball. Eric?

If ever, in her entire life she felt happier to see another person, she couldn't remember it. Her heart did backflips as she crossed the street. Tugging the blanket tighter, she told herself to be cool, but didn't think it could be possible. A literal heart-throb and from a distance, a good-looking guy, looked anxious to see her. Her, the homeless, shivering wet woman with squeaky shoes and messy hair.

"Linda, what happened?" he asked, as she approached. "I've been worried sick."

Though music to her ears, she kept a poker face, pursed her lips and shushed him by putting an index finger to her mouth. "Be quiet. I've got a whale of a story and a huge alteration, or call it a twist if you will, to our original plan."

Relief flooded his face. He beamed at her and stared into her eyes. "Okay, I'm just glad you're alive. When I noticed Grand Avenue and Main were both flooded out, I tried calling you. I kept on dialing your number and you never answered." He tried to embrace her but noticed the blanket and wet coat. "I bet you're cold."

"Ah, freezing. Can we go to your car?"

"Let's hurry." He grabbed her by the hand and pulled her towards a crowded parking lot located several blocks away. By the time they got there, he could see her quivering like a chihuahua in a blizzard. Eric started the engine, waited for the heater to kick in before asking, "So, tell me, what happened?"

# CHAPTER ELEVEN

Warm and safe, Linda sat on Eric's couch next to a lodge-style, wooden coffee table. He had made her a cup of hot chocolate. "Marshmallows?"

"Of course," she replied, watching him toss a handful into her cup. Earlier that evening, while Eric drove the two of them to his residence, she had filled him in on how her car had swept into the undercurrent and floated away, only to stop in a sink-hole. She described how she swam to the edge of what looked like a river, flowing rapidly down the road, and how a fireman had wheeled her to safety. Sharing the harrowing ordeal with Eric made the whole episode less intense and more like recounting a catastrophic soap opera.

The soothing and delicious cocoa calmed her nerves. "This is yummy, thanks." Linda could tell this wasn't your typical condominium. With views of the entire valley, the place would qualify as a bachelor pad for someone with a huge bank account, willing to pay enormous association fees. The luxu-rious home had high ceilings, skylights and shutters on the windows, and only shared one wall with the neighbor. When they entered through the kitchen, from the garage, she had noticed the latest stainless appliances, mosaic tiles on the backsplash, ivory cabinets with elegant handles and granite countertops. Eric's impressive condo took her breath away.

"So, your phone died in the flood?"

"It did." She wrapped all her fingers around the cup, inhaling the scent of sweet chocolate. "But that's not all that died. Listen Eric, I have this weird idea that might help." *Please, let him be on my side about this*, she thought in an effort to communicate or alert her sleeping guardian angel. Without Eric's support, she'd be in trouble; a fish out of water, lost in a sea of desperation; a melting marshmallow, dissolving, before it could bring happiness to others.

"Go ahead, I'm listening. You know I love your wild ideas." He leaned closer and planted a kiss on her cheek.

The kiss made her smile. It made the story difficult to tell, especially because she felt silly in Eric's loose-fitting, plaid, pajamas. "Look, this is serious. You can't tell anyone except the people involved with our 'happy war'."

"Happy war? Is that what we're calling it?"

"Sure, but that's not the thing." She paused, placed the cup down next to the spoon and reached for his hand. Silly looking or not, an unexpected burst of confidence shot out from somewhere within her soul, making her jabber like an animated canary. "Hear me out first, before you tell me I've flipped. I think this is the right way for me to proceed." Linda watched his eyes and wasn't sure if this would be too much to ask anyone, but she could tell, he found her entertaining. Maybe the pajamas made her look like one of those sad clowns at the circus.

"The only glitch I can see is my sister being in Hawaii, but maybe we can cross that bridge when we get to it." She let go of his hand, moved her arms erratically and pointed towards an imaginary future. The words in her mind weren't coming out the way she intended. The vision she wanted to share, locked and buried in a Pandora-like box. "I have to do this now. It's almost like fate weaseled into our plans, in a good way." She picked up the mug. "And don't forget; only our team can know about this."

Eric's face beamed with kindness. An expression that oozed love and acceptance but also confusion. He tilted his head and brushed a few loosened tendrils from her ponytail behind her ears. "You're beautiful, but I have no idea what you're talking about."

After stirring the bottom of the cup, she held up the palm of her other hand but looked down at her toes to gather her thoughts. *It was getting harder instead of easier.* "Eric, I don't have a place to live. My parents are hospitalized in Canada. I can't go to work. I have no furniture, and outside of some superficial friends at my office and a psycho ex-boyfriend, no one will miss me. You're the only human being who will know the truth about what happened to Linda Simpson." She licked the spoon clean and held it in front of her mouth like a microphone.

Linda compressed her lips and spoke like a broadcast journalist with a funny accent. "Last night, during the horrendous flood sweeping the area," she paused for dramatic effect, "this hardworking, single woman who grew up here, in our town, lost the battle with the biggest storm of the decade, and drowned. Rescue workers searched all night and are still trying to locate a body."

He covered his mouth to suppress a laugh. "You want to fake your death?"

"Why not? It's perfect." The spoon made a loud clink against the side of the mug.

"What about when your car turns up?"

"So, what if it does? That doesn't mean I didn't climb out and drown immediately afterwards."

"Didn't you say firemen were there to help? Won't they remember you?"

"Maybe, but I doubt it. It's not like they took a picture. The rain came down hard. Even if the fireman took pictures, faces would look distorted. You're in the clear too, because no one knows we're dating."

"What about your sister?"

Oh, jumping frog legs, this long-haired dude listened to everything she said. Her mind whirled with excitement but his question pushed her off the proverbial podium. Quietly, she stirred the sediment of sweet cocoa, sucking the syrupy chocolate from the bottom, as a diversion, while her mind pondered his logical question. As she slurped, and thought about what to say, he looked at his watch. For goodness sakes, did he understand how important this was to their plan? He had to take her seriously. This was serious.

She set the mug back down, "Okay, that's the only monkey wrench. They went to Hawaii for two weeks. My funeral would ruin all their fun. Can you imagine? I spoke to her after the accident and then we lost contact."

"You're right, that could be a problem, but she probably won't file a missing person's report until the two weeks is over, because you spoke to her. It's genius."

Relieved that he thought it might work, she exhaled. "My biggest problem is my bank account. I can't access any of my money. If I do, they'll know." Pointing at the flannel pajamas, she continued, "and though I love your taste in sleepwear, I need clothes, a place to live," she looked down at her feet, "and shoes. I need new boots."

"I love your enthusiasm." He reached for her and took her

into his arms. "I'm sorry but I like the way you think. Every word is driving me wild."

Embarrassed to have shared her crazy idea, she felt uncomfortable with the realization that she needed him. Sure, she wanted his attention and all the romance, but now she felt old-fashioned and out of place. Without a career and a home, she became another 'needy' woman looking for food and shelter. To hell with it, she thought, succumbing to his powerful arms and his bedroom eyes. "With Becca on the islands, no one will look for me for weeks," she muttered under her breath, hoping Eric was worth the risk.

"And by that time, let's hope our intravenous application of medication, into the veins of the world, will have taken effect. Meanwhile, of course, I'm thrilled to have a new roommate." His lips brushed hers and his arms tightened around her shoulders. "I could get used to having you around," he whispered. "Would you mind living here with me?"

Her eyes locked into his. *Please, she prayed, please be the man I think you are. Don't let me down.* "Can I take off your glasses?" His pupils grew larger when she lifted the tortoise-shell spectacles off his enormous, sexy nose.

"Sure, but I won't be able to see much."

"That's wonderful. I need you to listen. And listen well. I am a woman who has been in control of everything my entire life. Where I worked, who I talked to, where I vacationed, even the street I called home. I made my choices and slept in the mess of a bed I created. That being said, I am submitting myself to you, Eric Anderson, because to answer your question about living with you, I don't have a choice. I'm literally homeless." She put his glasses next to the cup on the coffee table. "Without those glasses you have to rely on me. I have power again."

"It's all about power, with you isn't it?" He nestled closer and his nose touched hers.

"It's the constant dynamic related to being female. Especially an educated woman who overthinks everything. We work hard to be independent, but if we want a relationship, we have to take a few steps back." In this case, there were no steps to dial back. Somewhere in her chest, she felt her heart sending up loud, repetitive messages about shutting her gargantuan mouth. At this breathless moment, she felt animal magnetism, the universe, the storm, and his caramel-colored bedroom eyes, all conspiring to take her down. Down a path of less resistance, less control, she swirled into a beckoning whirlpool of what could potentially be, true love. *Let it happen, she said to her herself. There is no net, no parachute or rescue team. Fall gently. Go.*

"Without my glasses it all makes sense," he teased." His lips touched hers and they kissed. "You'll have all the power in the world in about two weeks. In fact, you'll be the most powerful woman in the world." The next kiss was longer. His lips took their time exploring her mouth, in a memorable, romantic kiss that seized her soul. His warm hands moved up and under the loose-fitting pajama top.

Perplexed about the 'two weeks' comment, she put a hand on his chest, pushed him away, and took a breath. "Huh?"

"The Happy War, as you call it, begins in one week. I've done some research and you'll be meeting the team next week. Don't forget Etienne stayed here last night and he's coming back tonight around eight."

Impressed, but still bewildered, she rubbed her face where his five o'clock shadow had rubbed her cheek. "This is really happening?"

Pulling her close, he buried his face under her curls and mumbled, "Oh yeah, big time."

# CHAPTER TWELVE

They spent the next few hours in bed. At some point, Eric went upstairs to his home office to prepare for the meeting with Etienne. When he turned on the printer, Linda awoke to the hum of technology murmuring through the walls. What a difference a few hours had made. One day ago, she had slept on an uncomfortable cot, and now, she luxuriated like a spoiled housecat on high thread-count sheets, in a cherry-wood sleigh bed.

While his pajamas were comfortable, she hoped he had something different to wear. She moved to his walk-in closet, and the lights came on automatically. "Hello," Linda said, surprised by the motion-sensor lighting. Gray men's suits lined one side like Confederate soldiers, and on the other side, an entire row of white, long-sleeved shirts hung like friendly ghosts. In her search for jeans, sweaters and tennis shoes, she pulled open a drawer, to find men's underwear and paired socks. The next drawer had white tee-shirts. The bottom drawer had more flannel pajamas. On a lower shelf, she saw men's polished dress shoes, wingtips, penny loafers and slip-ons with tassels.

"Looking for something?" his voice made her jump.

"I'm just trying to locate casual clothes. Guess I'm not ready to face Etienne in your jammies."

He slapped his forehead, "Oh, no, I should have taken you shopping today. I promise we'll go tomorrow." He grabbed her by the hand pulling her into the next room, where an equally decked out, cedar-lined closet, had coats, sweaters, robes, jeans, and all manner of men's active sportswear, hanging from wooden hangers.

"Shopping? I'm sure glad we didn't shop this afternoon." The thought of his muscular loins, powerful hands and the way they had moved above her, made her giggle. When she recalled her own ecstatic moans, she blushed and turned to look at the clothes. "Right now, this should work. Would you mind if I picked out something to wear?"

"It's all men's stuff."

His comment made her heart sing. It was exactly what she had hoped, precisely what she wanted to hear. No residual women and their left-over outfits. No bottles of dried out makeup, old bras, pink razors or used, lacy thongs from one, or more old flames. Glad to know she didn't need to worry about stepping on any toes. Relief flooded, lightening her mood. "It's fine with me, if it's fine with you," she finally murmured, marveling at his exquisite taste. Her fingers fanned a collection of soft cotton. "I love these vintage flannel shirts."

"Wear whatever you like. You probably look good in anything."

Dying to try his designer jeans, she held up a pair and could tell they would never fit all her curves. Shoot, she thought, reaching for black bicycle pants. At least those had a touch of stretch. Topped off with a red, buffalo-plaid flannel shirt, she liked her reflection in the mirror. Today felt like her birthday. Today, her official new life as Eric's girlfriend would begin.

"Wow," he exclaimed, stepping back into the closet. "I can't believe those are my clothes. They sure look better on you."

"It's the freckles. People say they make me look younger than my age."

Enthralled with the vision in front of him, his mouth agape, he forgot to close his mouth. "Whatever it is, I like it."

His open mouth found her eager lips. "You are stunning," he whispered into her hair.

The kiss in the closet lasted several minutes. Finally, Linda reminded Eric of the time.

Eric smiled and shook his head. "Life can be so unfair. Come on." She followed him through several large, well-appointed rooms to the kitchen, where they stopped in front of a massive, built in refrigerator. "Do you want to help me put together a tray of snacks?"

"Of course, I'd be happy to help."

"Can I offer you a glass of wine?"

"No thanks, but bottled water would be great, I'm parched."

"How many bottles would you like?" He opened the fridge stocked with shelves of green drinking water.

She retrieved a bottle. "Oh, I like sparkling water."

"Etienne is from the exact town where it's bottled. But, being from France, he prefers wine."

"Don't generalize. Not all French people drink wine."

"Right," he said with a touch of sarcasm. He placed a platter on the center island and a cutting board. "We're having cheese, olives and wine for our snack tonight. "Later on, will you join us for a small glass?"

*Of course,* Linda wanted to shout. Her emotions were

bubbling all over the room like the effervescent water in the bottle. Everything seemed like suspended animation. A magical haze floated in front of her eyes, filtering out negative thoughts, creating the perception of ethereal happiness. Perhaps she had died in that terrible storm, and now, here she stood, in a parallel universe. Maybe even heaven. "Will you serve red wine? I think Frenchmen prefer red wine."

# CHAPTER THIRTEEN

Etienne listened carefully to Linda's tragic tale. He couldn't argue with her idea to remain missing. At least until their plans had moved into place.

Linda will need a new identity and a passport. "Eric, this won't be easy," Etienne noted.

"You're right. But I'm having her stay in the States."

"She'll still need a driver's license and a new name."

They sat at the dining table with the cheese platter in the middle. Seven, 8x10 inch photographs were laid out around the food. Eric picked up his glass and toasted Etienne, "To the Happy War." The glasses clinked, sounding like tiny bells.

"The Happy War," Linda and Etienne repeated.

"Linda," Eric set his glass aside. "We'll worry about your name and all that later. I want you to take a look at our team." Surprised to see her face among the others, she remembered he had asked her to stare at his cellphone for a few seconds before Etienne arrived. "Of course, this lovely mug is you, and your area is the East Coast of the U.S. I'd send you to Canada, but nowadays they ask for a passport. All the waterways, canals, and reservoirs will be in your hands." His tone sounded like a man giving a motivational speech.

"If you need to hire anyone, do it, but only if you think you can trust them. Basically, you'll have a week to reach each of the two major sections on your map. The more I learn about you, the more I think you can do this alone. And, in order to make things easier, I'll also be providing color coded documents that match the routes you'll be driving." He set her photo down and moved to the next one. "Keep an eye out for my neon sticky notes."

"As you know," he picked up his own photo and placed it next to hers, "I'm going back to the Middle East." Next, he picked up Etienne's photo and smiled. "Here is our man behind the Seine, the Rhine, and the blue Danube. He'll be taking care of all Western, Central and Eastern Europe."

Etienne reached over and took the photo. "Where did you get this? This is ancient." The picture showed a younger Etienne, wearing doctor's scrubs.

Eric waved him off. "I know it's you, and you know it's you, and that's all that matters. I've kept that photo for a long time. There's nothing wrong with looking like a young stud, my friend."

Etienne laughed and put the photo down.

"Next, we have Juan Garcia. My amigo from Italy is on his way. He'll be here soon. I imagine Giulia won't be thrilled, but he'll be back in her loving arms in about two weeks. I already mentioned that he's our West coast guy. He knows every waterway in the west, from the Columbia up north, and all the way south, as far as they go. With parts of the Rio Grande in drought, he'll be able to concentrate on the rivers in Venezuela, the Esmeraldas and of course the Amazon. Juan has many friends that he trusts, so he may need to hire guys that speak Spanish to help him out." He tapped the photo with his index finger. "It's a good thing Juan understands business and warfare."

"This is Sparky." Eric held up the picture and Etienne nodded. "Whacked out electrician, and amazing man. He'll have to figure out a way to handle some giant areas of China, Japan and Korea. I might be wrong, but I think he knows a little Mandarin. I'm looking forward to working with him again." Linda didn't see much in the picture of Sparky. The photo showed a grinning man in a floppy hat with black sunglasses.

"Well, he looks friendly", she surmised.

When Eric put the photo down and picked up another, she felt her heart do a back flip. *That old man? Are we desperate?* "This is Jack." He turned the picture towards Linda who tried not to laugh. With a serious expression on his frail, wrinkled visage, the old man in the photo looked as if he couldn't lift more than a liter of water. "He's going to Africa. In fact, we'll probably take the first leg of our flight together."

"Last of all, we have Milo, our techie. He's going to stay in one place, at a safe house, where we will be able to communicate with each other. Milo will keep track of all our messages. He'll be the heart, or the command central of the entire operation." He looked around and smiled at Etienne. "Well any questions?"

"Have you found a medicine with lasting results?" Etienne wanted to know.

"I think I did. Fluoxetine has a few issues. Suicide is one of them. We're looking to create peace, not global disaster. The SNRI restores balance. I'm sorry Linda, what I mean is, there's a serotonin norepinephrine reuptake inhibitor, as opposed to an SSRI. The SRIs block the action of the serotonin transporter, which increases the extracellular concentrations of the serotonergic neurotransmitters."

Etienne asked, "You're not talking about fenfluramine, are you?"

"Hell no, those cause heart-valve problems and act like a dopamine." Eric shook his head.

Linda looked lost and stifled a yawn. This part of the conversation sounded Greek to her.

"Fen-Phen used to be a fad. I'm sure you've heard of it. People used to think they'd lose a bunch of weight taking it. But that's not what we're using. Cocaine is an SRI but it's not selective enough. I'm fairly sure a generic version of an SNRI called valafaxine would do the trick. I'm also thinking of fast acting and plentiful ketamides, otherwise known as Special K, but everything has side effects. It has to be combined, so the neurotransmitters such as serotonin, are increased. Monoamines only work sixty percent of the time and nothing happens for over a week. Since some people don't react, and are resistant, we have to blend it with another pharmaceutical called modafinil."

Etienne nodded, "The Foreign Legion used that drug during covert reconnaissance missions. Not too many side effects."

"Good to know, doc" he sighed. "There's only one thing that reverses the effects within the frontal cortex, and that's Tryptophan."

"Mon Dieu. Could be a problem around Thanksgiving," he chuckled.

"We might have to take that chance. Hopefully, the U.S. will have learned to get along with everyone by then. Besides, that's almost a year away and tryptophan changes naturally to serotonin in the brain anyway. So, I think we're safe. I mean, you're the doctor. What do you think?"

"I think too much serotonin can also cause trouble. Confusion, diarrhea, and rapid heart rates: It's called serotonin syndrome and can cause seizures and be life threatening.

Pineapple, tofu, salmon, nuts, dates, turkey, dairy, fish, red meat, even chocolate has tryptophan. In normal societies people eat varied diets that include some or all of these things. Add in an SNRI and it might be too much."

"How much is too much?" Linda tried to interject.

"There are also people all over the world who take migraine medications or lithium, which increases serotonin levels too. I checked this out and did the numbers. The dosage we administer must be low. It can't interact with other drugs. An average dose for a depressed patient is 75mg. per day. Anything over 200 mg. will cause high blood pressure and other complications. Since we'll only have the one shot for every water supply, we also have to watch out for overlapping areas where dosages can double up. We're hoping for a long-term solution. Rome wasn't built in a day. It'll have to be a slow burn. I'm thinking very low doses will make a difference, eventually. It's the only way to be safe."

Linda nodded and felt more confused than ever. "Will we have different amounts for different applications? A small creek versus a bottomless lake?"

"Of course, everything will be clearly marked with a number that corresponds with the GPS coordinates on your phone. The latitude and longitude of every waterway will be easy to see. We're going after major rivers and large water towers. The parts per gallon will be the trick. Rivers fluctuate with the tides of the moon. Sometimes they are low from drought. A small creek has movement, but the bottomless lake stands still. We'll take all of that into consideration."

"Eric," Etienne interrupted. "I don't mean to be a killjoy, but do you think we should tone it down and use botanicals? There's Kava and Valerian in a lactose base. The worst that can happen are some skin rashes."

Eric leaned back in his chair. "I don't know. Those things

would need a much bigger dose. They work for some, and not for others. And lactose is cloudy. Not to mention, some people are intolerant. I'm almost thinking we could use passionflower and valerian root for places that aren't having major problems, such as Hawaii. Maybe Kava-Kava, as you suggest. They eat a lot of pineapple, and the islands appear to be a relaxed place to begin with." He waved his hand in a sideswiping motion. "Nah, let's leave Hawaii out."

"Australia?"

"We'll leave them out too. Besides, they are in the middle of a drought."

Eric's face looked distressed. This had to be a smooth operation. "Let's reconvene tomorrow after I do some math." He caught Linda's eye and looked up at Etienne. "I will be shopping for part of the morning but in the afternoon, I'm buckling down. No distractions."

Linda looked down at the table. "Don't look at me," she replied. Etienne burst into laughter.

# CHAPTER FOURTEEN

The next morning, Linda felt her heart jump at the sound of banging at the front door. The doorbell rang, followed by more loud knocking. Eric pulled back the covers. "I'll get it." Grabbing his robe off the back of the door, he moved to yank back the curtain, and spotted a non-descript, white vehicle. "This is too early, whoever you are," he grumbled, rubbing his eyes on the way downstairs. She heard the front door open, followed by a thundering male voice that reverberated throughout the entire condo.

"Buddy!" The ear-splitting yell shook the building, making the double-paned glass windows quake. "Hola, mi amigo!" Must be one of the team members. But she couldn't remember which one. The clock said 7:01am. Judging from the hullabal-loo, it sounded like friends who hadn't seen each other in decades. When the voices quieted down, she put a pillow over her head, closed her eyes and fell asleep.

What seemed like seconds later, Eric stood next to the bed with his friend Juan Garcia. *He's the one with the booming voice.* "Wake up sleeping beauty. Linda, you have to meet Juan." Eric grabbed the pillow and threw it onto the plush carpeting. Linda placed both arms over her face to cover her eyes, accidentally uncovering a breast. Juan's laugh sounded like a snort. She wanted to die. Eric and his friend were acting like fourth graders.

*Was this for real*? Before she opened one eye, she had to make sure the sheets covered all her personal parts. Embarrassed, she tucked everything under her body and looked up. A brawny, dark-haired man with full lips, and giant shoulders stood there, smiling a crooked smile. "Hi?" This wasn't any way to wake up on the first day of her new life. *Where did Eric find this creepy guy who seemed to ogle every inch of her bare skin?*

"Eric you dog," Juan shouted at the top of his lungs. Then a few decibels lower he added, "I mean Giulia is a peach, but would you look at this?" He waved his arms above the bed. "Is Linda a super model?"

Eric laughed at his friend. "Believe it or not, her sister arranged a blind date." Shocked at all this childish behavior, Linda's fists clenched the covers. They were having a conversation about her as if she wasn't even in the same room. Super model? More like a piece of salmon at a fish market.

"Of course," Juan nodded. "I can see that being the only way you'd get lucky enough to find someone like her. Wow."

Eric slapped his friend on the back and told him to stop drooling. "I'm making coffee. Linda don't forget you need clothes. We're leaving in an hour."

"Clothes? What does she need clothes for?" Juan asked with a clever smirk.

Eric laughed. "You calling me a dog, huh? You? Give me a break. You haven't changed a bit. Does Giulia know you're still a complete scoundrel?" Juan moved into the hall and followed

Eric to the kitchen. "Lovely Linda needs clothes because the storm washed away her entire apartment, her car, and everything else. Now remind me how you like your frou-frou- coffee. This isn't espresso and I don't have those tiny Italian cups."

"I drink mine Americano, which for your edification, is regular black coffee and no, I don't hold my pinky in the air when I drink it." He watched Eric fill a mug. "Not all Italians drink cappuccino."

"You crack me up. Garcia is not Italian. You were born in Long Beach. All of a sudden you're Italian?"

"Awe, shut up, I'm Italian by osmosis. You should hear me order the pasta dishes. Perfect pronunciation and I'm working on the hand gestures."

"Whatever, dude. Must be love."

"I heard about the storm. News said an atmospheric river swooped into Riverside County, even washed away some old WWII military jets at March Air Base. The TV meteorologist called it a 'Once in a five-hundred-year storm'."

(Over in the bedroom, Linda had no choice but to slip into the same bicycle pants she wore the previous day. This time, she picked a black-watch plaid, flannel shirt. She hurried to the sauna-like bathroom and turned on the shower.)

Juan maintained his military hairstyle even though he worked a civilian job in Rome as a fashion buyer for a major department store. Eric worried his friend may have softened up from too much of the dolce vita, or sweet life with Giulia. It was time to bring him up to speed on their mission. "Remember Fallujah?"

"How can I forget? If you want to make a two-hundred and fifty-pound, grown man cry, just remind me of that bleeping hell hole."

"Sorry, but I want you to know I'm going back. This time,

I'll have a different type of ammunition. No one will be watching my back. I'm going alone."

"All that hair on your head making you lose your mind? Didn't you suffer enough?" He shook his head back and forth, staring into steaming coffee. "Shit, I'm still sorry I couldn't save you the first time. Good thing that Frenchie guy was there. What's his name again?"

"Etienne," Eric replied.

Juan inhaled, blowing out a puff of air like a semi-truck releasing an air brake. It mingled with the steam from the cup. "Right, Etienne. Thank God for him. Can you imagine? You were losing blood like a butchered calf."

"Shut up Juan, I try not to think about it."

They sat slurping the hot brew in silence until Linda showed up humming a tune. She went straight to the coffee maker and poured herself a cup. The alluring aroma of freshly ground coffee filled every room.

"Linda, Juan used to be an ammunition specialist."

She looked above her cup and inhaled the delicious smell. "Sounds like the exact person we need."

"See, what did I tell you? You're a natural. We need someone who can distribute small, dissolvable chemical weapons into springs, rivers, reservoirs, aqueducts etc. All water ways. You're a pro at this Juan. With your background in WMD's, we need you on our team."

"Sure, that's why I'm here. But you still haven't explained your application. Didn't you say this is going world-wide?"

"It is."

"Why would you need chemical weapons all over the world? The war is in the Mid-East."

"Not that kind of weapon, Juan. Not that kind of war. In fact, it's not really a war. These weapons will contain a chemical that increases 5-hydroxytrptamine."

Puzzled, Juan moved his head from side to side. His facial features indicated he didn't understand. "Eric, in case you forgot, I am working with high fashion designers these days. I don't remember the chemistry and physics they taught me in the Army. You'll have to make it easier, maybe spell it out. My job is about trends in the marketplace and cutting-edge style. You know, silk stripe sportscoats with pocket squares that match. I can spot a Gucci sock and an Armani raincoat a mile away. I may not look gentle, but I'm a different guy. In other words, I'm not a soldier anymore."

Eric wanted to interject something, but Juan held up a hand. He didn't fly over the ocean for nothing and had a bit more to say. Quietly, he set the mug down, and placed a hand over his heart. "I may not be the guy you remember, but I have a vague idea of HT receptors. Don't worry bud, it's not like I'm dashing away with a tail between my legs. You know I'm not a pansy. If this is important to you, let's do the hokey pokey. I'm in--all the way." Juan pursed his lips and nodded, as if to seal the deal. "Reporting for duty, Sir." He shouted, adding a salute.

Linda found it all quite entertaining and had to smile.

Eric pointed at her and began to lecture. "Great. Okay, listen up. We have this idea about creating peace on Earth, with something similar to the world famous, mood-enhancing drug called, Woezap. I know you want to laugh, but don't. It's a big idea, and we think it's doable. The test-center at my work, lets me fool around with various chemical solutions. I've narrowed it down to a cocktail of FDA approved drugs that will work on all humans and won't harm wildlife or fish. My laboratory, and the biopharmaceutical company our firm purchased last year, has stockpiles of compounds and substances available for testing. They do trials with serotonin reuptake inhibitors on rats, monkeys, rabbits and mice. Trust me; my corporation, which is now called Pendalon, has the happiest animal test subjects in the business."

Eric took a swig of coffee and continued his enthusiastic monologue.

"We also work with foreign companies that will ship me anything I want, in any amount, on credit. My income is part commission, which means they wouldn't suspect anything. The dosages we'll use can't be too high either, or it also could raise a red flag. I'm thinking the max dosage on any of these pills is usually 200 milligrams. There won't be any dispersing explosives or large reservoirs to hold the agent. Including you, we'll have seven people prepared to dispense manual transmission of small batches. First, we have to figure out how much I need to order. If you can help with any logistical aspects, that would be great. The pills have to be distributed in a balanced, equal dosage worldwide, so that the obvious consequences can be felt by all populations at the same time. Since the Tigris and the Euphrates flow south, I figured that's an easy way to reach millions, right there."

"Wow," Juan's face looked impressed and he finally comprehended the situation. "So, we're going to spread attitude adjustment medication all over the world?"

Linda put her cup down. "Slightly unethical, but yes, that's the basic plan. We're calling it the Happy War."

"Hoo-ah," Juan yelled, his face showing excitement. "This is great. I'm thrilled to serve. "I think Giulia will help too. She can go sailing on the Tiber and the Arno. We have friends who keep begging us to join them on Lake Como."

Linda smiled, thinking of photos she had seen of Northern Italy. "Aren't Italians always happy?"

"Most of the time, but everyone has their days. Right now, there's a massive volcano going off and you can't blame them for being worried about it."

"Mount Etna, or is it Vesuvius this time?" she asked with a faraway look in her eyes. She had never travelled overseas, so her thoughts turned to the photographs in her collection of travel, architecture, and geography magazines. Wet and ruined magazines she'd never see again.

"Neither. This time it's some previously dormant, super volcano called Campi Flegrei, near Naples. Thank God Giulia and I don't live anywhere near it."

"Juan," Eric interjected. "Rome is only one hundred and thirty miles from Naples. That's close. But let's get back to the subject, so I can take Linda shopping."

Eric placed his cup into the dishwasher. "Dissolvable gel-caps with 200mg. of powder will have to do the trick. I'm thinking a million-gallon water tower would need fifty pills. We need to begin at the mouth of the rivers, dropping them in groups of twenty-five for each span of twenty miles. If it's rugged terrain, they can be dumped every fifty miles. We can drop them from the air, from bridges, balloons, planes and boats."

"Etienne's doing all of Europe and Russia, and I'm sure he'll be glad to have help in the south from Giulia. His rock-solid alibi is about going home to visit relatives. Right now, he lives in Paris, but he grew up near a water bottling plant in Vergeze. The guy knows the lay of the land and the natural springs like the back of his hand."

"Both of you know there are some problems in the Crimean Peninsula of the Ukraine. Etienne will need to make sure he gets into that area, but it might be dangerous."

"Linda will handle the Eastern states. Jack will be busy in Africa; Sparky will have his hands full in Asia. Milo will relay all our transmissions—both internal and external communications--from our safe house in Victoria, Canada." He pulled the cup from Linda's fingers and opened the dishwasher. "If we do this correctly, it will be untraceable."

"Juan, we've got to go. I promise to be back in a couple hours. There's cheese, olives, bread in there, and not much else. Help yourself or take your sexy rental car down the road to the burger joint."

"Are you kidding? Cheese, olives and bread? I'm feeling at home all ready. Have fun shopping."

# CHAPTER FIFTEEN

Driving back from the mall, Linda asked Eric to turn up the heater. "Winter feels like it's taking its time this year. Look at the trees, no buds, nothing."

"That's another reason we can't jump into this. Some of the rivers in the world are still frozen. We can't exactly add anything to ice. Plus, it'd be too dangerous for my team." He reached over and squeezed her hand. "Hopefully, spring will pop over the horizon, soon."

"So, once everything's in place, you're thinking two weeks?"

"Normally, I'd say two weeks. Our operation might take less in some spots, and more in others. Don't forget the dosage will be watered down in some places and ramped up in others. There's no way to keep it even. During normal warfare, annihilation evens things out. In this case, I don't even want people to sneeze or have an allergic reaction. Our goal of course, is peace."

Our goal? Linda liked the sound of it. *We are a couple now,* she said to herself. Eric was fully aware the whole crazy shebang was her idea. Meanwhile, her twisted dream had grown legs, becoming a monster of global proportions with various nefarious complications. A type of Machiavellian scheme, where a hopeful end, justifies the means. And, while the team members sounded qualified enough to pull this off, she wondered how Eric would be able to come up with enough of the product without jeopardizing his career.

"Eric, I'm worried about your role in all of this. You're the point man. The one who will supply each team member with what we need. How are you going to pull this off without getting in trouble, or losing your job?"

At the red light, he turned to look at her. "Linda, I care about you. More than I ever cared about any woman." The light changed. His eyes returned to the road. "I'm hoping this relationship will grow, because I like being with you. You're smart, considerate, and on top of all that, you're gorgeous." He spoke slowly as if every word mattered. "I admit, my history with girls isn't too impressive, mostly because I work hard and can't tolerate stupidity. Guess what I'm trying to say is: most women play ridiculous mind games...also called the feminine mystique or something. You, on the other hand are real. You have a refreshing attitude that makes me want to hug you while I'm driving. Too bad I can't."

Her stomach rumbled. He heard it and laughed. "Speaking of being real, we better stop and get something to eat."

"Sounds a bit arrogant. Are you're trying to tell me I'll never go hungry if I hang out with you?"

He laughed again. "Oh Linda, I don't care about the job or the money. I care about you."

"And we'll eat what?"

"How's pizza with goat-cheese and sundried tomatoes?"

"That's not what I meant."

"I know what you mean. A few more adjustments to my

401K, my offshore accounts and wait for it...." A sudden turn brought them into a busy parking lot.

Linda watched him maneuver into a tight space. Her eyes studied his movements and the quick rotations of the steering wheel. "Almost there," he huffed on the last turn. Once the engine quieted down, he twisted towards her and took both hands into his. The gear shift held up their clasped hands. "Early retirement. I'm planning to hand in my resignation at the end of our operation. Around that time, everyone in the world should feel better about everything." He sealed his statement with a wink, adding, "More importantly, I'll have more time to be with you." Finally, he exhaled, as if saying it aloud would make it true.

Though she liked what he said, she didn't know what to say. In fact, she loved what he said, but visiting the penitentiary wasn't her style and though asking for clarification felt unromantic, she needed reassurance. "Eric, aren't they going to notice missing shipments of pharmaceuticals?"

"No, they won't, because it's a blended concoction made up of different substances. Let me explain. Several employees will conduct a sort of trial run, intended for small batches. There will subsequently be a gigantic slipup, due to an assembly plant error. Everyone in upper management has access to the computer. While the capsules are created, the processing data can be easily adjusted. I forgot to mention that Milo is not only our IT guy, but he also works for Pendalon.

Even though we are going to use name brand medicine, nobody will expect the drugs to be blended into a new concoction. Once together, our quality control person will deem them unusable. It happens all the time. They will mark that batch hazardous waste, and move the canisters to a location out back. There's a special truck that takes them to a dumpsite. This time however, Juan will swap out the truck and drive all of it to my garage. The security detail is minimal and Juan is a talented guy. He can do it. Anyway, we then distribute the stuff to our team, and voila, we hit the road. The house will be sealed, and I'll inform our homeowner's association we're on vacation. It's a win-win."

The words 'Our homeowner's association' went straight to her heart. She was a member of a homeowner's association? It would take time to get used to this couple talk, but she loved it. "Are you sure you want to retire?"

"That's a loaded question my sweet. Let's eat."

# CHAPTER SIXTEEN

At the condo, it felt like a party. Juan sat at the dining room table playing chess with Etienne. Two other guys watched television from the couch and a third guy had his head in the Sub-Zero.

"Hey Jack, you looking for the Holy Grail? "Eric slapped his scrawny friend on the back and pulled him out of the ice-box.

The man placed a jar of olives on the counter. "Mercy, Mother of God, as I live and breathe--in the flesh--the one and only Eric Anderson."

"Good flight?"

"Are you kidding? "Pointing to a large stain on his dark shirt, he continued. "They put me by the restrooms, and some kid threw up on me a few seconds before the plane landed. Plus, they only served peanuts. I'm starved."

"Linda, come meet Jack," Eric shouted from the kitchen. "Please." Juan and Etienne were introducing her to Milo and Sparky, as if they had known her for years. They were complimenting her new sweater and wanted to see what else they had bought. "Linda," he repeated, noticing she liked the male attention. "Stop flirting with the team. This is business" he yelled in a militaristic tone across the room.

*Aye, aye sir,* she wanted to say. "I'm coming, sheesh."

Eric stood next to a frail, old man. Possibly an octogenarian, who looked weaker than the other team members. "Linda, look into the depth of your soul, because if you have any sins, this man will know all about them." He laughed and pulled her close. "This is our resident, retired priest, who just flew over eight thousand miles to take part in the adventure of his life. Jack, let me introduce you to Linda, the softer, gentler side of our operation."

Jack glanced back and forth between Linda and Eric and nodded his head. "So far, I like what I see. Nice to meet you Miss," he chuckled, with a deferential bow. "Does your mother know you're hanging with the likes of these fellows?"

"She's already on a respirator from smoking all her life. Knowing too much about my troubles would finish her off." Then, in a softer tone she winked, and added, "Jack, let's keep her alive, okay?"

"Don't know how you do it, Eric." He grabbed the bottle of olives and moved to open a cupboard, searching for a bowl to dump the contents. "The higher ups appear to find favor with you, my old friend." After closing and opening a few more cabinets, he shrugged, and waited, until Eric handed him a dish.

"Higher ups? My boss approves of my work," Eric teased. "Maybe I'll get a raise."

"Oh, you know what I mean." Jack pointed at the ceiling. "Let's take these olives out to the chess champions." The elderly man moved towards the intense competition at the dining table.

"Checkmate," said Etienne with a chuckle. Linda sat down and introductions were made. When the game wrapped up, Eric dived into the basics which included general locations, the medicine, summaries of the larger rivers and details involved in the massive process.

"Any questions?"

Sparky broke the proverbial ice by asking the first question, "Can we use drones? Wouldn't it be more efficient? I'll be near the Himalayas working on the Yangtze and the Mekong. The Yangtze alone is over thirty-nine hundred miles long."

"If you know how to operate a drone at a professional level, without being seen by the government, it sounds good. Don't forget there shouldn't be anything to trace. The capsules dissolve immediately. If you take unnecessary risks, no one will come bail you out of a communist prison. Sparky, I imagine that's the last place you'd want to end up. Right?

Maybe hire one of those Sherpas. Put the caps into a flower and tell them it's a sacred ritual for someone who tried hiking Kilimanjaro. Think big and creative. You were selected for this assignment because you can think out of the box. By the way, the Nile is longer, bud."

Sparky swiped his arm through the air, as if to dismiss any argument about the length of rivers, and the behemoth scope of the upcoming project. "Jack has a better gimmick than all of us."

"That's what you think, eh?" Jack asked, popping an olive into his mouth.

"Sure," he pointed at the ceiling. "You've got the big guy on your side."

"True, but I plan on doing real missionary work while sailing the length of the Nile. There's also the Blue Nile, you know. There are plenty of rivers on the African continent and dense jungles filled with wild animals, giant man-eating ants, spiders and snakes. Don't worry about me Sparky, the big guy as you call him, and I, will both be busy."

Linda leaned over to Eric. "Do you think we should serve something with those olives? How about those delicious gourmet cheeses you served the other night?"

"Wow, I should have thought of that, sorry." He jumped up, and minutes later returned with a serving platter heaped with wrapped cheeses, a handful of knives and a loaf of crusty bread.

Etienne slathered one of the softer cheeses onto a slice of bread, then sipped water from a clear glass. He chewed slowly, swallowed, and said, "Eric, before you got back from the store, Juan and I worked out some details regarding dosage amounts and transport. We kept worrying about how to convey everything from one place to another, and finally came up with a nifty idea. Take a look." Etienne yanked a plastic bag from his pocket. "See this sandwich bag? This is made of rice paper. It dissolves immediately upon touching water. They come in different sizes, but we only need the gallon-sized, and these small ones. "Check it out." He pushed the bag into his glass of water where it disappeared, immediately. A collective gasp met Etienne's proud Gallic features. The water in the glass stayed clear. No residue, nothing cloudy, not even a lonesome bubble, fogged up the goblet to indicate a trace of the baggie. Finally, he drank from his glass and smiled.

Linda sized up the team as they beat on the table and whooped like a bunch of naughty kids. Eric and Etienne were the obvious brains behind the group. Juan seemed all muscle and brute strength. Sparky had a mouth that wouldn't quit, while geeky Milo looked reserved and calculating. Of course, Jack had the heart and soul thing down to a science. Though he looked physically weak, she felt better having him around. It was quite a group. They were the elite, strong-willed soldiers assembled to fight the Happy War. She felt proud to be part of the group.

Juan and Sparky called Etienne's demonstration a clever magic trick. Milo asked to look at the glass with his delightful Bohemian accent. Jack smiled, and Linda was impressed. "Perfect," said Eric. "That is perfect."

# CHAPTER SEVENTEEN

The next morning, she found out everything she needed to know. Eric provided overwhelming answers, preempting anything she might want to ask. Seven thick piles of paper sat on the dining room table. Each with designated itineraries and attached envelopes, waited next to a croissant, and an empty mug. Her stack included tickets to Newark airport, rental car confirmation numbers, hotel reservations, and the lockers, where she'd have to switch her empty, gray luggage for the filled-up luggage. She couldn't take any clothes, other than the ones on her back. If garments were needed, they would need to be purchased locally.

A neon green sticky-note, reminding her to wear comfortable shoes, was stuck on two tickets for the sightseeing harbor cruise of Manhattan. Taking the tour twice would help her reach different areas and allow her to be discreet. This crucial section covered the East River, Harlem River, Hudson River and more. During the duration of each boat tour, six small bags would need to be deposited in the various waterways. Another note said, 'distract onlookers by sneezing, coughing and acting'.

'Use diversion techniques by pointing in a different direction'. 'One bag can be flushed down the bathroom toilet during any water voyage'. The detailed documents included daily activities, even a restaurant guide.

The following day, according to the itinerary, she'd be driving north to Connecticut, visiting many rivers, possibly water towers. The instructions indicated that she'd need to find the Farmington, the Norwalk and the Connecticut rivers on her drive towards Massachusetts. A new driver's license was attached to the documents with a paper clip. One small bag every twenty miles will work on these rivers, the directions said, but don't stress about being exact. Do your best.

Bridges were circled on the enclosed maps, with red ink. Eric's plan sounded like fun. The first week-and-a-half, included boat trips on the Ohio River, the Potomac, a hot-air balloon ride, and a fishing expedition. Plus, there was a simple mapped out day-hike, luxurious riverfront hotel reservations, picnics and several festivals throughout the East Coast. It looked like a blast, but sounded exhausting.

Throughout her journey, no matter how entertaining, she had to remember two essential, but basic things. Eric highlighted these important items with yellow ink. First, communicate only through Milo, no matter what, and second, don't forget to leave behind the special, therapeutic gifts. Her eyes scanned the rest of the route, the maps and the tickets. It looked like a complete, detailed package. She'd be flying home from Atlanta.

All the reservations and the name on the license said Nancy Mulligan. She didn't care for the alias, and didn't think she looked like a Nancy. It didn't matter, turning back wasn't an option. She had a new identity. No one would find her. Not even Wayne, her worst choice in men. His threats had haunted her dreams for years. Now, with Eric, she had the opportunity for a new life. Everything was possible. Even world peace.

The last few pages had a ticket to Disneyworld attached, with a luxurious stay in a lakeside resort. Eric had clipped two photos to the printout. It looked gorgeous! From there, she'd be on her own, driving routes along the Caloosahatchee, Withlacoochee and Kissimmee Rivers, all the way to Wakulla, the world's largest, freshwater springs. The lodge paperwork and brochure, indicated this was a naturally protected nature reserve, where all sorts of creatures, including vultures and crocodiles, roamed around the property. Crocs? Yikes. Maybe she needed her coffee before the others woke up.

When she stood, she flipped through Eric's itinerary. He'd be flying into Cairo with Lufthansa. His return trip brought him home to San Diego from Erbil. It looked like he had two weeks to cover Jordan, Israel, Lebanon, Syria, and Iran, while he traveled over one thousand miles north. A large envelope contained bus tickets, visas and other documents, and yet his pile was almost the same size as Milo's. No Disneyworld for him. In fact, his journey looked rather dangerous.

Snooping a bit more, she flipped open Milo's document folder. He had the good fortune of going straight to the safehouse in Canada. That's where he would have to set up his computer and all telecommunications. Eric wanted to make sure they always had a way of reaching each other. Milo would have to intercept every call, even personal messages. All telephone calls would be routed to Milo's number. The team would receive special cell phones that only reached Milo on speed dial. In an emergency, Milo would have to dispatch help and assistance. His airfare had him going round-trip into Seattle, with a ferry-boat connection to Vancouver Island.

The sound of someone padding down the stairs, made her jump. "Good morning gorgeous," said Juan. He wore long underwear and a navy-blue robe. "Did Eric make coffee before he left?"

"Doesn't smell like it, but I can fix that situation faster than you can rifle through your itinerary. Check it out. Looks thorough; Eric probably didn't sleep a wink." She moved into the kitchen and turned on the water to fill the pot. More voices filled the dining room. Sparky greeted Juan, followed by the sound of Jack, Milo and Etienne grumbling about how they had to have coffee. "Good morning everyone," she said cheerfully. "The black brew is almost ready. Anyone use cream or sugar?"

Juan yawned like a hungry lion waiting for a hyena to pop out of the brush. "No, we all drink it black, except maybe our friend from gay Paree." He took a large bite of the croissant and chomped on it loudly. "Can we hurry it up? I'm gonna choke over here."

"Don't listen to him, Miss Linda, I take it black too," Etienne replied, with a shake of his head. "Take your time. Obviously, Juan is not a morning person."

"Thanks Etienne. I hope you can all be civilized while Eric is gone," she said, sounding like a reprimanding den mother. "The coffee will be ready soon, and he'll be back this afternoon. I'm sure he wants you to read your itineraries and study that gargantuan atlas." She pointed to a stack of books in the center of the table. "Maybe you should take photos of the pages that relate to your specific journey."

Sparky started to complain. "Except half the world is in my area. I'll be lucky to make a dent in this plan. Looks like he wants me to concentrate on the Han and the Yalu and let's see..." he mumbled inaudible curse words under his breath while flipping through most of the stack. "The train sounds good, through China and Korea. There are boats and bridges. Most of it looks like I'm camping or staying in youth hostels. Come on, Eric, this is crazy. After that, I'm heading to

Shanghai and the mouth of the Yangtze. Last on the list is the Ganges. I'm exhausted just reading this."

Linda went to get the coffee. She poured a cup for Juan and asked Sparky an innocent question, "Have you ever been to Asia?"

"You're kidding, right? Just because my dad fought in Vietnam, and just because he brought my mom all the way from Cambodia, doesn't mean I have visited, or had any desire to visit. I don't even like sushi. People are always profiling and having preconceived notions of who I am. My family members are all flag-waving U.S. citizens and proud of it."

"Whoa, have some coffee, Sparky. She just wanted to know if you've been there." Jack spoke up in her defense and smiled. Linda filled all the cups before she returned to the kitchen to make another pot.

*What a strong group of odd characters,* she thought, her hands shaking as she scooped the aromatic grounds into the filter. *I can handle this.*

At nine in the morning, Milo left for an hour. "Linda, I'll be back soon." He waved goodbye and an hour later, he sat back down to read a book about radio frequencies in third world countries.

The team studied the books, made notations, and worked hard to understand the geographic routes they planned to take. None of their trips included luxury hotels. Around noon, Juan received a call from Eric, asking him to meet him near his work, at the Pendalon Pharmaceutical Company. Juan dressed up in designer jeans, topped with a sporty, but fashionable hoodie, and promised to bring back dinner.

Linda sat on the couch, studying a map of the Eastern seaboard. The rest stops and gas stations were clearly marked, so she placed a red dot where she planned to stop. Etienne sat across from her in a soft leather chair. Though he knew most of

Europe like the back of his hand, he wanted to study crucial locations by doing internet searches on his phone, matching them up with Eric's atlas, and putting notes in the margin of his itinerary. Being a connoisseur of delicious delicacies, he hoped to synchronize this extreme trek with excellent eating establishments. According to the itinerary, he would be travelling through narrow inlets that flowed into massive rivers, and over charming small bridges, which were hotspots for fine dining. He set his sights on waterfront towns with the finest, most impressive cafés in Europe. His most difficult task, involved the Volga River in Russia. Unfortunately, it also had the least amount of gourmet dining, but he held out hope for a farm to table restaurant near the Caspian Sea.

"Can I turn on the television?" asked a bored Milo. Everyone nodded in unison. Eric's condo had plenty of cozy nooks for quiet reading. With the remote in his hand, Milo surfed a few channels and stopped on the local news. They showed pictures of the flood and cars being pulled from the mud. When a picture of Linda's face came on the screen, he jumped up and pointed at the television.

"Look at this," he yelled in an unexpected booming voice. Excited, he turned up the volume. The somber faced announcer said, 'After an exhaustive search, the local woman, Linda Simpson, is presumed to have succumbed to the high waters, during the flood. Other casualties took place in the north end of town. Throughout the entire city, several buildings collapsed, including apartment houses, displacing hundreds of residents. Linda Simpson had lived in one of the apartment buildings destroyed by the storm. The hospital also had evacuations. Several patients on the lower floors were transferred by helicopter to a nearby hospice.'

'This young woman, Linda Simpson, local councilman Fred Sanderson, along with retired librarian Bernice Hellman, brings the number of presumed dead, and missing, to five. Two bodies remain unidentified.' The camera zoomed in on Linda's car being towed down the road, followed by a picture of her face, and headshots of the two other victims. 'A spokesperson for Mr. Sanderson's family told our reporters that he loved this community until his last breath. A breath and a life shortened by falling debris, when the storm hit his modest home.' The announcer followed the short quip about Mr. Sanderson's life with a touching tribute to the librarian, while all three of the victim's faces remained posted on the right side.

*That old photo didn't even look like her,* Linda thought, shaking her head but glad it didn't resemble her at all. With that photo, they'd never find her. She wanted to laugh, because it was, *without a doubt, the worst driver's license picture of her life.*

'If you, or anyone you know, has any information regarding this woman, and can help investigators find out what happened on that cold March evening, please contact the downtown police department. I'm Sandra Beck with your—best local news channel.'

"I know what happened," said Etienne, smiling at Linda.

"We all know," said Sparky. "What if there's a reward?"

Linda rolled her eyes and returned to reading a brochure about a riverboat cruise.

"Jack, I'm not religious, but isn't it a sin to withhold information?" Sparky didn't want to let it go.

Considering what they were all about to do, it seemed like the lamest question, she ever heard. "Sparky, can you please, shut up? There's no reward. No one cares except my sister, and she's in Hawaii." He had the audacity to bring up sin, when they were going to dump chemicals in the world's water supply? Sure, she knew it wasn't right. But her heart was in the right place. This was for the children of the world, and those who were weak and marginalized. She was just a pawn on the giant chessboard of life with the job of future superhero. Her soul wasn't an issue. Not right now, anyway, she'd have to deal with that later. Whether misguided, or not, the mission was to complete her task, in order to help save humankind. And, she had to believe it would work. Any room for doubt could mess up the entire team.

Fortunately, Eric walked in from the kitchen, so she didn't have to get into it with Sparky. "No one cares about what?" He looked worn out. Disheveled hair, he seemed different, maybe because he had also removed the earring from his nose. He placed a large shopping bag filled with drab olive-green clothing on the dining room table, picked up the remote, and turned off the television. A sudden quiet filled the room.

After a few short seconds Sparky's annoying voice cracked into the silence. "Linda was on the news," Sparky informed Eric. "They're looking for her, all over the place."

"They have no idea who they're looking for. They think that's her, but it's not." It sounded good when he said it. The unflinching, professional, sales-like attitude he used to deliver his message, sounded confident. A born leader, Linda felt in awe of his commanding presence.

Sparky shook his head in mock understanding. "Mistaken identity, huh?"

"Exactly. Now come here and find something that fits. I spent an hour at the Army-Navy store trying to pick out comfortable, worn-out fatigues for all of us. There are two more bags in the car and they're all marked small, medium, large and extra-large. Tomorrow, rain or shine, we're going to finalize the plan. Speaking of extra-large, is Juan, back yet?"

"Not yet. Isn't he getting dinner?"

"Dinner? Ah, that must be the delay. Juan's bringing us the modified capsules. All we have to do is portion them out, divide the lot of them, and store them into those water-soluble baggies. Finally, we'll scoop them into our gray luggage. Then, those six suitcases will be shipped overnight, waiting at the different airport lockers. I have a friend who works in shipping. He told me to pack the suitcases into brown boxes and he'll pick them up with his white, unmarked van tomorrow morning. Each box will be labeled with the correct airport name and the corresponding locker number. Six, ex-military friends from all over the world will be picking them up from baggage claim and putting them into your locker. They are being paid to do this and are enthusiastic about assisting us with our grandmother's ashes."

Sparky made a face. "What?"

"It's a white lie, okay? I had to say something. Plus, it also explains why the luggage is lightweight. Now, don't forget, your own luggage has to remain empty because you're switching it. Whatever you leave in your luggage will end up in an airport locker. Did everyone get all that?"

Etienne, Jack and Linda nodded.

Sparky shrugged but looked amused. "Cremated?"

Eric pointed at Milo. "Except you Milo, you can keep your own luggage and of course you don't need to switch it."

"That's good," Milo replied. "Because my grandmother's doing just fine and has Tango lessons every Friday."

# CHAPTER EIGHTEEN

At exactly six p.m. that evening, Juan walked through the front door holding white bags filled with warm sandwiches. Sparky jumped from the couch, almost tackling Juan. The unmistakable scent of cheeseburgers filled the entire condo.

"Food," Sparky yelled, yanking a bag from Juan's overloaded arms. "Let me help. I smell French fries."

"Eric," Juan shouted over the excited voices. "I came by earlier with the truck and unloaded into the garage. Then, I went back to get the burgers and my rental car. Did you see the stuff?" He dropped three more greasy bags onto the dining room table before the two of them headed for the garage.

Giant metal drums, with yellow and black hazardous waste markings, filled the two-car garage. Eric ran a hand over his head in an effort to maintain his cool. "Oh no, we have to open these to make sure they are the capsules we want." He chewed on a lower lip, taking shallow breaths while thinking and trying to figure out what to do.

"Are you sure these are capsules, Eric?"

"No, right now I'm not sure--but they should be—they better be. Was it hard to unload all alone? You had a house full of team members with nothing to do, why didn't you ask one of them to help?"

"The truck had a lift. It was easy to unload. That's what scares me. The barrels feel empty."

"Pills aren't heavy Juan. Sounds like the correct shipment, but I have no idea how to open these canisters."

Juan pulled out his phone to do a search. "Well it needs something better than a can opener." Hold on a second. "Here's one site, says you need an air chisel or a cutting torch."

"Oh man, this adds a complication I didn't think about. Delete your search."

"Don't worry, pal. I'll get them all open by tomorrow. If you're thinking delay, don't worry about me. Giulia can live without my love for another week. You know, all that 'wherefore art thou Romeo' stuff. and how distance makes hearts grow fonder? Maybe my being here will make her appreciate me, right Eric?"

"Totally," he answered, nodding, gazing at the filled garage and thinking of the overwhelming tasks ahead. "You're worth the wait, buddy."

"Besides, every extra day will bring us warmer weather; except in Patagonia where winter is on its way. Let's hope these contain what we need," he added, kicking one of the rusty drums."

"Tomorrow morning, come upstairs and wake me up as soon as you get the first one open. Let's eat."

The team sat in front of big juicy burgers and cooled off fries. Linda sat at the head of the table, holding a can of soda.

Eric wondered why they hadn't started to chow down. "Why aren't you eating? The cheese is congealing."

"Eh, your friend, Jack thought we should wait. After all,

this is our last night together," Linda replied. And, Etienne suggested Jack should say the same prayer he said over you that time you almost died. Isn't that thoughtful?"

Eric pulled out a chair and sat next to Sparky. "I don't know. Sparky, do you mind hearing our prayer?"

"No, I was raised in a multiracial household of Baptist and Buddhist, and now I'm the ***bad-dest,*** he giggled like a naughty schoolboy. "I love diversity. Ask the others. What about Milo?"

Milo tucked his chin length white hair behind his ears. "I was raised in a Jewish family, and I love God. End of story. There's nothing more to say."

Jack and Linda felt they needed a moment of silence, words of encouragement, a blessing or something. Jack said, "You know, I think it's nice of Etienne to remember my words. That was a long time ago and those prayers tumbled, quite naturally, out of my mouth, straight from my heart. Since Etienne served as the medic, and worked with the Red Cross, he thought you might need last rites. It was an ugly mess, but in the end, it all worked out." He inhaled and continued to speak slowly. "What I said back then, wasn't a memorized prayer, simply my authentic way of asking for help. I turned my personal request into a custom plea to the Almighty. Good thing He listened, and continues to listen. Eric, you were passed out and didn't hear any of it."

"No, I didn't, sorry." Eric cleared his throat and looked at the scrumptious meal set in front of them. "Let's just eat. You guys must be starved." He felt embarrassed for delaying everyone's dinner with Jack and Etienne's sentimental memories. The point was, he survived a disastrous nightmare and had learned to move on. Talking about it felt weird.

"Wait, wait, wait, something came to me. Let's join hands above the table," Father Jack suggested. "I know a prayer that is meant for this occasion. My friends, we are all being called to serve."

Linda put her can of soda down and reached out a hand. In unison, they all clasped hands around the dining room table, bowing their heads. Jack, Eric, Milo, Sparky, Juan, Etienne and Linda, formed a united, throbbing conduit of intertwining fingers. Symbolically, the team united as one peace-loving group of positive energy, their hearts and collective thoughts all anticipating success.

"You don't have to say anything or repeat the words, but listen. I think you'll like it," said Jack. "It's the prayer of Saint Francis of Assisi:" He paused, and looked around at the group before he began the prayer. "Lord, make me an instrument of your peace. Where there is hatred, let me sow love; where there is injury, pardon; where there is doubt, faith; where there is despair, hope; where there is darkness, light; and where there is sadness, joy. O Divine Master grant that I may not so much seek to be consoled, as to console; to be understood, as to understand; to be loved, as to love. For it is in giving that we receive, it is in pardoning that we are pardoned. And, it is in dying that we are born to eternal life."

Eric said, "Amen", and the others followed his lead. "Thanks for that Jack. Your words describe this mission to a tee." He picked up his burger and smiled. Can we eat now?"

## CHAPTER NINETEEN

Late that evening, Linda asked Eric about Michigan. "I noticed you didn't have it on my itinerary. They have a lot of lakes."

"Oh that's because of Flint. They are having so many issues with drinking water and the water is being tested every day. I figured it might be good to leave them out. Just a precautionary measure, that's all."

She nodded and pulled up the covers. "I understand. That's a good idea. What about Chicago? I know for a fact they need some attitude adjusting up there."

"Based on the rise in homicides this year, I'd say you're right." Eric climbed into bed. "I made a small mistake. Civil engineering made the Chicago River, the only river in the world, to flow backwards from its original course. In all my scheming, plotting and map reading, I left it out. At first, I had hoped your Mississippi deposits would flow right under the Michigan Avenue Bridge and then I remembered it went the other way. We might need to make a detour somewhere."

"Wait, that's right by the Tribune Tower, which is the parent company of our local paper. Maybe, when I'm finished with my two weeks in the East, I can visit my old boss. I'm sure she'd love to have lunch. After a stealth riverfront restaurant deposit, I'll be waiting for you right here."

His expression changed. "That's a horrible idea. Aren't you supposed to be...?" He couldn't say it. "You know?"

She knew what he meant. Of course, she had to be dead as a doornail, and the more she thought about it, the more she began to get cold feet. "Yes, but maybe I can turn up in a couple of weeks? It wouldn't hurt. You know I liked my job, and there's Becca who will be coming back from Hawaii. The timing will work. When they ask where I've been, I'll say I've been comatose. Maybe I'll say my boyfriend brought me to his house, and I slept the entire time."

The wheels in his head were turning. He seemed miles away, as if staring out to sea at some distant island. When he opened his mouth to speak, nothing came out. It had to make sense to both of them. They both knew she would eventually want her old life back. She needed her job and her family. His fingers reached for hers, and his eyes returned from faraway. "Linda, you have to do what makes sense to you. We're about to begin a huge, global undertaking that is supposed to help the entire world, and all of it stems from your idea. You're a brilliant woman and I want you to know I'll back you up, no matter what." Moist, amber eyes reflected the lights, as he gazed at her with an incredible intensity. "You mean more to me than anything."

"I feel the same way," she said. "Can you imagine how worried I'm going to be while you're traipsing around Iraq?"

"You can't think about that. You have to focus. We all have to focus. One slipup among the seven of us could bring on an international crisis. Remember, if anything weird happens, you have to find Milo. Don't come here. No friends, no family. Right now, and for the next two weeks, it's a good thing they think you're gone. By the way, I'm sorry about the name on your tickets, but I had to think of something fast."

"I wondered why...."

Eric began to hum and sang, "I'm going to marry the one I love," followed by more humming. "Guess I forgot the lyrics." Fluffing his pillow, he moved closer to Linda and continued to hum the catchy tune. "When I went to get your driver's license, they played it on the radio. The song made me think me of you."

She kissed him. "I love you too Eric Anderson, not as Nancy Mulligan, but as Linda Simpson. One day, a few weeks from today, when the world has turned into a better place, Linda will reemerge like Lazarus." She put the pillow on her head, pulled down on both sides to mimic a head covering, and made a somber face. In a flourish, she tossed the pillow aside and said, "I'm alive. I'm alive. It's a miracle."

"Ooh, Biblical drama. I like it. You'll have to make a real splash of an entrance. Part the Red Sea, or cut off my hair. But first, we need sleep, tomorrow is a big day." Encircling her waist with one arm, he spooned up close and began to snore.

"Goodnight," she whispered, rehashing Eric's admission of love. How was she supposed to sleep? Maybe she was supposed to feel like Noah's wife, tossing and turning in anticipation of a giant deluge that would change the world. Good thing she slept light because at two in the morning, Juan strolled into the bedroom, shaking Eric awake. He held up a small bag containing pills. Linda pretended to sleep, peeking from one eye. Tan and muscular, Juan stood near Eric wearing nothing but worn jeans. "Is this the way they're supposed to look? The capsules. You told me to get you up."

Eric sat up, turned on the light and put on his glasses. "Let's see them." He studied the markings, took a cap out of the bag, sniffed it, twisted it open, tasted it and smiled. "It looks good. Time for mass distribution."

# CHAPTER TWENTY

For a career woman who used to wear colorful suits with hand painted silk scarves, one plain outfit for two weeks, didn't seem fair. Though sensible, she didn't like it. Her get-up consisted of long underwear, olive green pants, a brown tee shirt, a warm jacket and hiking boots. A small backpack contained a change of underwear and socks. The side pocket held all her paperwork, such as the tickets and maps. Eric had also provided lip balm, mosquito repellent, toothpaste, and a small first aid kit. She added ponytail holders, floss and a small comb. With the television blasting her photo, she thought about coloring her hair, but there wasn't time. Once she pulled her hair back, she could pass for anyone. No makeup, no lipstick and the plainest outfit, made her look like a young college student out on break. Nancy Mulligan had to fool everyone.

There was a palpable buzz in the condo, accompanied by the delightful aroma of fresh coffee. Milo woke early and left quietly for the airport. Juan and Sparky slept late, because they had opened the canisters, filled up the dissolving bags and distributed everything into team luggage, all before the sun crept over the horizon. Still before sunrise, they packed the boxes, labeled them, and distributed the locker keys by clipping them to each member's personal suitcase.

Jack, Etienne and Linda looked eager and prepared. A delivery guy came at nine in the morning for the boxes. Jack mumbled prayers and tied his boots. Etienne sipped his hot brew and talked about his two kids, Lana and Lea. He explained to Linda how the thought of seeing them, before he embarked on this complex endeavor, helped alleviate any anxiety. Plus, he knew his wife Suzanne would be waiting with hugs and kisses at the baggage claim.

"Mon amour," he said, closing his eyes, and inhaling the steam from his cup. The accent, or maybe his expression, made Linda blush.

The international flights were scheduled from LAX, so Jack and Eric would also ride in the same shuttle. With her flight not leaving Ontario airport until late in the day, Linda would need to lock up and drop the key in the neighbor's mail slot. Yesterday, Eric told the neighbor he'd be gone for a few weeks. He had asked her to keep an eye on the place, and though reluctant at first, she even agreed to water the plants on the patio.

Awake and moving quickly, Linda listened to Eric's loud voice fill the condo. His hair slicked back into a tight, damp ponytail, he looked military from every angle. "Are you guys ready?" Eric asked, heading for the door. "I think I hear the shuttle." Jack and Etienne came over to bump fists, as they filed outside to the van. Eric grabbed Linda's hand. "Be careful." Quickly, he kissed her on the lips and turned to go. "See you in two weeks," he said with a pinched expression that pulled together his eyebrows. He tossed his backpack onto the seat of the shuttle and climbed in next to Jack. Etienne gestured a thumbs up sign. She waved goodbye and slid the van door closed.

*Bang. The door sounded so final. He'll be back. Be brave, she heard a voice in her head. No tears. Her heart wanted to jump out of her chest to follow Eric.*

Inside the condo, she heard steps descending the stairs. Linda went to get a couple mugs of coffee, and handed them to Juan and Sparky. "They just left, but the coffee is still fresh."

"Thanks, I heard them leave. Eric can yell, man." He yawned. "Look at us, it's like we're back in the reserves," Juan commented, between sips of the hot beverage.

"You look like a lean, mean fighting machine," said Sparky.

Linda had to agree. "You guys look great." She admired their camouflage patterned tee-shirts. Juan had a navy-blue bandana tied around his neck. "You both look like soldiers ready to win the Happy War," she said, with a small giggle. "Are you waiting for a shuttle too?"

"Nope. I'm driving all over California, Arizona and Nevada, on up to Idaho and Montana. Most of the time I'll be camping in a tent or renting an RV."

"Sounds lovely but kind of chilly this time of year."

"Good thing I love the outdoors. This will be one giant road trip. I'll have to hire a team at the border. Next week, I have a flight to Bogota. This afternoon, I'm taking Sparky to the San Diego Airport. He can rest while I drive."

"I guess you like driving?"

"Are you kidding? Do you know how beautiful it is up by the Snake River? I'll be a kid in a candy store with those magnificent views, breathing fresh, mountain air in God's country."

Sparky yawned. "I'm sleeping on the flight to Beijing."

"Maybe we should get our lazy butt's going, huh?" Juan set the cup down and walked over to Linda. "Hey, pretty one, you stay careful out there." He gave her a bear hug and moved towards the door. "Come on Spark, we have a job to do."

Sparky, moved rather sloth like, and not quite ready to seize the day. He handed her the mug, slipped his backpack on and said, "Sayonara, Miss Linda, I hope we meet again."

Seconds later, the condo fell into complete silence. It felt like the last day of school when everyone rushes home, the buses are gone but one responsible person, the hall monitor, has to stay behind to lock the doors. It made her sad to think she wouldn't see Eric for two weeks and yet, she wanted to sing songs of joy about the upcoming changes. A glorious hope filled the hole in her heart. *Eric will be back,* she said, while placing coffee cups into the dishwasher. *I have to think positive and focus on the task ahead.*

*Like a specialized team of rugged angels, these are the toughest guys on the planet with one thing on their mind: Peace on Earth. We can do this,* she shouted, dancing a happy dance around the living room. "By the grace of God, help us with our crazy plan." Out of breath, she sat down to pray. "Amen and Hallelujah! Please, let this work!"

# CHAPTER TWENTY-ONE

The weather cooperated. The jet flew above clouds and cornfields without a hiccup of turbulence. The only excitement Linda experienced had to do with the romance novel she picked up at the airport. The heroine had to save a bunch of kooks from a mad drug dealer, while looking for her true love. Meanwhile, the handsome Prince had wandered off, right when the main character needed him most. What an idiot.

When debarking the plane, she left it on the seat, unfinished. Maybe the next reader would appreciate it. The novel made her think of Eric and how she'd have to face uncertainty, and risk getting caught. A high wire act without a net. Too bad she had sent him off, smack dab into the middle of a real war. But did she? Why did she feel guilty? Eric and his inner demons acted like they needed to go revenge the wounds of war. His conscience weighed on her heart, as if she had pushed him out the door, and yet, he seemed only too eager to return to actual battle sites, hoping to right the wrongs brought on by ancient history. Whether the prince saves the day or not, life isn't a romance novel. Things had a way of being much more complicated.

Back on terra firma, she hurried to the baggage claim for her own empty suitcase. After rolling it to the lockers, she pulled out the key and the number corresponded to the year of her birth. A sort of subtle reminder from Eric that he cared, and wanted to hold her hand during this debacle. *Play it safe,* she told herself. *Act natural and nothing will go wrong.* She switched the suitcases, closed the locker, and threw away the key.

Out by the curb, taxis stood in line waiting to transport passengers to awaiting hotels. Her watch said midnight. Though tired, her mind raced around wondering about the rest of the team. Jack and Eric somewhere in the air on their way to Cairo. Milo setting up his computer in the safe house, and Etienne and Sparky, far above the planet, but soon to be navigating foreign baggage claim areas. Lastly, she thought of Juan, with his male bravado, muscular biceps and incomparable confidence. Each member possessed amazing qualities, most likely more than she knew, or could ever imagine. These were incredible people, tackling chores involving a myriad of moving parts. They had rehearsed, studied and attempted to synchronize almost every step, in order to orchestrate world intervention, without a note of detection.

When her cab stopped in front of gold-rimmed glass doors on a circular driveway, her thoughts returned to the moment. Linda paid the driver and waved goodbye. A few people milled around in the elegant lobby; music wafted from a bar in the hallway. The check-in area had a long walnut counter, marble floors and enormous tropical plants. *'Impressive', she whispered, thinking Eric had good taste when it came to hotels.* Eric's own bed had sumptuous, 1000-count thread sheets and a magnificent down comforter with a satin duvet.

"Excuse me?" A serious looking woman in a beige uniform asked, "May I help you?"

"I have a reservation for three days," Linda replied, still daydreaming about Eric and his massive, dreamy bed. When a bellboy came to take her luggage, she told him she would prefer to carry it herself.

"Name?"

"Lin—Nancy," she hesitated. *It's about to begin.* Heat rose from under her arms and she tried to smile. "It should be under Mulligan."

"Oh, here it is. May I see identification, such as a passport or driver's license?"

Linda presented the driver's license. The lady stared at the photo for what felt like an uncomfortable amount of time. The photo Eric took on that first morning they had made love. The messy hair and his red checkered shirt, still looked better than her real driver's license. At least Eric's quick snapshot made her appear human.

Finally, the lady softened. "Nice photo," she said with a smile. "You look good in red. Here's your key card. We serve a complimentary breakfast from six in the morning, until nine. Your room is on the third floor." The woman pushed a piece of paper in front of Linda. "The room is paid for, but I need your signature for any added amenities you might need."

She signed Nancy Mulligan for the first time. *Of course, she looked good in red. Especially, after having wild sex with Eric.* Anything was better than the plain brown tee-shirt she had on, which made her look pale. "I don't plan on using the mini-bar, but I understand."

"We have several wonderful amenities, including a spa and sauna, a work-out gym, and of course our gorgeous lounge, which you passed on your way to our desk." The woman pointed over Linda's shoulder. "They serve spectacular drinks and appetizers, plus there's live music every night. We also have a world-class, award-winning restaurant on the top floor, concierge services and more. I hope you enjoy your stay Ms. Mulligan."

"Breakfast is down here? Right?"

The woman nodded. Linda put her water-resistant wallet away and moved towards the elevators. A handsome businessman in a blue suit, wearing a yellow tie, entered the same elevator and nodded. "Hello-oo," he seemed to purr. There was no denying he had a powerful presence and good looks, but his eyes and demeanor, immediately gave her the creeps. The elevator acted lethargic so she looked at the buttons to deflect his intense gaze.

"Hi," she raised one hand and waved.

"Business or pleasure?" the man asked with a lopsided grin. Linda tried to figure out what she didn't like about him. He had the know-it-all air of a politician, or a self-important businessman at a conference. Tall, thin and blonde, his piercing, glacier blue eyes kept staring. Undressing her with his eyes, hungrily moving up and down each one of her pant legs, he paused for a second at her wrinkled crotch, pursed his lips, and began a slow, upward climb. Inch by inch, he went slow and stopped at her nipples. The elevator was cold. Three simple floors felt like a hundred, when finally, his eyes returned to hers.

Embarrassed and not wanting to talk, she looked down at his cordovan wingtips and back up at the lit numbers on the inside of the door. "Sightseeing, I've never seen New York."

Finally, the elevator jolted to a stop.

"That sounds like fun," he answered with a wink. When the doors opened, she moved swiftly down the hall, rolling her suitcase like a Ferrari on a racetrack.

# CHAPTER TWENTY-TWO

The next morning, she stuffed handfuls of the pharm packets into her backpack, wrapped the rest into her long underwear, and shoved the remainder into the wall safe. When she pulled the curtain aside, the sun peeked through cumulus clouds. Linda needed sustenance. Figured she'd check out the breakfast buffet before beginning her role as a genuine tourist. While tying her boots, the phone rang. "Hey Miss Linda, this is Milo. I'm supposed to make sure you arrived safely."

"Oh wow, hi Milo. Nice to hear your voice. So far, everything's fine. And you?"

"This is a great island. I might check out Butchart Gardens today."

"You're already set up and everything?"

"Done, done, and done. Don't forget I left before you, had a shorter flight, and I'm an overachieving techno-geek."

Counting the hours ahead on her watch, she stared at the dial and wondered if Eric and Jack had landed in Egypt. "Have you heard from anyone else?"

"Juan called to tell me Sparky's flight is delayed because of some typhoon. I'm glad he told me but I checked the computer and the storm is going south. Juan is headed up 395 towards Tahoe, and the Carson River. Eventually, he'll be in Seattle. I think we might be able to have lunch one day, towards the end of the week. We'll see."

"Oh right, he'll be up there near the border. I bet lunch will be fun. Nothing to report on my end but I haven't left the room yet. Wish me luck."

"That goes without saying. My next call is to Etienne, his plane landed this morning."

"Thanks for calling Milo. Take care." She disconnected the call, locked the room, and put the 'Do Not Disturb' sign on the outside door handle, before heading to the lobby for breakfast.

Mere seconds after stepping from the elevator, the unmistakable smell of burned toast and cinnamon wafted in her direction. She took a window seat, but her line of sight had the ugly, backside of the airport, filled with gray office towers, shipping containers and semi-trucks. Down below, the hubbub of busy workers, the size of ants, reminded her of all the things she needed to do. Today, she'd rent a vehicle and take her first boat cruise, but first, she needed coffee and pancakes. The server set a stainless carafe in front of her.

"We have bottomless coffee," the woman said with a Jersey accent. "Buffet's self-serve, but I can get what you'd like...."

"No, I got it, thanks." The coffee didn't taste like the good stuff Eric had at the condo, but right now, taste didn't matter. All she needed was a jolt of caffeine; strong, black and bitter to help charge her engines. Pancakes doused in a liter of syrup might also add to the sweet kick her body needed.

While stabbing her last piece of syrup-covered pancake, a dark, uncomfortable cloud floated into the restaurant. Eric's plan had seemingly covered everything. They had role-played various scenarios where she might have to abort certain locations, where stagnant water, currents, toxic cesspools or hazardous conditions could put her in extreme peril. What Eric forgot to mention, was potentially the most dangerous of all: the human element.

The entire team would understand if she couldn't hike to a high elevation to reach a waterfall, or if she skipped a location because security was tight around a reservoir. The rule, in a nutshell, was to do the best she could. A nervous reaction caused an undesirable dampness under her arms, when she realized there were variables they hadn't considered. The discomfort kept her glued to the chair like a deer on a highway. Vulnerable, and unsure of what to do, she swallowed the last morsel with difficulty, followed by a swig of the bitter brew.

The man approached. Slowly, she turned to look outside, away from him, and his ogling eyes. The pompous voice, "Hey, it's the lovely lady from the elevator."

Immediately, she pegged him for a liar. Without lipstick, blush and fashionable clothes, she didn't feel lovely. Especially after spending the previous day on a long flight. "May I?" He pulled out the chair across from her, and set down an enormous helping of bacon and eggs. The swooshing sound of blood rushed through her veins and echoed in her ears. *Keep cool,* she told herself. *You're done eating, just say goodbye. Pull out your chair and leave.* Not knowing what to say, she smiled.

"I dabble in photography, and noticed how the light from the window made a picture-perfect frame for your beautiful profile."

One hand clenched the tablecloth. Her mind traveled back to the fiction book she had read on the plane. *Eric's face flashed in front of her. Where were her heroes? Where was her knight in shining armor? She felt alone in a room full of strange hotel guests.* No Prince would be hopping off his stallion, to save her during times of distress. The man's hypnotic eyes bored, or rather drilled into her being. *Breathe, Linda. Breathe.* He wore the same suit he had on yesterday, this time with a red-striped tie, and a pale blue shirt. Someone at the buffet line had burned the toast. Linda sneezed into her napkin. *Air, I need air.*

"Bless you," the man said. "My name is Mark, and your name?" He reached across the table to shake her hand.

Hesitating, but trying to remain nonchalant, she let go of the tablecloth and shook his hand. "I'm Nancy, nice to meet you--again."

"Anyone ever tell you that you have gorgeous eyes?"

She shrugged and replied, "Sometimes, but not lately."

"Nancy, you really are stunning." He kept staring, forgetting about his meal. "You are both delicate and regal; frankly, you take my breath away."

She pointed at his food, "I think your breakfast is getting cold."

"Nonsense. Cold or hot, it doesn't matter. I'm sitting next to a classic beauty. If I was a painter, I'd ask you to model. I've seen the work of the master's at The Louvre, The Smithsonian, The National Gallery and the Uffizi. Faces I hope never to forget, and your glorious face, which I hope will be etched into my permanent memory--forever." Mark picked up a piece of bacon and munched on it, while leering. Linda felt like puking pancakes.

Time to flag down the server. *Where's the server? I need to tip her well so I can get out of here.* Linda stood and looked around for the lady from New Jersey.

"Wait, don't go." His tone pleaded, and his eyes zoomed up and down her body, while he licked the bacon suggestively. *Disgusting pig!*

It would look strange if she ran across the dining room.

*What had she done, she wondered, to encourage this man?* "Sorry, I have tickets and can't be late."

"Tickets?" He bared gleaming teeth and his eyes grew wider.

She needed to lie, but worried he'd be able to tell. As if, in the big scope of things, it would matter what this stranger thought. Still, she didn't want any complications, and her sister always told her she wasn't a good liar. Bad enough she had to use an alias. "Just a harbor cruise...."

He pushed the dining room chair back. "I've always wanted to do that. May I accompany you? Please?"

"Aren't you part of some convention?" *Why couldn't she say no, absolutely not?*

"I was the keynote speaker, and that part of the program is over. A few more days before I fly back to Denver."

"I can't, I have to go." Linda scanned the entire room but the server wasn't around, and she never came by for the tip.

"Nancy, I think you'll like having me around."

Now he had become an arrogant pervert. "Take care, Mark." She moved decidedly through the coffee shop, and had almost made it to the door, when she felt his hand grasp her arm.

"I'm coming with you."

"Please don't," she yanked herself away. Obviously an intelligent, fine-looking man, he had lowered himself into something strange and unusual. He evoked a nightmare about a giant parasite, she couldn't shake off. Being keynote speaker gave him a few extra points, only adding to her vulnerability, because she didn't want to alert hotel security about the poster boy for unacceptable convention behavior. *Think, think, think; this guy is a gross waste of my time. I have so much to do. How do I get away?*

Surprising even herself, she said, "Fine, I'm taking an

Uber." Before taking the first cruise, she had planned on picking up the rent-a-car, but with Mark hanging around, asking too many questions, that would have to wait. Rather than risk him knowing too much, she had to take baby steps and proceed with caution.

"No, you're not. I have a limo at my disposal."

She couldn't call the cops. Not with Nancy being her assumed name, and a room full of pharmaceuticals. "Okay, let's go." She'd rent the car tomorrow. Linda sighed, knowing she couldn't drop too many pills with this person around anyway.

"Can I change first?" He pointed to his suit and smiled a photogenic smile. "I brought some nice casual slacks and a sweater. Would you mind?"

*Yes, dimwit, I would mind!* Dimples or not, of course she'd mind. "No, not at all," she lied. "I'll wait in the lobby."

And there it was: he heard her lie. Becca had told her many times, not to lie, because she couldn't do it right. When she attempted to lie, it almost always, showed on her face. Sometimes her eyelid would quiver, her voice cracked or her nose twitched at the wrong time. Of course, she would have skipped out, leaving him in the dust, faster than a longshot horse at Belmont. "Nancy, if you stay down here, you'll take off on me, huh?"

"I guess there's that chance." She answered, with a confidant looking grin.

"Wow, that smile," he inhaled, squinting his eyes as if smelling a rose. Grabbing her hand, he pulled her toward the elevator. "Please, wait outside my room. I'll change fast." When he pushed the button for the twentieth floor, her smile disappeared.

All the way up she stared at his shoes while trying to figure out what to do. His large hand still clamped onto hers. Silently, they rode up without anyone stopping to enter. Meanwhile, she wondered how her loose pants, man's tee-shirt and hiking boots had attracted this strange man. Without any makeup, mascara, blush, or lipstick, this guy had carried on as if she were the freaking Mona Lisa. Finally, after what felt like ten minutes, the bell dinged, and they stepped into the corridor. He took out a keycard and opened the door to his room.

"I'll wait here," she tried to say, before he forced his lips onto hers, pushed her into the room and locked the door. His moves were sudden, unexpected and rehearsed. He had done this before and knew what to do. With brute strength hidden under his fancy suit, he picked her up and carried her to the bed. Strong arms pinned her down while he moaned with desire. His tongue kept trying to get through her clenched teeth. She could tell he was aroused. Because of her own situation, her name-change and the contents of her wall safe, she couldn't scream to alert the staff. Though she felt helpless, she was not going to surrender.

*This must be what's meant when people say they painted themselves into a corner, she thought.* Her mind raced, her body squirmed and her legs kicked under Mark's roaming hands. There had to be a way out of this, without killing him. After all, she had traveled here on a mission of peace. When his hand moved under her shirt, she slugged him on the back, and kicked one of his legs as hard as possible. "Stop," she said, firmly, but he didn't flinch. In contrast to her petite frame, this attacker had large bones, and bigger muscles, as if he worked out daily.

"Nancy," he whispered. "You don't know how much I need you. The minute I saw you, I knew I wanted you, and had to have you." She couldn't move. Stuck like a bug in a museum entomological exhibit. At least he still had his pants on. By pinning her to the bed with his body, he couldn't pull off her pants and long johns, giving her a few seconds to formulate a plan. Pretty soon she'd have to kick him in the balls, but she wanted to wait and see if there was a better option. If he alerted hotel security, she might be stuck in a he-said, she-said situation. This man looked important, and at this moment, she looked like some sort of camo-wearing anarchist.

With all her strength, she tried to push him away. "Mark? What's going on, I thought you liked me?" Maybe she could reason with her attacker. "I thought you wanted to go on that cruise? Can we at least see the Statue of Liberty?" She wanted to add, *'You know, like civilized individuals rather than animals?'* Instead of answering, he pushed his lips onto her mouth, blocking out her words, making her gag. "Air, I need air. Let me breathe."

"I am so hungry in lust for you. Never have I felt such a strong desire for anyone. I know I'm acting crazy, but there's something about you that fuels a fire, deep within." Again, his hands moved under her shirt, almost reaching her breasts. This time she pushed him away with more force.

*Fire my ass; more like a hormonal imbalance.* How he managed to come up with such unbelievable hooey, boggled her mind. "Well this isn't how most relationships begin, Mark. You said you liked me, right?"

"Are you kidding, right now, I couldn't live a day without you," he mumbled, his face smashed against her throat. His wet tongue swirled around her ear, his manhood hard, pushing aggressively through layers of fabric. *Revolting*!

For one second, she managed to push his forehead, shoving his head away. "That's good," she said. "We're making progress. So, it's not like you want to rape me, right?" His head relocated down to her chest, and though she still had on the shirt, it felt strange to feel his warm, damp breath in such a personal place. Her mouth felt sensitive and raw. Wanting to scream, she worried she'd expose the entire crew and ruin everything.

Determined, she wasn't going to allow one maniac to ruin their entire mission.

When he tightened his grip, something felt hot and damp. Blastoff. It seemed Mark would need a dry cleaner. "Mark, let me go. I want to go now." *Gross, forget the cleaner, go buy a new suit! Blech!* This monster had attempted a rape and it failed. A wave of guilt washed over her. For some reason she couldn't help feeling soiled, dirty and disgusted for coming near his room. Someday, she'd have to cry about this day, and when that day came, she would also mourn for other victims of violence, while nursing her inner wounds. But that day wasn't today. Today, she had important work to do and this atrocious individual wasn't part of the plan.

The evil, satiated attacker leaned back and smiled. At that instant, Linda pushed him hard and ran for the door. When she swung it open, a member of housekeeping stood next to a cart filled with soap and small bottles of shampoo. Linda swiped up a few to use as weapons in case Mark followed her to the elevator. Fortunately, he didn't. Linda went to her room and packed her bags. The time for early checkout had arrived.

# CHAPTER TWENTY-THREE

The boat sailed down the Hudson River towards Ellis Island. It made her think of all her relatives who came to this country for freedom. They came, because in other countries they were told what to believe, and how to believe it. They escaped political unrest and famine. They left harsh conditions, where war and terrorism had created a culture of hate. They called the U.S. the New World. Linda looked up at the Statue of Liberty and thought Lady Liberty represented a sort of mother of protection. 'Mother of Exiles' wrote Emma Lazarus. A proud, but tired mother, with children running amuck all over a huge, bustling country, the statue a symbol of love, amid strife.

Linda sighed, as if the weight of the world rested on her shoulders. She rubbed her bruised arms, thinking of her foolish gullibility. *Someday, Mark, when you least expect it, karma or something like it, will surprise you. It will knock the wind out of your sails, teach you a lesson, and for some strange reason, you'll know why bad things are happening. And though I will move on, I hope God helps your sorry soul.*

The salty mist tingled on her skin. *I can't think of Mark anymore, I have more important things to do.* Stalling, she waited for the right moment. She scanned the group of passengers. Right when everyone turned to look at the Brooklyn Bridge, causing a perfect distraction, she tossed the bag overboard. Coincidentally, the ship's bell clanged seconds after the first dosage of happiness went over the side.

A man spoke through a loud amplifier about the Empire State Building, the USS Intrepid, the United Nations and the One World Observatory. Skyscrapers gleamed in the afternoon sun. The buildings reached towards the heavens in a colorful array of glass and steel. Wall Street, Times Square and Central Park, were all part of the tour. Gut-wrenching history, and awe-inspiring beauty, captured her attention and held her heart.

A tear rolled down Linda's cheek. She had to help the children, the widows, women who stayed alone in hotels, men who worked for nasty bosses, the disenfranchised, and the marginal populations that included scores of repressed, bullied humans who shared the same planet. With solid conviction, she tossed another tiny gift into the wake of the boat. Soon, it would be a new awakening for the descendants, and the great grandchildren of the huddled masses. Those who trusted, that this new place, the United States of America would offer their families solace and hope. There was no turning back and no cold feet.

As the boat headed back to the Brooklyn Cruise terminal, Linda thought about her next trip on the Staten Island ferry. Jack had told her about his church in Fairview New Jersey, near the edge of the Palisades, overlooking the Hudson. As pastor, he had held Mass there many times. One chilly January morning, he left the rectory after the service and looked out onto the ice floes while praying. The colors above, and around him, were gray, blue and white. At first, he heard geese, followed by an airplane swooping low. An automatic reflex to continue his prayers kicked in like a second rinse cycle. Jack had explained to her how he saw the Airbus on that fateful day, in January 2009. For good reason, the courageous pilot, a hero, landed the plane on the river, while an astounded Jack watched from the shore. Jack meanwhile offered up intense, heartfelt prayers, perhaps assisting and saving those hundred and fifty-five souls. It was apparent Jack believed his words had traveled to God. His unshakeable faith made his eyes twinkle when he talked about it.

The connectivity of everything made sense, giving her goosebumps. Atoms and air molecules are invisible and yet they touch, they bounce. Not everything is visible to the human eye. Did she underestimate the power of something theologians have addressed for thousands of years?

She reflected on prayer, a subject she had avoided most of her life. Perhaps she attempted to pray when her car sank. Had a small prayer saved her from Mark? Had her sister prayed for her to love Eric? Was prayer the secret weapon? Rarely did she step into a church, and she didn't think of herself as religious, but, as she gazed over the aquamarine-colored water, she felt a spiritual stirring in her soul. Linda knew that medicating the world's water supply was a form of playing God. A loving God who would not approve. Still, she felt loved and protected at this moment, more than she ever, and didn't feel alone. But, like an obstinate child who does something naughty right in front of dad, or perhaps the oxymoronic Christian soldier, she needed to plow ahead and deal with the consequences later.

A lot had changed in the New World, and a lot of bad things had happened on American soil. Of course, that didn't meant things couldn't change for the good. The Hudson had a few nice doses of the pills now; step one, and at least three hundred more to go. Mark had inadvertently pushed her to have faith in her dream. Though Jack gave her a few words of inspiration, Mark had made it personal. This day had filled her bruised body with hope, more than any day of her life. Today, she might make a dent, and she wasn't giving up until she ran out of packets.

They disembarked on the pier and the Captain took her hand to assist her step onto the gangway. "Did you enjoy our tour?" He had a rugged look and sparkling emerald eyes that mimicked waves on the Atlantic Ocean.

"Breathtaking," she answered. "Maybe even life changing."

## CHAPTER TWENTY-FOUR

Jack and Eric said goodbye to each other at the Cairo airport in Egypt. Eric would travel north, and Jack would be travelling south on the Nile. In this case, as in the case of anything worth doing, there were complications. The locks, dams and reservoirs would be stopping Jack's boat every once in a while, and while inconvenient, it would give him a chance to disembark, making it easier to sprinkle capsules from bridges near the shore. He also knew he'd have to wait until he reached the southern point of his journey before unloading larger quantities, because the Nile flowed north.

Jack had friends who sailed the Peace Boat, also known as the Voices of Peace, an international outfit, that proclaimed impartial news in Arabic, English, French and Hebrew. Set up with a microphone and large speakers, the old white vessel traveled throughout the Middle East, spreading positive messages in an effort to ease tensions between religious groups. Five years had gone by since Father Jack had been on board. He had spent many months, travelling and preaching on the ship with a crew of nineteen, and their Captain John. Just like old times, the boat and crew waited for Jack at Port Said.

Jack looked forward to sailing down to Lake Victoria, to the Congo, and finally to the Zambezi river. Time permitting, he also wanted to get to South Africa and the Orange River. He'd do all he could, then turn around, since some West African areas were dangerous. The Peace Boat was too large to navigate all the rivers, but he could hitch a ride on other fishing vessels and rafts.

A small rice paper bag in his pocket, awaited the first drop. Wanting to release the capsules near the shore before boarding, he set the suitcase down, blocking the view from shore, and tossed the bag of capsules into the water. The event hidden by loose-fitting khaki pants to anyone observing from the boat. As the concoction bubbled and dissolved, a smidgen of hope fired up his personal crusade for peace. Though a twisted way to push people into kindness, he felt it had a good agenda; one he couldn't argue against.

Forgive me Lord, he mumbled under his breath, at the same time he heard his name. "It's Jack, its Jack," one of the old crewmen hobbled down the gangway. "Oh Jack, it's great to see you, sir." The toothless, shirtless man attempted to assist Jack with his featherweight luggage.

Recognizing the man, he chuckled at the man's excitement and shook his hand. "It's fine Gamal. I got it." Jack smiled at the beaming old sailor and trudged up to the deck. "How's everyone doing on the old Peace Boat?" Classical music streamed from the speakers, the temperature soared into the eighties, and he noticed tourists milling around the pier, waiting to embark on one of the Dahabiya luxury cruise ships to Aswan. Far in the middle of the placid river, a felucca sailed in the distance.

Captain John came over to shake his hand. "Welcome back

Padre. I'm ready to take you wherever you want to go." A stained, white and blue striped shirt coordinated with the unkempt beard.

"I'll go wherever you take me."

Everyone laughed. "Gamal, get Jack something to drink." The Captain ordered in a pleasant, but authoritative voice. Gamal, smiled and limped toward the galley. Captain John turned to face Jack. "Same cabin, same old stuff. We just need you to come up with something inspirational. I think they're starving for it. Even my pathetic crew needs your words of wisdom. I suppose, I do too."

"A reasonable request good Captain, and the reason I'm here." Everyone's ears would soon be overflowing with hopeful messages. First order of business would be to write a new sermon. He'd read it out loud the next morning, as the boat traveled south. "Who was sent here last?" Jack's question referred to his fellow priests. He wondered who came before him because everyone had a unique style when it came to delivering the Good News.

"It's been awhile. We've read small segments from the New Testament or Psalms, but most of the time we play music. I can't remember the name of the last missionary."

Gamal handed Jack a soda. "We read some of Charlie's stuff."

John nodded and looked sad. "Yeah, we read Charlie's old poems. They always lift our spirits."

Jack thought back to the hero who emulated Jesus more than any man he ever met. "Remember his favorite psalm?"

"Sure, we play a recording of Charlie's voice reading it. Psalm 29:3-4, --The voice of the Lord is over the waters...."

Jack recalled the amazing priest who began the Peace Boat. Anchored in New York harbor, the old, worn out ship began a new life as a missionary vessel, hoping to spread messages of love and peace. Charlie's poems made people listen. His poems filled sad hearts with joy. *Maybe, thought Jack, I'll try my hand at poetry too.* "What about news? Do you even dare broadcast any news?"

"Not lately," John answered. "There's too much going on and too many factions. The people still get a kick out of seeing and hearing us, even when the only thing we're broadcasting is classical music. Music unites, like a special language that reaches into their hearts." John slapped Jack on the shoulder. "Wow, five years. You're looking good, Father."

"Long time, huh?"

John shook his head and pulled on his scraggly beard. "I know you're tired, but join us for dinner. We're having Gamal's famous fish soup."

"Jack laughed and licked his lips, "The Tagine Samak with that amazing tomato sauce? Sure, can't wait."

Gamal smiled from ear to ear. Such a hardworking, humble man thought Jack, watching the old man shuffle back to the galley. Gamal wore old white linen pants that were rolled up at the hem and doubled down over the waist. A rope held them up, and though wrinkled, they looked clean.

A vibration made Jack jump, "Oh dear, I'm receiving my first phone call. Excuse me John," He wandered to the side and looked at the buzz of the milling crowd on shore. There were the obvious tourists that stuck out like a sore thumb. Pale legged men in linen shorts with white socks, accompanied by women in wide-brim hats. After snapping hurried pictures of the boat, they returned to the massive throng of humans. Fast little boys darted in and out of the crowd, as if playing a game. Some would stop at the shore to take a quick breath. They waved at Jack and took off running. The noises, smells and screams of babies made the entire scene electric, vibrant and alive. A colorful caravan of camels stacked high with packages, bounced along in the distance. Delighted to be back, Jack smiled. *Let the journey begin,* he thought, answering the phone.

"Hello Milo, we landed safely. We're about to set sail."

"Wonderful. We're on schedule. Did you see Eric get on the bus?"

"Last I saw, he was heading for the bus terminal."

"Good. Don't forget you have a little less than two weeks to cover a continent. Do the best you can."

"I understand."

"We won't be communicating, unless there's an emergency. Stay safe, and I'll call again before you head home."

A nostalgic and melancholy moment washed over Jack when he thought of his old friend Charlie, his passion for the Peace Ship, and his incredible desire to do the work of Jesus. *Africa needs this type of missionary work.* Even though he had retired, and even though he had worked hard his entire life, he felt a reawakened strength, a sort of zealous renewal, that would help him continue to preach the Gospel. "Okay, buddy," he replied. "Remember God is with us."

"Where else would He be?" Milo said with a laugh. "Take care."

# CHAPTER TWENTY-FIVE

Sparky didn't like the lady who took his passport. She stared at his picture for what felt like five long minutes. After the excruciating and painful wait, she stamped it and asked where his parents were from.

"California, my parents live in the Silicon Valley. Can I go now?"

"Who are you visiting?" She snapped the question, like a police interrogator.

Fortunately, he had read up on the sights. The plane had a travel magazine listing the top ten sightseeing destinations. "No one, I'm a tourist and plan to see giant pandas in Chengdu."

She nodded but remained serious. "And after that, what do you plan on doing?"

*The pandas should have been enough. Didn't this woman have a heart? Why would I hurry away from cute little bear cubs?* "I'm going to see a famous pagoda," he replied with a touch of sarcasm. "Then, maybe a waterfall." Silently cursing, he now wished he had memorized all the famous spots.

"Jiuzhaigou?" she asked with a frown.

Of course, he had to see Jiuzhaigou. Not only because it happened to be a breathtaking place, but more importantly, because it was home to over one hundred and fourteen lakes, eleven or more rapids, eighteen groupings of waterfalls, and several tributaries of the Yangtze. Tomorrow, he planned to take a bullet train to Xian. As he shook his head in the affirmative, she broke into a small, unconvincing sneer. Sheesh, if anyone needed a dose of Woezap or whatever, here, right in front of him, stood the ideal candidate.

"Earthquake in 2017," she said. "No individual access--must take river cruise with tour group to Jiuzhaigou."

He focused on a dark brown mole situated in the middle of the woman's forehead. Her outfit consisted of a standard navy-blue uniform with decorative slanted stripes on the sleeve of the jacket. The authoritative woman wore no makeup and on her short hair sat a brimmed, military-style hat with a matching band of stripes. The hat sat tilted far on the back of her head, looking as if it the slightest breeze could knock it off. Sparky wondered whether she knew a black hair had sprung from her beauty mark. "I don't have time to go on some twelve-day cruise. I have reservations in Thailand." *Count to ten,* Sparky, he told himself. After which, he began counting to one hundred, albeit slowly and silently. When he reached the number twenty, she interrupted....

"Sorry, sir, you need to speak to professional travel agency. We have desk in airport." She pointed above a sea of bustling people.

"Fine." He shoved his passport into his pocket. "Thanks," he said, moving past her desk, and holding up two fingers in a peace sign. Inhaling deeply, he longed for fresh air. Between the long flight and the crowds at the airport, his lungs felt stifled. Maybe getting away from this robotic soldier woman would make him feel better. *She really needed to have a doctor look at that mole.*

Before speaking to the cruise desk, Sparky wanted to at least locate the lockers. No way, in any version of hell, could he waste a week traveling down the Yangtze. Even the thought made his skin crawl. He imagined a bunch of rich tourists talking about the buffet, and their couple's massages. The whole idea sounded painfully boring. Besides, he had enormous areas to cover. He had to visit the Yellow River, the Mekong, followed by the Ganges, all in two weeks. If time permitted it, he would also travel to the largest oasis in Saudi Arabia. Asia was enormous. He'd do his best.

In the distance, on the other side of the vast building, his eyes caught sight of a green sign pointing towards lockers. *Well, let's see what these people say first,* he muttered, as he moved through loud groups of people, pushing luggage and pulling children in various directions.

A pretty, young lady, sporting a different uniform, directed visitors to offices that were located behind a long information counter. When Sparky mentioned he wanted to visit Jiuzhaigou, she directed him to a small office, immediately. A heavy-set gentleman with a short-sleeved shirt and tie, sat down across from him. The man told him about the quake. Without any emotion, he explained the structural damage that occurred to bridges and buildings making travel unsafe. He also described the devastating financial losses, tremendous casualties, and how going alone was out of the question. It sounded like a memorized script he repeated hundreds of times a day. After his speech, he placed three brochures in front of Sparky and told him to select the one that sounded best. They were all excursions going to Jiuzhaigou; consisting of a four-day tour, a seven-day tour, and a twelve-day tour. Sparky selected the four-day tour, paid for it, and went to trade in his luggage. Sadly, the four-day trip wouldn't take him to the Chengdu Research Base for Giant Panda Breeding.

# CHAPTER TWENTY-SIX

Once Etienne reached home, he didn't need to go far to make a deposit into the Seine. He walked across the Pont Neuf, and dropped a few small bags into water flowing toward England. Crowds of people made him confident. Spring in Paris meant tourists. Not just any tourists, but kissing and hugging tourists, staring obliviously into each other's eyes, while they blocked Etienne's movements. The next morning, he would take the train through the Chunnel to the Tower Bridge, above the Thames. But, right now his stomach growled and he needed sustenance.

"Bonne après-midi," said a kind server at Etienne's favorite café.

While in America, Etienne had missed one of his favorite French meals, typically consisting of pate, French bread, gherkins and the obligatory glass of red house wine. Though he didn't leave home too often, when he did, he missed pastries, and the aroma surrounding the bakeries in his neighborhood. As he looked outside, he noticed the blossoming trees and thought back to the deluge he had suffered through in California. Sparkling sunlight poured through the massive French doors of the river view restaurant. Trees blossomed everywhere. The scent of the local trees had lifted his spirit. He watched flower petals catch a breeze, land on the water, bobbing colorfully down the river, seemingly giggling in clusters, riding currents until floating out of view.

It seemed Etienne had a newfound appreciation for Paris. He had earned his stripes by serving in the military; he had volunteered with doctors without borders, the Red Cross and Greenpeace. Life in this exquisite area was a small slice of heaven and a gift he felt he deserved. Hunger pangs reminded him Paris was meant to be savored, one delicious bite at a time.

"Will your wife be joining you?" The server carried a placemat in one hand and a pitcher in the other.

"Oui," replied Etienne, "and my children."

She set the pitcher down and set the table for four. "Voila," she said. "Bon Appetite."

"Daddy, daddy, the children shouted as they ran to the table by the window."

"You already ordered?" His wife asked, placing a small kiss on his cheek. She pulled out a chair and told the children to be quiet and sit. The two little girls continued to chirp like spring finches, while playing with their napkins.

"No, I ordered an appetizer. Please join me. American food made me crave this stuff." Suzanne's delicate features, her stylish haircut, and perky nose were, très French. Once a nurse, now a fashionable wife to a semi-retired doctor, Etienne inhaled her perfume, and admired his adorable kids. Both girls wore parochial school uniforms with stretched out, white socks and dusty sneakers.

"Ah, American food, I've heard some stories," she said with a laugh. How's Eric?"

"Good, I think he might have found a girlfriend."

"Ooo-la-la," she squealed with delight. "I'm so glad. It's about time! Did you have a good trip?"

The server returned for their order but noticed they hadn't had time to study the menu. "I'll give you a moment."

Etienne answered his wife. "It's not over; I have to go to a medical conference in Prague. I'm also stopping in Zurich and Budapest. It's an unusual case and they want my perspective. Every time they come across that article about the fungal infections, they call me."

Sadness, depression and anger didn't have anything to do with mycological airborne viruses, and yet a poet might argue they could spread from broken hearts. A mushroom cloud over countries with bad weather, strange governments and too many wars. Yes, special injections were necessary, he reasoned, and only he could administer the medication to the despondent and forlorn patients. It only felt like half a lie. Maybe not even a lie at all.

"No, daddy, no," the girls said in unison. "Please, don't go."

Etienne reached over to tickle them, but anticipating his movements, they ducked under the table. "Come back little monkeys, I have good news."

Suzanne leaned closer to hear his version of good news, and the giggling children climbed back to their seats.

"We're going to Grandma's by train in two days." The quirky small town had been Etienne's boyhood home. The little girls loved Grandma and had fun with her cats. Suzanne loved her cooking, even though she complained about putting on a few pounds, every visit.

Lea and Lana jumped up and down on the café stools. "Can we go with choo-choo?"

"Yes, choo-choo, that's what daddy said." Suzanne reached for his hand. "You don't need to attend anymore medical conferences, my love."

"You're right my sweet, crepe Suzette, but there's more to life than éclairs and macarons. This symposium will cover stem cell research and pharmaceuticals. The hospital visits are related to preventing an infectious disease from spreading."

"Not again," she mumbled. "Be careful and wear a mask."

He squeezed her fingers and brought them to his lips. "Don't forget mon chéri, I love you always." *My disease, he thought, is being head over heels for this gorgeous woman. My symptoms, he thought, include loathing every moment I am away from my family. My cure will be to finish this heartfelt task for Eric, so I can feel good about staying home, forever.*

"Tomorrow you pack. When I come back, we'll be ready to go to Vergèze. I'm traveling to Prague, but only after I know you're comfortable at Mom's."

From there, Etienne would be travelling near rushing brooks that feed into bottling plants, and he'd visit different springs near Switzerland, before crossing into Germany to the Rhine. He'd spend a day floating down the Danube on a water-taxi, followed by a plane to Kiev to the Dnieper, where he planned on photographing seven famous bridges. Before returning to Paris, he'd make the most difficult journey to the Moscow Canal and the Volga Baltic waterway. He could take a short cut and begin at the mouth of the Valdai Hills but he hadn't decided. Eric told him to do his best. Maybe hiking in the upland regions would work better. There were many things to consider, and he needed to sort out the details. It was exciting to think that with one gigantic deposit of magical tablets, the Moscow leaders might learn to be nice. He could only hope.

"They have school, dear."

"True, but there's nothing like spring in the South of France. Remember the lavender? Besides, our girls are smart, they'll be able to catch up, won't you?"

"Yes, daddy," Lea replied. "Can we pick grapes too?"

"I don't think they're ripe yet, but there might be strawberries."

Lana looked at Lea and they screamed, "Strawberries!" at the top of their lungs. The girls loved strawberries in everything. They loved it better than chocolate. They loved them dipped in powdered sugar or pureed and layered as cake-filling. Strawberries made everything better. One bowl of strawberries could cheer them up after a long, hard day at school.

The server came around with a wine glass for Suzanne. "Are you ready to order?"

"Oui," Etienne answered, "We'll have the French onion soup, the coq au vin, and the girls want the croquettes."

"Can we have strawberry tart? Please?"

"We'll see, said the blind man," Etienne answered, staring into his wife's emerald eyes. Leaving her, and the children, for even a day, made him feel blind and crazy. Blind enough to take part in this wild idea that gave him secret powers. This opportunity jolted his manhood, his life's work, his testosterone, his ego and filled him with a drive he hadn't felt since he was a young legionnaire. Etienne knew the consequences of prescription drugs, their repercussions, and side effects, and had never taken any, electing to suffer through dental work without anesthesia, even toughing out backpain and headaches. Clinical analyses of medications were his forte. And yet, at that moment, he felt as if he were drinking caffeinated beverages mixed with little blue pills of manliness, rather than the mild table wine in his glass. Instead of feeling like a blind man, he felt a youthful, unstoppable virility.

The unrest with Brexit, the European Union, the civil unrest due to refugees, terrorists, bombers, and a plethora of madmen who drove vehicles into crowds of innocent civilians, had turned the country upside down. Maybe, just maybe, he could take this negativity out of his country, off this continent, and out of the world. If ever, there needed to be a time to come together in harmony, this would be the time. He hoped with every fiber of his being, that travelling to the prescribed far-off villages, with remote rivers and reservoirs would make a difference. Sadly, when he thought of the entire world, he knew the diluted dosages would scarcely make a dent. He thought of himself as a happy man with a happy family and wanted everyone to experience similar levels of happiness, or even better.

"You're not blind daddy," Lea said.

Etienne closed his eyes. "What about now?"

"No," Lana and Lea kept giggling as the food arrived. "Do you smell the food, daddy?"

With his eyes still closed, he pulled Suzanne closer, planting a kiss on her cheek. The server watched and smiled. It was, after all, spring in Paris.

## CHAPTER TWENTY-SEVEN

Linda drove miles and miles through congested cities and lush forests. Her goal was to make it up to Vermont, where the longest river in New England begins to flow south. She traveled along the Adirondacks, past the Green Mountains, and enjoyed a small picnic at Lake Champlain, where she stayed overnight. She then headed east, towards Bellows Falls, and the Moore reservoir, which continued south as the Connecticut River. During her travels, she met campers, fishermen and hikers everywhere who were kind enough to share their knowledge of the area. Soon, she learned to follow signs to bait and tackle shops, which led her right to river front campgrounds.

When fishermen asked why she traveled alone, she'd hold up a notepad and say something about being a travel writer. It sounded plausible. Fortunately, no one asked her to elaborate. Heading south through Massachusetts, she turned right for a two-hour detour to Saratoga Springs. There, while on a guided tour, she dropped small packets of the pharma-gold, before she drove south to Connecticut. The tour guide faced forward and didn't see anything unusual. Near Farmington, she looked forward to the balloon ride Eric had planned. It sounded fun and exhilarating, even dangerous. Lately, danger seemed to fuel her adrenalin.

Early the following day, the pilot of the hot air balloon lifted off with Linda, and a pair of newlyweds. The balloon company made it into a special event for romantic couples and sightseers, by serving mimosas, cinnamon rolls and fresh fruit. At two thousand feet, he pointed out areas familiar to the local couple. Majestic mountains circled around the horizon. Large homes became small dots. Backyards with turquoise swimming pools sparkled like giant jewels below emerald treetops, and freeways shined like molten, stretched glass. As the gondola floated higher and higher, she began to feel like a bird. For a short time, the trees looked like broccoli, until they changed into a green blur down below.

They crossed over the Farmington River a few times, but she couldn't drop anything without being obvious. Never one to fail, Linda had an idea. Hidden by her jacket, she slipped a packet into her champagne, where it dissolved immediately. The new concoction, also a blend of tangerine juice and sparkling wine, filled the flute to the brim. Now she needed to wait until their guide released a small amount of propane to fuel the balloon. The loud noise and unexpected blast from the flames would surround them for a few seconds, camouflaging her behavior. Her timing had to be impeccable. Plus, the hot air balloon and the sudden combustion had to be in sync, above the river, for the entire diversion to work. The unexpected noise would make her jump, signifying she had delicate nerves. At that precise moment, she'd toss the contents of her glass over the side, and hopefully, everyone would laugh. End of story.

"Isn't this incredible?" the female passenger asked Linda.

Linda nodded, somewhat surprised that the woman wanted

to converse. "It's breathtaking," she responded, as the balloon neared the river. "By the way, I meant to congratulate you on your wedding."

Mesmerized by the beauty of her surroundings, Linda held her drink over the edge of the basket.

"You ought to drink that before you spill it," the woman said, pointing at Linda's glass. "It's so delicious." The newlywed's eyes zoomed in on Linda's cocktail.

The husband turned from gazing at the view. "Oh, she's going to make a toast to us, the wonderful couple, from Albany." He raised his glass, expecting Linda to raise her glass. When she didn't, he shrugged, drank everything in his glass, and planted a sloppy, wet kiss on his new wife's cheek. "Isn't this amazing?"

"Miss," she addressed Linda with a smile. "If you don't like that drink, I'd be happy to take it off your hands."

The balloon drifted over the river, but the pilot still didn't need to add any hot air. They had descended from a high altitude to see the reflection of the balloon on the water. The newlyweds made Linda nervous, especially, when the bride reached one of her manicured hands towards the plastic flute.

"I might drink it later," Linda said, holding it firmly. Finally, the man in charge reached for the propane tank, releasing a shot of gas into the sky. Above them, a flare-up of golden flames filled the balloon. They were at the edge of the river. Linda jumped like a nervous colt; it was now or never. Most of her drink went over the side, but a warm current brought some of it back, splashing onto the newlywed couple.

The couple laughed. "I didn't mean like that," the young lady said, licking a drop off the back of her hand. "What a mess."

Linda felt horrible and it showed on her face.

The husband reached into his pocket for a napkin, wiped

the orange concoction off his jacket, but continued his hearty laughter. "Well it isn't holy water, but we appreciate your blessings anyway."

Embarrassed to have sprayed some of her cocktail in the wrong direction, she stared into her empty glass. "Hey, I promise to buy both of you a new one when we land. Sorry about that."

"Oh, that will be fun. We love to make new friends," the lady chirped like a little bird. "Do you live around here?"

The pilot circled around a field. It looked like they were about to land. Linda pointed at the distant horizon as if speaking to a child. "Way over there, I live far, far away."

# CHAPTER TWENTY-EIGHT

Juan took a right in Gardiner, Montana to the North entrance of Yellowstone. He climbed out of his rugged red jeep and walked into a river rafting office, hoping to sign up for a float tour.

"We have a four-person minimum and the tours don't begin until May."

"Then why are you open?"

"Tee-shirts, souvenirs, hiking maps, overnight permits and fishing licenses--we sell a little bit of Yellowstone for everyone."

*Isn't that special?* Juan rolled his eyes and reached into his back pocket. "Look, I'm ex-military, the water is thawed out and I'd love to see the scenery and the wildlife. I'll pay extra." He flipped open his wallet to show his Military identification card.

The young man standing behind the counter didn't like Juan's attitude and didn't appear impressed. "Buddy, it's not up to me, but thanks for your service anyway. The Park Rangers around here monitor who goes down the river. There's a winter moratorium in effect until May first." With a quick glance at his watch, he looked up and smiled. "I guess that means we'll see you in four weeks. Can I interest you in a baseball cap with our embroidered logo on it?"

Colorful fishing lures and reels filled one side of a display case near the cash register. Frustrated, and left without options, Juan looked down at the brochure taped onto glass and said, "No, but I'll take the overnight camping permit."

"That's twenty-five per night and includes a backcountry use permit."

"What's this about an annual pass being only twenty-five? Shouldn't I get one of those instead?"

"Probably not, because annual passes are for advanced purchase only. They require you to watch a safety video about bears, fires, and food storage. The paperwork takes a long time, and they are only available at the Central Backcountry Office."

Juan hoped a grizzly would chase this guy down tonight and make him supper. "I'm aware there are rules and regulations, and I'm traveling solo. Cut to the chase. Give me a hiking map too."

The man moved towards his cash register and pulled some paperwork from a file. "Are you staying at one of our lovely campsites or out, under the stars?"

"Why? Is the campsite an extra charge?"

"Of course, mi amigo, that's called capitalism."

Strangling this little know-it-all, sounded good about now, but then he'd have to forget about the entire mission. Maybe the volcano in Italy put him on edge. Every time he thought of Giulia, he imagined her shouting for help on their balcony, while hot magma flowed down the cobblestone street. *Mi amigo, huh?*

When his fingers began to roll into a fist and his biceps

unintentionally flexed, Juan inhaled. He tried to think back to Jack's prayer about understanding. They were calming words he needed to hear again. Words from a saint might help him keep his cool. His mother, and all her church-lady friends had prayed to saints. She told him the saints talked to God, and intervened to help with everything. Right now, he needed help, but couldn't remember a single sentence of any prayer, and would never admit he didn't even know the Lord's Prayer. *Mom, can you help me? Can you intervene? I bet you're the best angel they have up there. This weakling behind the counter deserves a kick from my hiking boots. I bet you'd think he's nice. You'd offer him cookies. Mom, I don't have cookies. He's a son of a....* Juan kept trying to settle his nerves by thinking about his mother. *He's so scrawny, I bet he doesn't eat cookies.*

He rubbed his eyes. Tired from driving and making deposits along the Snake River all day, he didn't feel like fighting. His anger-filled days were supposed to be in the past, along with dusty bandages on a battlefield, or empty casings on the streets of L.A. "Right, I didn't think it's free, but I'm sleeping in my Jeep." Though he planned a few nights in a tent, he hoped to postpone the risk of being vulnerable to bears, indefinitely.

"The campsites fill up early. Your extra fifteen dollars will allow you use of the showers, fire pits, picnic tables, wireless internet, a coin operated laundry room, and daytime use of the tot lot playground."

Juvenile thoughts made him want to take the punk to that play area, where he could push him headfirst down the slide. "Fine, I'll take it and that hiking map." Juan handed the man a hundred-dollar bill and waited for his ten dollars in change. "I think you owe me a ten-dollar bill."

"Nope, the taxes and fees took you up to ninety-eight dollars. Here's two dollars." The guy also handed him green sheets of paper, a map, a small cardboard permit for his wallet, and a parking sticker for his car. "No pets, right?"

"No."

"Place this in the front window. It's good for three days."

What a peach. Juan began to feel bad for the miserable little guy. Thin and underfed, he wore an oversized rafting tee and baggy shorts. There weren't too many women in the area, no fun restaurants and winters were colder than summers on Denali. On top of everything, the owner of this business probably didn't pay him too well. "Were you born in Montana?"

"Nope, born and raised in Massachusetts."

Juan thought back to the one time he went to Boston, and wondered how a guy, who grew up in such a huge city, would acclimate to the outdoor life.

"Is this your summer job?"

"Dude, what's with the questions? You should find a campsite before it gets too crowded. Let me show you a couple of wooded areas that haven't been worn down by those gargantuan RVs." He opened a map and circled a few things with a black felt pen. "There's a small gravel road here that goes to the river, but it's quite a hike to the restrooms. There's this dead-end over here, that's too small to back in, or pull-through, for any RV, but just right for your vehicle. Plus, it's nice and remote, and still near most of the facilities."

Juan nodded, and took the map. "Sorry, if I sounded a bit short earlier, but had my heart set on a raft trip."

"No worries, I know what it's like to have your heart set on something, and not get what you want. In my case, things are working out better than I thought they would." He smiled from ear to ear, grabbed a baseball hat and handed it to Juan. "To answer your question, I was a Harvard law grad, but my, ah—you know—lifestyle, didn't help me pass the bar. So, here I am--bought this place--got sober--even met a hot babe up in Billings.

Life is good, bro," he said with a laugh. "We're having a June wedding right next to Ole Faithful."

Juan put the cap on his head. *Boy, had he underestimated this guy*. "Wow, congrats."

"We're cool Juan. And hey, thanks again for your service. This time I mean it."

# CHAPTER TWENTY-NINE

The long flight gave Eric a throbbing headache. After a short layover, he caught a bus heading to Israel, where he planned to visit a nature reserve at the Ayun River, in the Galilee Panhandle. The Nahal Lyon springs originate in Lebanon, and flow southward into tributaries of the Jordan River. Filled with picture-perfect waterfalls and rushing streams, he had looked forward to some of the prettiest parts of this adventure. Right now, however, his head felt wedged between the bus axle and the tires. And, though he had enough medicine to drug several nations, he didn't even carry an aspirin.

Taking a nap would be a fabulous idea, but he felt uneasy surrounded by strangers speaking a variety of languages. More importantly, he needed to figure out how to transfer to the bus going to the Jordan River. The rumors he had heard indicated that getting to Amman would be difficult, and that getting to Bagdad, Iraq, could be extra challenging. Folding the map, he looked out the window at the distant hills and thought of

Linda. Soft lips, bright eyes and voluptuous curves were there, wrapped in crisp clean sheets, far on the horizon--a mirage, beckoning him to close his eyes and come to bed.

The bus lurched to a stop, waking Eric. After long delays and some yelling, more Arab travelers were allowed onto the bus. Dust billowed in through the windows. Eric closed his eyes again. The aching feeling of missing Linda contributed to his headache. Plus, he worried he had pushed her too far. *Heck, it was her idea,* he thought, his fist hitting the empty seat in front of him. A horrible feeling made him sweaty and guilt-ridden for egging her on. *Accept it Eric,* he told himself. *She's tough--we're two of a kind. That woman is a mirror image of my very soul. If something goes haywire, I have to be ready to take the blame. Well who else? I've always accepted responsibility. My boots will soon be on the ground.* The sound of a bumpy gravel road drowned out the rumbling in his stomach. *I guess I'm ready to serve again.*

When the bus stopped in Tel-Aviv, he ran to buy a bag of snacks. While in the store, the bus filled up with a diverse group of singing American missionaries. The cheerful choir were headed to Nazareth. One after another, they sang deeply moving spirituals and uplifting gospel songs. Eric sat in the only seat available, and though his hands were full, he made a clumsy attempt to shake hands with his seatmate. "Hello, it sounds like you're from the states, I'm Eric from California."

"Well God bless you," the heavy-set man said, pulling a napkin out of his pocket to wipe his brow. "They told me it'd be warm as Palm Springs around here, but I've never been to Palm Springs." Out of breath from singing, he used his hat to fan his face, stuffed the wet tissue into his breast pocket and offered a clammy hand. "Name's Stokley, a pleasure to meet you."

Eric liked the man's gregarious personality and wanted to

know more about the tour. Stokley tried to get Eric to join in the singing, but Eric preferred crunching down on chips instead. Food might help him be more responsive. The plane ride, the time differences and the oppressive heat were making him dizzy. Hearing the heartfelt songs made him feel better, even the headache seemed to be disappearing.

A song ended and the man leaned closer, answering Eric's earlier questions. "We're going to Canaan. We are almost there," said Stokley. The man looked at his watch. "One hour and we should be there. I'm so excited, I feel like a squirrel playing in a pile of woodchips. Eric, my friend, this has been my lifetime dream and it's about to come true. Can you believe it?" The man chuckled, and a smile pushed his cheeks into shiny, pudgy spheres.

Inspirational and talented voices, with varied, harmonizing parts filled the bus, like a free concert of professionals or a mysterious choir of angels sent from heaven above. The bus passengers and tourists, bobbed their heads or tapped fingers on the seats, as the group sang, "And there will be no sorrow, there in that tomorrow, we will be there by and by; milk and honey flowing, there is where I'm going, Canaan land is just in sight." A euphoric feeling filled the air. Eric wanted to stick with the religious group for as long as possible. If for nothing else, it helped his headache. But when they reached Nazareth, the group disembarked and headed for a shuttle to Canaan. Still singing, Stokley tipped his hat and waved goodbye.

"Wait, Stokley, when are you leaving here?" The group filed off the bus and Eric ran after them. The driver waited, but revved the engine.

"Oh, I'm glad you asked me that brother. We'll see a few sights around here and have lunch. We'll be traveling to the Jordan in four hours." He waved an arm in front of him to encompass all the singers. "We're all getting baptized. Now you tell me, if that isn't that the most amazing thing you've ever heard? We'll be consecrated right there, with the same water, where John the Baptist, and Jesus stood. "Lord, I am not worthy," the man shouted over the obnoxious noise of the bus as he turned to go. Some of the others cried, "Amen," in response. "Anyway, take care, of yourself, young man."

"I want to go with you," Eric yelled over the commotion. "I should be here when you get back from lunch. Will you baptize me?"

Stokley chuckled again, "Well Hallelujah brother, that's the best news I've heard all day. I'd be happy to help make sure your soul is on the highway to heaven." Stokley waved again and lumbered to the end of his church group. A man dressed as a reverend, sat on a shuttle, waiting for the singing missionaries. Eric returned to his bus to the Ayun River. He had to hurry if he wanted to make it back to this station in time. The one-hour trip, the drop, and another hour back depending on the bus schedule, would cut it close.

Thank you, Jack, he mumbled to himself as he slouched into his seat. Jack always told him it was God who helped him survive the bombings in Fallujah. But what about Etienne? He had literally saved his life with medicine, tourniquets and gauze. *Was he being stubborn?* Had God worked through his French friend? Eric had always credited Etienne for saving his life but something made him think he might have been dead wrong.

A bright lightbulb seemed to go off in his head. Chaplain Jack had been right, all along. Eric leaned forward, clamped his hands over his ears, hearing the beating of his heart, while he succumbed to what felt like the love of God. A weight lifted from his shoulders. No one sang, only a child screamed, after which two men argued in a foreign language and a baby cried. As the bus rumbled down the road, his burdens and guilt floated down an imaginary river. *Jack you're right about God, he whispered to himself. I've been a fool and I'm sorry. Thanks for everything.*

# CHAPTER THIRTY

Meanwhile, Milo kept intercepting calls from Giulia who complained about the rugged climb she had to make near ancient Roman bridges. Mostly, they were rustic ruins and not easily accessible. When she called to complain to Juan, even though Milo tried to explain Juan was unavailable and hiking around the Rocky Mountains, she unleashed a stream of Italian words that Milo didn't understand. One day, he tried to research some of the words online, and found out, in Italy they call the Tiber River the Tevere. She often repeated the word volcano, which made him worry, but he could only reply with a concerned sounding, 'Si'.

Usually, he'd sit at a small desk, play computer games or read eBooks, while waiting for communication from the rest of the team. He'd leave to buy food, come back, and sleep next to the phone. The days were quiet, the shutters were closed and at night he heard nothing but the melancholy sound of a foghorn in the distance. Milo, who slept light anyway, began to look forward to her emotion-filled, intrusive morning calls. Sometimes he surprised her by learning a short phrase, such as

*Buongiorno.* It never occurred to Giulia that eleven in the morning her time, meant two o'clock in the morning in Canada.

The lilting sound of her irate voice, screaming in Italian, about how she needed to talk to Juan immediately, because a nozzle broke in the kitchen sink, made Milo smile. The plumber, Giulia had contacted, had made things worse, leaving Milo to ponder the perplexities of life. He hoped Etienne would hurry toward the mineral water bottling plant in Lombardy. This woman needed something to calm her nerves, and he thought, *perhaps they had a solution to her problems. Most likely,* he reasoned, *she drank Chianti.* Even the freshest wine, right out of the barrel, wouldn't have the lasting properties of their water elixir. Milo knew that mixing antidepressants with alcohol, though not a good idea, resulted in fewer inhibitions, and not much more.

"L'uomo e un bastardo," she screeched into the phone.

The curtains were closed. Dawn or daylight were somewhere in the distant future. "Who? What?" Milo's computer had a few blinking lights that allowed him to feel his way to the desk. Quickly, he translated the word 'please' on his browser. "Per favore?"

More Italian curse words rolled off of her tongue. *Seriously? What is Juan thinking? This woman better be hot, thought* Milo, as he ran fingers across the keyboard in order to search for a profile picture. *There she is*: big hair, nice cleavage and that Mona Lisa-type smile. *Not bad, but I doubt this dame is worth the drama.*

"Giulia, I'm on your side, what's going on? I'm here alone and I'd love to help. Can you try to talk to me in English?"

Was she crying? Milo wasn't sure, but it sounded like sobbing. "Oh, Milo, I'm so sad."

"Why, what happened? Did you have trouble in Florence?"

"No, I broke the heel of my shoe at the Arno and ran out of pills."

Good, he was thrilled she had dumped all her doses. Maybe this meant she wouldn't be calling him anymore. "That's not a reason to be sad. I'm sure Juan will buy you a new pair of shoes." Thank goodness she had finished her promise to help. If it wasn't three in the morning, he'd do a happy dance around the room, to a music video.

Milo had worried about her from the beginning. A woman he had never met, and didn't know anything about, had been entrusted to a highly secretive job. Eric allowed it because of Juan. Without credentials, a good background check and some sort of vetting, Milo felt she was a gamble. But, by some miracle performed by the local Roman gods, she had completed the task. *Arrivederci, lady and don't bug me anymore.* Of course, he knew this needy, insecure woman would continue calling at all hours of the night. At least until Juan climbed, hiked or sailed within the frequency range of a satellite tower.

"Milo, you're not listening. Those were designer shoes."

"Yeah, bet they cost a fortune."

She sniveled on the other end. "Milo, I am not sad because of the shoe. I am sad because of the plumber." *What an unusual woman.* At least he found her entertaining.

Milo sighed. How could a sink cause this much emotion? "Maybe you should call another plumber? Have you thought about a handyman?"

At the word 'handyman' she cried even harder. What the heck. "I'm sorry, I'm trying to help."

"No, you don't understand."

"Oh, come on, I'm trying to help."

"You cannot. No one can help me."

*That's probably the truth, thought Milo. She had hit the nail right on the proverbial head.* "I can't reach Juan right now. He's out in the American wilderness where there's no cell reception."

"I know, like John Wayne."

"Kind of—look—I have a computer right in front of me. Tell me what's wrong with your sink and maybe I can troubleshoot some ideas. Then, I can order the parts. By the time they get to your place, Juan will be back. Give me the make or a model number. Do you know what company made the sink Giulia?"

"Juan is wonderful handyman but the plumber...." She stopped talking and he could hear her voice quiver. At least she wasn't whimpering anymore. "He screwed in a new pipe," she whispered.

Milo sighed in relief, "Okay, so it's all fixed?"

"Yes, I am in love."

"Amore, see I learned a few words, just for you. I'll tell Juan." *Did she just say what I thought she said?*

"No, please. Don't tell him. I am packing my things and leaving for Scotland."

"What?"

"I am going to Aberdeen with the plumber."

Milo knew Italian opera when he heard it. And, at this moment he had become part of the cast. Would he sing or shout a poignant reply? Sundays, his mother played sad arias over and over on an old record player. *He remembered his mother's tears rolling down her cheeks, and as a young boy, he wondered how a fictional story could repeatedly make her cry, and, why she didn't opt for something happier such as a Broadway musical.* "Tragic," his mother whispered, her body shaking with emotion. "*Yes, Mama," he had replied, snuggling close. "Don't be sad.*"

"Right," he drawled out the word into three syllables, almost a song. "Now I understand. Have a good time. Are you going back to Rome?"

"No, we are moving."

This was exhausting. "Bye Giulia, I have to go now," he said with a yawn." *Screwing in new pipe, huh? Sorry, Juan buddy, it's time to find a new home. Milo hoped Juan wouldn't take it too hard.*

"Goodbye Milo, Grazie." When the call disconnected it felt final, but he still wasn't sure about her sink. The dripping had stopped and Giulia had left Juan for the plumber.

## CHAPTER THIRTY-ONE

Linda turned off the highway at the Great Falls Tavern visitor's center, in Virginia, so she could hike next to the Potomac. Today's capsules were supposed to flow towards the White House. A fact she found both humorous and brilliant at the same time. Anticipation made her grip the steering wheel even tighter, as she turned into the gravel lot.

While parking the car, she thought about the previous day in the Appalachians where she had stayed in a riverfront log cabin and attempted to use a rod and reel for the first time. Too bad she ended up knee high in a marsh.

Though she thrived on adventure, the damp clothing and wet boots made her crank the heat up in the car. She couldn't wait to get out of the car to stretch her legs. Yesterday, she had slipped off a moss-covered rock, and it caused her to laugh hysterically. The sudden dunk into the cold river had felt invigorating and exciting, best of all, the water seemed to knock some humor into her serious mission. At the time, she was out of control, and couldn't stop laughing. After a few minutes of the icy bliss, a cranky fisherwoman heard the commotion and made her stop. "Shush, you'll scare away the fish," the woman yelled in a scolding tone.

Bruised, but not ready to quit, Linda crawled out and continued to fish. She kept trying different lures and floaters to no avail. One soft-spoken old fisherman suggested a whipped concoction of cheese, another old codger told her to use worms. All of it made her queasy.

The fishing experience reminded her of wading out of her car, during that freaky storm. There seemed to be a connection brought together by water. A strange turn of events had dumped her into a rushing stream. As if the universe conspired, by conditioning her, in a sort of prep, so she'd fulfill her dreams of world peace. *It had to be related--every drop that splashed on her, or rained on Eric, felt like a type of embryonic fluid--gluing the world together. Water that gives life and water that drowns life could also be the water that changes, strengthens and cools the molten iron. The world needs cooling.* Linda didn't have many excuses, except in her desire to be iron-like tough, she felt humbled, and found she sucked as a fisherperson.

That evening, she planned to return the rental car. But first, she wanted to walk along the North River Trail to Riverbend County Park. Tomorrow, she'd ride the train to Orlando, rent another vehicle and go up to the panhandle. From there, she'd head for the airport in Georgia, and back to California. The days slipped by, and she had a lot to do. Eric had thought of everything, even squeezing in a day of fun at the amusement park.

At the Great Falls, visitor's center, the park ranger gave her a hiking map and told her not to walk on the Aqueduct dam. The message about the danger of the low flow threshold was posted on trees, trash cans, and rocks. Apparently, the powerful hydraulics could be fatal. Check-mark-point taken--she wouldn't walk on the dam. They told her she might see beavers, herons, bald eagles and blooming wildflowers on the trails. They also warned about mud, downed trees, and told her to bury her trash, in case she couldn't find a receptacle.

What they didn't warn her about came hours later. While Linda ate her turkey sandwich and slurped soda from a can, she admired the flowers and cute little birds that wanted crumbs. She sat on a rock next to the breathtaking Mather Gorge, enjoying the view. A blue butterfly settled on a nearby rock. Across the river on the other shore, she noticed a deer and her fawns retreating into the foliage. After a pleasant, idyllically situated lunch, she hiked down to rinse her fingers in the ice-cold river and to release a small packet.

A gruff sound came from the forest behind her. Slowly, she turned and saw a black bear. Goosebumps, or maybe just the hairs on the back of her head came alive. Though the animal wasn't large, Linda figured the Ursus americanus had relatives nearby. Maybe many relations were coming together for a family reunion. Her mind raced. *Don't they say a person should freeze in place? Forget that,* she thought. Frightened, she flew down the path, running like a rocket, zipping past planet-like boulders and massive conifers.

Behind her, the lumbering sound of heavy breathing and grumbling, huffing noises approached. One, maybe more, bears gamboled after her. No way, was she going to look. In front, a downed tree blocked the trail. *Could this get any worse?* Linda climbed over the log, but it slowed her down. Her scratched palms and ankles began to bleed. Two, growling black bears had smelled Linda's sandwich, and were coming fast. They had spent the winter hibernating and acted like they wanted turkey filled tourist-hold the mayo.

The trail rose to the top of the cliffs, above the gorge. Miraculously, she remembered something strange from girl scouts, about making oneself bigger. She pulled off the backpack, grasped it with both hands, set it on her head, and marched forward. Her eyes and ears on guard, listened for the grunting that seemed to cease back at the massive log. Outside of the thumping heart in her ears, and the sound of a rushing river, she didn't hear anything else. Perhaps the log had been filled with juicy, gourmet termites. Somehow, she had outrun her would be attackers.

Linda exhaled, and continued to hike, albeit faster than usual, toward the parking lot. One scream, and the ranger would have asked too many questions. What she didn't understand is why the park service didn't warn hikers about hungry bears? They warned about slippery rocks, snakes and the dangerous dam, but they didn't warn her about frightening, black bears. *Maybe someday she'd write them a letter.*

At the car, she took out her first aid kit, and placed bandages on her wounds. Her work on the Potomac, fourteen miles upstream from the leader of the free world, was complete. Hopefully, this terrifying experience, and each drop of blood, would end up being worth it.

And, while she didn't think bears should hang out in close proximity to the White House, the experience made sense, as a way to strengthen and prepare her for the future. If she could handle being chased by a bear, she could handle anything. *Floods, attempted rape and black bears, were now chapters from the historical pages of her life. Not only would she possess a resume worth reading but someday, she could write a memoir with a ferocious bear pictured on the cover.*

*Laughing at the idea of having an exciting page-turner on the bestseller lists, she drove toward the mall to find warm, dry socks. In the back of her mind, she wondered about those future lessons and obstacles that were sure to come her way. 'I'm ready', she yelled inside the car, at the top of her voice. 'Linda's ready for anything, but what about Nancy Mulligan? Time to toughen up lady!'*

With an hour to kill before driving to the train station, she wanted to stop at the mall for a new shirt, pants and dry boots. Her cell phone rang.

"Linda," Milo shouted. "Before you go to Orlando, destroy your identification. They are double-checking all park entrances and ramping up security. Shred it. Throw out your driver's license. Got it?"

# CHAPTER THIRTY-TWO

On board the snail-paced vessel, the river locks and the gentle currents made traveling laidback. No one hurried, no one could get anywhere fast, and the hot, humid weather only added to the lazy atmosphere. Jack planned to get off the boat at Luxor, and from there, he wanted to fly to Uganda. With the Nile flowing north, he didn't dare drop too many capsules until he reached the southernmost point of Lake Victoria. The heat made him sluggish. The crew, and the captain appeared to be in a continual, zombie-like state of lethargy, even though they blasted Beethoven's Fifth Symphony over the speakers most of the time. Jack thought he woke the pharaohs with loud, fervent sermons, as they sailed over calm water. The onshore crowds were sparse, but the prayers, faith and hope offered from the vessel remained simple and steady. Sadly, after a few days, Jack had to say goodbye.

Gamal handed him a heavy bag filled with canned sodas. He stared at his bare feet. "We are glad you came, Jack."

"Look at me," Jack said. "Look me in the eye. You are an

incredible human being and I'm honored to have served this community, here on the Nile, with you."

The humidity, coupled with the heat, made the cook's face shinier than usual. An unmistakable tear glistened on Gamal's cheek.

"Plus, Gamal, listen to me," Jack said. "You're a master chef," he added, touching his stomach. "Those delicious smells coming from the galley will linger in my memories, for a long time."

The boat stopped in Luxor, where a cab would take Jack to the Luxor International Airport. He made a vow in his heart to return, but right now they had a deadline, a deadline to save the world.

"You will be surprised when I come back," Jack said, trying to cheer up his gnarled, old friend.

The captain looked over the rail. Disheveled hair stuck wildly from his cap, and his former white tee shirt now sported a medley of perspiration and stains. "You said that hooey five years ago. Let's see if you can come sooner."

"I promise. God is your witness," Jack pointed at the sky. The sentimental goodbyes were breaking his heart. *It had to be a guardian angel or his old friend Charlie, because in his head, he heard the undeniable repetition of the words, 'go Jack go'. Would Jesus have time to urge him on? Clear as drinking water, the lucid message repeated: 'go Jack, go'*. He turned around and saluted the captain. "Ma'a Salama," he shouted and waved to everyone on the ship. Words that translate as 'with peace' but are used as goodbye.

The slow-moving boat had set his schedule behind. Dashing down the gangway, he hoped for youthful joints and a spry step going down the gangway to the cab. From Luxor, Jack would take a flight to Entebbe International on the shores of

Lake Victoria in Uganda. The biggest hotels were right on the shore. Jack would be able to walk around in a bathing suit from the swimming pool, to the edge of the lake, where he hoped to release a large packet of capsules. Retired, but not yet feeble, he had to finish this journey to the best of his ability.

The following day, weather permitting, he would take a small boat trip to the Kenyan side of the massive lake. After that, he would have a couple days left to visit rivers in West Africa. He had a confirmed flight to Conakry International in Guinea and another ticket back to Cairo, where he hoped to return to the Peace boat; that's if, Captain John wouldn't mind having him there permanently. Deep inside his heart, Jack knew it was his calling. The truth stared him down, like the bust of Tutankhamen gazing wide-eyed from under a gold striped nemes. Jack couldn't deny it any longer. Transmitting the Good News along the peaceful banks of the Nile was his life's calling, and he had to stay in Africa, for the rest of his life.

The wind had picked up. He looked out the fifth-floor window of his hotel room and thought back to Gamal's native recipes. The mere thought made him hungry. The last time he came to Lake Victoria, he had kabobs and curried potatoes for dinner. Tonight, at the downstairs restaurant, he hoped to duplicate that memorable feast.

Anticipation and hunger moved him toward sensational aromas that swirled from the dining room. Though his stomach churned more than usual, the hunger pangs went beyond the desire for food. Every step on the flower fringed stone path, reminded him of his goals. After years of wondering where he'd retire, the answers were projecting clear messages into his head. *Spend your retirement on the Peace boat.* A voice in his head seemed to say: Spread the word, write your poems and don't ever abandon your friends. *Go Jack go.*

"Just do it for the Lord." That's what Charlie would say, and that's what he heard.

A waiter handed him a menu, and as the sunlight set into the far-off hills, he watched a boat bobbing in the sparkling reflections caused by twilight. *"I will, Charlie. I will," he mumbled, before whispering a mealtime prayer of grace.*

# CHAPTER THIRTY-THREE

The skeptical looking steward considered Sparky's luggage. "Do you have more than backpack?"

"No, this is it." The high-speed bullet train sped towards Hong Kong.

"Can I look inside? It is for security purposes." The man set down his clipboard and reached for Sparky's pack.

"Yes, but they already checked it at the gate."

Sparky had put his last remaining pouches into his pockets. Besides a change of clothes, his backpack contained nothing but a first aid kit, bug repellant, deodorant and a shampoo bottle from the river cruise.

"No but. Backpacks can carry bad things such as explosives. I need to see inside."

Patience wasn't Sparky's thing and he was tired. He handed the man the bag. "There's nothing to see except my stinky clothes."

The man kept eye contact with Sparky while searching through each pocket of the olive-green canvas bag. When the man yanked out a pair of wrinkled pants, a small plastic bag filled with four capsules fell to the floor. The man bent down, picked up the bag and held it close to his face. "What is this? Narcotics?"

*Oh no, how did I forget about those?* "No, those are for seasickness," Sparky lied. Shit, shit, and more shit. This could be bad.

"You go on boat?"

"Yes, I just got back from Jiuzhaigou." He pointed to the shampoo. See? This is from the cruise."

The man nodded but didn't look convinced. He squinted, wanting more details, while asking more questions. "Did you see the Nuorilang waterfall and the lakes that are bluer than any blue in the world? It's like a painting."

"I did, hold on." Sparky took out his camera phone and flipped through several stunning pictures of the falls cascading over rocks and plants. Another photo had a turquoise blue lake called Tiger Lake. "So, you've been there too? Isn't it gorgeous?"

"Yes, I went many years ago for honeymoon." The man smiled, returning Sparky's clothes into his pack. "Okay, I see you are tourist."

Sparky sighed with relief. Maybe this man wouldn't bother him anymore. In an attempt to be friendly, he said, "Guess they had a seven-point earthquake over there a few years ago."

Now the man looked sad. "Yes," he nodded. "Many people die."

"I'm sorry; I shouldn't have brought it up."

"You drug addict?"

"No." Shocked at the question, Sparky worried he may have sounded defensive.

The man on the train shook his head and smiled. "Have nice trip."

"Wait, I need my motion sickness pills. Can I have them

back?" Sparky reached out with his hand, but the man shooed it away.

"No, I must give to senior engineer. You done with boat ride, no?"

"I plan on taking another boat ride to the mouth of the Yellow River Delta. He pulled the location up on his phone. "Look at this photo of the waterfall. Isn't that breathtaking?"

"This is high speed train to Hong Kong. We will stop near Yellow River in Jiangzhuang."

"Right, that's exactly where I'm going. Sparky took out the map and stared at it. "Jiangzhuang," he repeated to make sure he pronounced it correctly. Bluffing and taking another risk, he said, "I think the boat ride is near there."

"No," the man answered emphatically. "Not there, you will find Delta in Dongying."

The man looked weird again. Sparky had thought they had bonded over the pictures of waterfalls. He had smiled when he mentioned his honeymoon. Honestly, Sparky didn't want to go on another boat trip, but he had to find the Yellow river, make the drop and move toward the MeKong. That stupid four-day cruise had changed his schedule.

All the midnight buffets in the world were not enough to make him say he liked the cruise. Guys like him thrived on leisure, but only after they finished what they started. He didn't need towels shaped like panda bears, ping pong tournaments and cigar bars. What Sparky craved had to do with his own faraway mattress, his video games, his funny bobblehead dolls and a well-worn plaid quilt. More importantly, he couldn't let this frail, train-dude take the pills that could be used as evidence against him. Getting arrested had not been part of the plan.

The man had the pill-filled package clipped to the top of his clipboard. Sparky began to cough. "Sorry, I have allergies," he said to the man. "So, which stop should I take if I want to go on the boat trip, to see the waterfalls?"

The man flipped through some papers with names of the various stops along the way. Meanwhile, Sparky coughed again and reached for his water bottle. After taking a small sip, he aimed the spout under the turned pages on the clipboard, pushing the bottom of the bottle like a turkey baster. About eight ounces of water spurted out, dissolving the rice paper bag, immediately followed by disappearing capsules. "Man, I'm so sorry," said Sparky. "Did I get you wet?"

"Sit down," the man spat. "Row six, near window." The surprising splash of water went all over the man's hand and dripped down to his shoes. Sparky tried not to laugh, but knew he had to get off at the next stop, no matter what. If he stayed seated, the senior engineer would want to check his pockets. Absolutely no way, was he going to end his life in a communist jail. Sparky kept his eyes on his interrogator, who began to cross-examine a young pregnant woman. "Where is your husband?"

The train stopped. Sparky ran the other direction hoping to find an exit. Small musical dings were alerting passengers to be careful, as the doors opened and closed, somewhat fast. At the next car, he leapt off the train, and ran as fast as he could to blend in with a crowd.

When he turned the corner, he caught his breath and looked both ways to see if anyone had followed. "*Thank you, Mom,*" he whispered to himself. "*Thanks for being a caring, sensitive and wonderful mom. I'm thankful beyond words for our cultural identity and Asian heritage, because without it, not only would I not fit in around here, but I'd stick out like a sore thumb.*"

# CHAPTER THIRTY-FOUR

Drinking beer, instead of wine, didn't suit Etienne. After riding trains across Germany, taking leisurely boat rides and ferries, he zoomed down the autobahn in a luxury rental. Yawning but sober, he didn't understand why the locals seemed to prefer the beverage made with hops, rather than the luscious fruits of the gnarled vine. Most of his riverfront stops were close to famous breweries that took pride in using only the best, crystal clear water. Great water and fresh grains aside, he couldn't relate to the area's historic devotion to the bubbly brew, even though they bottled the stuff for over a thousand years.

Exhausted, he decided to take another boat tour on the Rhine because it advertised a stop at a winery. *His daughters would have loved this trip he thought, looking toward ancient buildings, fortresses, churches and photogenic castles.* After a few hours of superb wine-tasting, he found a nice hotel room nearby and passed out.

The next day, he planned to visit the Rhine-Main-Danube

Canal. The Captain of the Rhine boat had said there were water taxis going down the Danube towards Vienna and Budapest. Over the border in Hungary, he planned to enjoy his favorite Hungarian meal, consisting of Chicken Paprikash, which is served with handmade noodles and a side of sweet, yet tart, cucumber salad. First, he'd enjoy a glass of their famous, red wine, and for dessert he'd indulge in a slice of Dobosh Torte. The multilayered chocolate cake, his personal reward for a job well done. Anticipating the upcoming feast, made his mouth water and his stomach growl.

Over the years, he had become, what some folks call a 'foodie'. Perhaps unusual, the only food he craved outside of French cuisine, happened to be Hungarian fare. Rather than wanting gourmet, Parisian-inspired fusions blending the two cultures; he preferred ancient Magyar, (Hungarian) recipes, exactly as they originated. These were authentic, unique meals, not influenced too much by invaders who brought in Austrian, Russian, German, or Turkish tastes. Best of all, his hankerings were only 1400 miles away from home, which amounted to a long, scenic drive, with delectable eateries, and bed and breakfasts, along the way, or, a short flight. Maybe one day, he'd take the train and bring Suzanne. Either way, Etienne loved Europe, and all of its amazing, gastronomical decadence.

Hearty, satisfying, dinners in Hungary, are often served in the classic style, on wooden plates, with Roma musicians playing Braham's Hungarian Dances in the background. Incredibly memorable meals, similar to ones served to herdsmen on the plains, (the puszta), and comparable to feasts served to the aristocracy, that used to gaze from castles, onto the blue Danube. The tradition of soaking in hot baths, evident in the natural spas throughout Budapest, and all over Hungary, reminded Etienne that the minerals in the water, may make the difference in the taste of the food. *Would he, be skewing with the taste of the delicious food? Banish the thought!*

Real food, before the celebrity chefs arrived. He kept thinking of all the delicious choices waiting ahead. Meat dishes, such as cured Mangalitsa bacon, or fried turkey breast stuffed with foie-gras, spicy sausages and various types of salami, accompanied by warm shredded potatoes, stuffed turnips and sweet or hot peppers. He had tried many of the first course entrees, which consisted of chilled cherry soup or pureed zucchini, a delectable cream of mushroom soup, or a simple cheese spread on rye. His memories included side dishes, such as, dilled carrots, red cabbage stewed with wine, crisp cauliflower with toasted breadcrumbs and fabulous pickled vegetables.

*The walnut crepes are different--in some ways better--than the crepes Suzette back home. Generously stuffed with a hearty portion of sweetened ground nuts, they don't need a flambe or sauce to be magnificent.* He sighed, thinking about plum dumplings, beef goulash and the stuffed peppers served with grain bread, or a garlicky, fried bread called ***langos.*** All of it, made Etienne excited. *Oh, if I wasn't French, I'd want to be a Magyar!*

Other countries eat similar things, but the Hungarians create unique flavor combinations that go beyond the ubiquitous paprika. A few hundred miles away, neighboring countries use fresh herbs such as rosemary, oregano and basil, while the Hungarians prefer, parsley, dill, and caraway seeds. After a bountiful meal, everyone is offered a shot of apricot brandy, and serenaded by heart-wrenching gypsy music, which brings on misty-eyes, even for those who don't understand a word. Finally, trays of pastries are passed around. Some are layered with vanilla, chestnut cream or chocolate, and are served along with strong, sobering coffee. Most evenings end in laughter, kisses and hugs. In a small way, because of Hungary's difficult past, every day is considered a sort of celebration.

This would only be Etienne's fourth trip to the capital city, and he planned to make it memorable. First, he needed the wine list. He loved the dark red wine they call Bull's Blood, from a town called Eger. It has a deep, lingering flavor, similar to a Cabernet. Instead of one measly glass; he finished off the bottle. Somehow, he managed to amble out of the restaurant with a full stomach and a smile. *That was heavenly,* he thought straightening and attempting to place one foot in front of the other. *I'm too full for the water-taxi but I'll buy souvenirs for my girls.*

That afternoon, at the spectacular Chain Bridge, he threw some capsules over the rails. As they flew through the air, he heard someone yelling. "***Nem Szabad.***" (Not Allowed) Of course Etienne didn't understand the words. The officer thought he was littering. A forceful hand grabbed the slight Frenchman and pulled him along the sidewalk, shoving him back to the concourse, entering the bridge.

"***Be vagy rugva***?" (Are you drunk?) Befuddled at Etienne's behavior, the policeman kept repeating rules about littering, adding the various fines associated with throwing things into the river. Rambling in Hungarian, the copper kept saying ***tilos or forbidden,*** *but* Etienne didn't understand the language, unless it had something to do with food. "Francia," the cop said into his radio. Fortunately, he had to go fight some real crime, and had to leave.

Strolling, perhaps staggering along the river, he hoped to find another place that served the delightful red wine. Tomorrow, he'd take the train to the Vltava in Prague. After that, he'd visit the Chorna in Crimea and the Volga in Russia. At that moment however, he felt dizzy and wanted to find a good place to take a nap. Maybe after a short rest, he could find a place called a ***Csarda***, where they served more delicious, authentic food. *Despite the blasted police, Etienne loved this place, and planned on bringing his family back soon.* Fortunately, by morning, *he* wouldn't remember a single negative thing that happened.

# CHAPTER THIRTY-FIVE

A constant mist falls like angel dust in Kauai. Island breezes and sunshine make the flowers not only bigger, but blooms emit a sweet, alluring scent. The plants, lava rocks and the blue-green ocean, are only part of an unendingly picturesque display that includes: waterfalls with prisms of rainbows, mountains, fields of sugarcane, coffee plantations, volcanoes, unspoiled beaches and golf courses.

While Gary tagged along behind a few semi-professional golfers on a Princeville golf course, Becca decided to take pictures at the Botanical Gardens. The wind tousled her hair while she focused her camera on a large blossom, inhaled the intoxicating scent and snapped the photo. When her reggae ringtone began to play, it startled and jolted her upright. The phone indicated that the call came from the Riverside County Sheriff's Department.

"Is this Becca Wood?"

Hesitating, she answered, "Yes, and who is this?"

"Are you Linda Simpson's sister?"

"That's me. Is something wrong?"

"Well, I'm sorry to inform you, but your sister is missing. This is the Sheriff's Department. We had a giant flood around here, searched for survivors and waited a few days before calling, just in case she'd turn up. But we haven't located her, or a body. A manager, from her office, called us to see if we had heard anything. Did you hear about the storm?"

Becca didn't want to laugh, but she remembered, quite clearly in fact, the last conversation she had with her sister. "I'm sure she's fine. I'm on vacation and I'll be back in a couple of days."

"How do you know she's fine? Have you heard from her?"

"Not recently, but she called me the night of the flood and told me a fireman had rescued her."

"I see," he responded, flipping through papers. "Guess I better interview some of the firemen and first responders again. Must have missed something. Sorry to bother you. I hope you're right and she's alive. Our department put out a BOLO--which means 'Be on the lookout' and an APB. The television news reports keep showing her picture, every day. No one has come forth."

Becca remembered what had happened. The hospital had been in complete chaos. She didn't have time to listen to her whining little sister. "Dang, I can't imagine why she isn't at work. She likes her job. The night of the crazy storm I was at St. Francis Hospital. I work in ICU. I put her on hold, and by the time I came back, the call disconnected. I'm sure you know we had to relocate people from the bottom floor. One of your Sheriff's helicopters helped."

The mist turned into rain. Slowly, Becca moved down a paved path toward the parking lot and the rental car.

"Did you know her apartment building collapsed?"

"Oh, that's right. I heard everyone got out. Thank God Linda wasn't home when it happened."

"Right now, our department presumes she's dead. I'm sorry Ma'am. If I hear anything, I'll call you back."

*Dead? These people are mixing things up.* "Thank you, Sir." At the car, she contemplated the unsettling news. *Linda, I have three more days in paradise and you better be alive.*

Nurses saw it all. They either held hands with suffering family members or avoided them altogether. There were comatose patients, with miles of tangible wires connected to beating hearts, and intangible hearts praying in the hospital chapel. *Bad things happened to all her patients, but under no circumstances were horrible things supposed to happen to her.* Turning out of the gravel parking lot, she wanted to shout, "God, please find my sister." But the words stuck in her throat, and her tears blended with rain on the windshield.

# CHAPTER THIRTY-SIX

Paco promised to meet Juan at the El Dorado International Airport in Bogota. From there, they had to take a flight to Leticia, Columbia. They planned on taking a tour boat upriver to the city of Iquitos. Since they wouldn't have much time, they opted to stay one night in an eco-lodge. Buried in jungle in the middle of the Pacaya National Reserve, they'd have to fly back to Lima, and head to Los Angeles, where Juan still needed to conclude his drops in the L.A. River. *Those would be his final stops, before heading to LAX, where he'd board an international flight, and return to the most sensuous Italian woman on the planet. Every spoken word from her cherry lips, a romantic song. He day-dreamed of her soft, ebony hair, sparkling eyes, her Spumante like giggles that bubbled over when excited and, though intoxicating, those thoughts kept him going every day. Soon Giulia, I'll be in your arms again.*

"Hey Boss," Paco called out from the window of a compact car. He waved at Juan and grinned. The short and slender man looked exhausted, but had to come along because he knew how to pilot a small plane above dense jungles.

"Hey Bro, how was your trip to Venezuela?" Juan slipped into the passenger seat and watched his clever friend maneuver his way out of the main terminal to an airfield, a few miles away.

Paco's smile faded. "Not so good, but I made it. Even dropped deposits in the Orinoco. Remember when we met in El Paso? You gave me two extra packets and a lady saw you handing them over. She told me she needed them for her starving baby and if I don't give it to her she goes to police."

"Please tell me you didn't."

Shocked at Juan's comment, Paco laughed, "No, of course not." He waved his hand in the air as if flagging a taxi. "She thought they were expensive drugs to could sell."

"Never mind, we'll use them in the Amazon." Yawning, he felt as tired as Paco looked, maybe more so. "Are you as tired as I am? Man, I hiked up one river and trekked down another. Everything is sore." They boarded the small plane, turning the door handles into the locked position, and were on their way.

Paco's face showed more than mere exhaustion. A twinge of guilt spread over his haggard eyes, reminding Juan of a kid who stole the last cookie. "Mijo, please understand, I had to put them in the Rio Grande, because she was shouting for the Federales and the American Border patrol. What a big mouth. She kept yelling and pointing. The packs dissolved fast."

"That's okay," Juan replied, his drooping eyes drifting into sleep mode. "Wake me when we get there," he mumbled. But, after landing, he realized the two extra packets might cause trouble. He remembered Eric saying something about how too much, may cause Serotonin Syndrome, resulting in strange symptoms such as: diarrhea, rapid heart rates, tremors, confusion. It could even be life threatening. *Shit.* Juan grabbed his backpack and proceeded to exit the plane. *Too much of anything can be fatal, he thought with a shrug. Maybe even too much love.*

*Giulia. Her crazy, passionate kisses and her unending, physical desire for what seemed like a fathom of endless love. Every night, after demanding days at work, she needed him, and pounced all over him. Relentless in her sensual cravings, he tried hard to satisfy her longings, but she never let him sleep. After a wild night, and a long, grueling day at work, he'd step inside the front door and there she was, holding a glass of wine and popping out of a snug fitting negligee. No man in his right mind would complain, but he needed sleep.*

*'Wakeup', he said to himself, trying to refocus his thinking on the extra two packets. Maybe, because of the recent winter storms, the water would be higher, and there would be enough water to dilute the active ingredients in the medicine. One could only hope.*

"Come on Paco, time to bring peace to the jungle."

# CHAPTER THIRTY-SEVEN

Eric decided that since most of the current fighting involved Syria, he'd avoid that region. And, while Baghdad still didn't look peaceful, the Iraqi officers and aid workers were side by side, ensuring safe passage to diplomats, journalists, and residents. Eric's business card said, Pharmaceutical Supply Chain Manager. Soldiers were everywhere. Armored vehicles passed him as he hiked to the Fourteenth of July Bridge over the Tigris River. Somehow, he remembered which way to go, and he also recalled how the bridges had been destroyed during the fight with extremists. Everything looked almost normal. Outside of a little trouble getting a visa, he didn't have too many dramatic moments, and relied on a tiny book filled with translated phrases.

In his backpack, Eric had a picnic lunch he wanted to enjoy on the banks of the historic river. While he noshed, he thought about the other team members and hoped they were completing their tasks without any trouble. *By now, Linda should be in Florida, Juan, on his way back from the Amazon, and Etienne would be heading home from a high elevation in the Carpathian Mountains. Jack should be winding down his African adventures and Sparky might be finished at the Ganges.* This father-like anxiety of seeing them, would soon be over. Military planes and helicopters flew above him. Practice drills and earthshaking blasts could be heard in the distance. Each distant thud a sad reminder of war. He shuddered, counting the hours until he could tell Milo to go home.

The word 'home' sounded dreamy, but there were loose ends, and a bit more to do. He wasn't a soldier anymore, nonetheless, he still had to think like one. His personal mantra brought back the old days: Ready on the left, ready on the right, eyes wide open, boots on the ground and ready to rock. Reflecting back, he thought of the kind missionaries who baptized him in the river Jordan. They gave him good civilian advice about places to sleep, places to avoid and sent him off with caring words that helped him stay out of trouble. Most of all, he appreciated their prayers because he needed more than luck to get through all of it.

Tomorrow, he'd find a way to the Euphrates. The following day, he'd catch the flight to Erbil which would take him home.

Reeds and tall grass edged the river. The thought of going home put him in a good mood. Sitting on a large boulder, he skipped a pebble into the river when his phone rang. "Hello Eric, it's Milo, can you hear me?"

The special satellite phones made clear communication possible anywhere. Of course, the local military bases had put up cell towers, making reception with the states sound like a call from next door. "Wow, Milo, it's great to hear your voice. I was just thinking about you. What's up?"

"Sorry to bug you but this is serious. Juan hired a pilot over the Amazon to help him distribute from the air. I guess they tied each bag to a small rock--er--I don't know--something like that. Anyway, the aircraft ran out of gas—well we don't really know what happened—they had nowhere to land, guess they lost control.... Some witnesses heard the plane sputtering before it went down in the densest part of the jungle. A rescue team from Peru went out to search the area and couldn't find the wreckage."

Eric didn't know what to say. "When did you find out?"

"This happened yesterday. I have an App that allows me to zoom in with over 180,000 megapixels and I still couldn't see the plane. I saw the rescuers, but the rest is a massive green blur."

"And? What about those witnesses?"

"Indigenous locals who don't speak Spanish or Portuguese. One of them indicated they heard the plane, that's all."

Finally, today, the rescuers found Juan and his pilot, a guy called Paco. The plane had turned upside down and they were dead. They found Juan's waterproof phone—the one that leads only to me. Don't worry, I jammed the connection and disconnected the line. Anything incriminating dissolved on contact with the water. The jungle floor had recent rains and floods. They nose-dived into a marsh-like bog. I know he's your friend and I know you were close. Oh man, I don't know what to say. I'm so sorry."

Eric looked up at the cloud streaked, azure sky. A tear rolled down his face. "Milo, I can't believe it." Mouth agape, he sighed and words came out in slow motion. "Milo, this is so unexpected. Are they sure it was Juan?"

Milo made a small sound of agreement.

"We're almost finished with everything. I'm here in the birthplace of civilization and you're telling me the grim reaper came after my best friend. This can't be happening."

"I know, I know, but it happened. I feel your pain, bud. At least he checked out doing something honorable. Dude is a hero. I didn't know him too well, but he had cool down to a science."

Eric continued to throw rocks into the Tigris River. "What was the other guy's name?"

"Paco. I only know this because Juan told me about him piloting the plane. Poor fellow. They have no way of identifying him because he didn't carry I.D. The authorities down in Peru called before I disconnected Juan's phone. Paco didn't even have a phone. Told me they have no way of finding out anything about him. I didn't think I should offer any information, so I didn't volunteer his name. It's so freaking sad."

"What about Juan? Did you call Giulia?" Eric strained to listen, but the phone went silent for a few seconds. "Milo?"

"Oh man, like most good stories this one has a twist." Milo bit his lip before blurting, "Giulia called a week ago, said she's in love with some other guy, and she's moving to Scotland."

Eric threw another pebble and watched the concentric circles ripple in the smooth flowing water. "That bites," he said wiping tears with his sleeve. "That bites worse than a mouth full of habanero."

"Yup, at least Juan didn't know about it."

"You didn't tell him?"

"No, why should I break his heart?" Milo replied, "Figured he'd find out soon enough."

"Good call, my friend," Eric said with a sniff. "This is bad. Putrid and rotten, rolled into an old cheese sandwich and stuffed into worn gym socks bad."

"That's pretty bad. It looks like you're trying to look at the bright side. Be careful out there in the war zone."

"No war right now but you're right, anything can happen. Anyway, I'll be landing in San Diego in two days."

"Bet you're glad for that."

"I'm not sorry we did this. Minus one, we're still a team. Cross your fingers that it all works out as planned. And, you're right Milo; Juan is my hero whether it does, or doesn't."

# CHAPTER THIRTY-EIGHT

Like a forlorn Cinderella, Linda daydreamed atop her bunk. Though she had no delusions of being a princess, she thought back to the incredible sights and sounds she had enjoyed at Disney World. Though she only rode a few rides, she had fun experiencing all the various lands, where she tasted different foods and saw cute shows, while thinking of her own handsome prince, far away, on another continent. *The park is an unreal, magical place, where fantasies become possibilities, and on some level, exactly what her team wanted to instill into a world filled with hate. The only problem is, reality keeps getting in the way. If ever she, Linda Simpson needed rescuing, this was that moment. Eric!*

The dank, ice-cold cell felt like a refrigerator. The place smelled like old cheesy socks and used baby butt wipes. Some drunk moaned in another holding tank. Footsteps approached.

"Sleep well Miss Mulligan?' The voice came from a rotund female officer.

Linda looked down at her own wrist, remembering how they took her watch, her shoelaces, and executed an embarrassing body cavity search. "I was tired," she yawned. It was six in the morning, and she had arrived two hours ago.

"Detective Vega wants to talk to you."

"Right now?"

"Well," the officer glanced at a clock in the hall, "I think you have time."

"I'm supposed to catch a flight from Atlanta."

"You should have thought of that before you were caught. Now come on." She unlocked the door and accompanied her to the questioning room. "Sit here. You want coffee?"

Linda nodded, and thought back to the previous evening when she drove from Orlando, stopping quickly to make a deposit at the Kissimmee River, before heading north to the Panhandle area. Twilight fell as she entered the Tallahassee area. Eric had made reservations for her at a place called Wakulla Springs.

Nightfall had come faster than she thought it would, and once she exited the highway, the way to the resort took a circuitous route into a pitch dark but foggy nightmare. Embraced in a bear hug of lush tropical vegetation, the road winded around tall trees, no stars, no moon and only the headlights on the car. Danger seemed to lurk behind the trees. *The sound of tires on asphalt competed with the thumping of her heart. An uneasy feeling of being lost made her nervous, and the lack of other cars made her think she should turn back.* Finally, she noticed a rustic wooden sign, 'Wakulla Lodge, Up Ahead'.

By this time, she could hardly keep her eyes open.

After navigating the extra-long driveway, she saw a group of buildings that would have been a perfect backdrop for a movie set among Army barracks, circa 1930. A meager bulb lit the stairwell next to her downstairs unit. It was past 11PM, but a sign on the building said the custodian would have the key, after hours.

The dusty room had looked like a monk had occupied it, many years ago, perhaps in the Middle Ages. There were no fancy hotel extras, no minibar, no desk with stationary, in fact nothing but a bed, a nightstand and a wobbly lamp. It all kind of looked like her current accommodations. A giant moth fluttered under the shade. One towel in the bathroom looked like it had visible germs. She remembered how she had collapsed onto the squeaky bed.

*At midnight, she woke up, worried because she had to leave early for Atlanta to catch her flight. Two weeks were almost over. Hooray, she wanted to celebrate, to fall into Eric's arms, and make love all night. Maybe, she'd cook him breakfast every day for the rest of their lives.* The resonating, deep sound of an owl pierced the silent compound. Ominous looking turkey vultures wandered around outside her door. *Focus, she told herself. This last drop of pleasure-filled medication could make a big difference in the lives of important, influential people.*

Blinking several times, her eyes were having trouble adjusting to the dark. At least she could make out basic shapes in the distance. Through the mess of tangled vines and immense trees, she saw a bridge, several boats near the water and the silhouette of more turkey vultures. *Maybe, she thought, it looked pretty cool in the daytime.* A chorus of frogs filled the damp night air. The springs were located a small distance from the buildings and the parking lot, at the end of a flower-rimmed, paved path. Had she found that walkway, it could have saved her.

After a few minutes she had landed in sludge. Soft, gushy mud that felt like it would suck the sneakers off her feet. Each step a sloppy chore, she dragged herself to the edge of the water and hunched over to make sure she wouldn't slip into the quicksand like goop. When she tossed the packet, it had set off the motion detector flood lights and the surveillance cameras.

Though she couldn't be sure, a large crocodile splashed his tail and moved in her direction. That's when she had screamed.

In her possession were four more packets meant for Georgia and Chicago. *Guess she wasn't going to be meeting her friend at the Tribune.* Dodging behind a tree, she had tried to move as fast as possible toward the car. Out of breath, she pulled the last four packs from her pocket. The lights didn't bother her as much as the crocodile. She stomped the pharmaceuticals into the slimy mud, hoping the croc wouldn't catch up and eat her. Seconds later, her face met the wet muck, when two security guards grabbed her, wrestling her to the ground.

# CHAPTER THIRTY-NINE

Milo had to reach Eric to tell him he saw Linda on the news. The grainy video showed her throwing a small bag over her shoulder, while running from an alligator with gigantic teeth. The newscasters referred to her as a terrorist wanting to plant plastic explosives. A dive team had been summoned to locate the substance in the bag, but found nothing. As if it mattered, the reporters called the toothy beast a crocodile. And, either way, Linda was in trouble.

Held for questioning until further notice, they identified her as Nancy Mulligan from California. When he heard the words Wakulla County Sheriff's department on the television, Milo sat up and listened. Police detectives kept leaving him voice mails that came through on Linda's phone. One message from Homeland Security said she would be held without bail until their team of experts found out what she threw in the water. After several nerve-wracking messages, Milo destroyed all traces of the line. The next time someone called, they would reach an untraceable general telephone company recording, about a wrong number.

There were so many things Milo needed to tell Eric. For one thing, Etienne slipped on ice at the Volga, and though he wasn't badly injured, the bruises made him head home to Paris. And, he wanted to tell him that Jack had decided to ride out the rest of his days on the Peace boat, going up and down the Nile. So, they wouldn't be seeing Jack back at the condo. Then, there were a few depressing details about Juan's upcoming funeral, and now this fiasco with Linda, which could potentially be the worst news of all. If they find something, or she says the wrong thing, they could all fall into the proverbial toilet, flushed and forgotten forever.

Unfortunately, however, both Sparky and Eric were unreachable. Both, were in the air and flying home. Both, were supposed to hire a shuttle from the airport. Milo had promised to meet them at Eric's pad, and Linda was supposed to greet everyone with cold brews. This craziness was her idea in the first place, and now, things were getting messed up. Milo felt like a nervous baker holding a five-tiered wedding cake, while running from a growling Doberman. In two weeks, everything had changed and the future looked bleak.

*What a cluster of unimaginable consequences. Juan had been a decorated military man and an ammunition specialist, with a chest full of medals to show for it. He should be the last man on earth to be piranha chow in South America. Maybe, thought Milo, he could arrange a service for Juan coinciding with the arrival of the others. The idea alone made him feel better. He'd do a search and find out about his family. He'd contact a pastor at a non-denominational church, print out large photos of Juan, both in uniform, and doing other things he loved. Naturally, Eric could say a few words. He wondered whether the pictures of Juan in Rome should include Giulia. After all, the bitch dumped him for some other guy. And yet, he remembered Juan's words about how much he loved his Italian beauty.*

*Amore aside, maybe she'd have to be in the photos, but she wouldn't be invited to the memorial; no way, no how. Not over his own dead body, and that was final.*

# CHAPTER FORTY

"Hope you like it black," the officer said. She placed a paper cup in front of Linda and turned on the television. "Vending machine is out of creamer and we don't have a cappuccino machine."

"That's fine," Linda replied. The officer's attempt at humor didn't phase her and she didn't smile.

"Detective Vega will be here shortly. I'll be at my desk but you can ring for room service." The officer opened the door and her laughter echoed down the hallway.

*Still not funny*, thought Linda. She yawned, and watched the news report. A man and a pretty female reporter sat behind an enormous blue desk. The woman said, "Thank you for watching Weekend Recap. I'm Adrienne Brae and this is Conner Names. So, Conner, what do you make of this strange food poisoning alert down in El Paso?"

"The country has had enough with the romaine lettuce recall, right?"

"Officials are fairly certain this isn't e-coli, which has fever and vomiting associated with it. The CDC is certain these mild cases of diarrhea and nausea are simply what they call Montezuma's revenge, down in that part of the country."

Conner chuckled, "So, just some bad tacos, huh?"

The woman, Adrienne, put her hand to her mouth, in a mock effort to conceal agreement with the politically incorrect question posed by her cohost. Wanting to change the subject, "I guess they have to do more research." She shuffled a few papers and pulled out another report. "Then there's this frightening scene in Florida. Have you seen the video going viral?"

Linda's mugshot, flashed on the screen. *Oh Eric. Where are you?*

"Yup, Adrienne, I've seen it and it's quite a shocker. Officials have identified the possible terrorist subject as Nancy Mulligan, from California. Take a look at this surveillance video taken at Wakulla Springs, which is a national treasure, and a natural habitat for wildlife. As you watch, notice she's throwing something over her shoulder. You can see it right there. Subsequently, she screams, and runs from a pretty dangerous looking crocodile."

"Ooh my gosh." Adrienne looks horrified.

"The authorities have studied the footage. They believe it looks like a type of plastic explosive. While her motives are unclear, Miss Mulligan is being detained for questioning. They have dispatched bomb-sniffing dogs, and scuba divers to the scene hoping to locate the explosives before they detonate."

"Wow, Conner, that's scary, I wonder what would motivate her to throw explosives into a crystal-clear river?"

"This all happened at midnight, making some locals think she had some sort of diabolical worship situation associated with it, perhaps a cult. Certain cultures practice witchcraft at late hours. Those who practice voodoo also have opinions on this subject."

"You mean she might have thrown an eye of newt or something?"

Conner nodded. "Yikes, huh? Think about it, Adrienne. Nancy Mulligan doesn't look like a Unabomber."

*Linda yawned. If love is a cult, she's guilty as hell.*

The woman smiled, shook her light blond hair as if to dismiss the shock of it all, and picked up another piece of paper. "Finally, we have the man running for office, who probably won't be governor of Colorado."

"Adrienne, you must be talking about the sensational story regarding Mark Shegg. If you haven't already heard about the scandalous rumors and the charges of sexual misconduct against Mark Shegg, you will hear them now. Three women have come forward accusing the ex-Boulder Mayor of harassment and sexual assault."

*Mark? Linda looked up at the television and couldn't believe it. Her assailant's face flashed on the screen in the first photo. They also showed him in his trusty blue suit, shaking hands with constituents who were supposed to vote for him. What a disgusting pig!*

Short clips of three attractive women were shown. They all emphatically accused Mark, and all three looked, and sounded believable. None of the accusations surprised Linda. In fact, she had a notion there were many others.

Mark had accosted them at his office in Denver, at a nearby dining establishment and at a hospital fundraiser. 'Allegedly, there are other victims', the newscaster said. Both announcers urged women to come forward if they had any undesirable contact with Mark Shegg. *There might be hundreds,* thought Linda.

"In a surprise twist in this scandalous race for governor, Mark Shegg's attorney told our sister station in Colorado, that two of the women are making things up, because Mark was in New York two weeks ago, speaking at a political fundraiser."

"What about the third woman, Conner? You mean she wasn't making things up?"

"Apparently, they know she's not lying, because, listen to this, Mrs. Shegg, who left him a week ago, has phone records and receipts as evidence."

The two newscasters made a sad face, followed by a quick smile. "What a weekend," Adrienne said. "Thanks for joining us for Weekend Recap."

# CHAPTER FORTY-ONE

Detective Vega walked into the room and threw a folder on the table. He muted the television and pulled out a folding chair. "Nancy? I'm Joe Vega."

Linda nodded at the slick looking detective who wore a violet shirt under a tan suit. The top buttons to his shirt were open, displaying a gold medallion.

"Do you know you're being charged with a very serious crime?"

She shook her head. "Beats me--I didn't do anything wrong."

He pursed his lips and paused, as if thinking of some sort of strategic way to pose a question. "Then, why don't you explain to me what happened?"

"I did. I told them everything. Don't you have it in that report?" She pointed to the manila folder on the table.

"Sorry, but I have to hear the whole story again."

Linda sighed. "Whatever, not much to tell.... I didn't get to the resort until it was super late and, after a long drive, I needed a walk. My legs felt like pretzels. I spent the whole day driving up from Orlando, where I visited amusement parks. Since I was checking out in the morning to go to Atlanta, figured I'd do some late-night tourism. Looks like an interesting place, but as soon as I saw the water, the lights came on. That's when a croc came after me, so I screamed. Guess I woke up the security people—the park ranger—the sheriff's department and whoever brought me here."

"How does that explain the bag of explosives?" Vega asked with a sneer.

"I heard some reference to explosives on the television news. Have no clue what you, or anyone for that matter, are talking about. Me? With explosives, that's a laugh. I'd probably kill myself."

He tried a different tack. "Lady, why would you go to an amusement park all by yourself anyway? You're a pretty girl. Don't you have a boyfriend?"

"I do." *Any more information and she'd need a lawyer. Things weren't looking good, but she didn't think they had anything on her. Those weren't explosives, and she didn't have a trace of anything in her bag, or her pockets. All the pills had been sealed in the rice-paper bags. Gone, like magic, and her lips were sealed.*

"But, why doesn't he travel with you?"

She shrugged.

"Tell me this, what's with the Band-Aids on your ankles and the scratches on your arms? What happened?"

She shrugged again.

"Look lady, the camera doesn't lie. The clock said midnight. There you are tossing something over your shoulder and screaming like a banshee. Copies of the video are in the hands of homeland security. This is a serious matter. We looked at that tape several times and the object flying through the air glistens in the floodlights, but we have no idea what it could be. It's hard to assess the density and the material properties on the footage, because it's like a flash of light."

"Did you see the giant croc? I didn't know it was so close until I saw it on television. Why don't you assess the properties of the wild beast, with enormous molars? If he ate me for a midnight snack would your department feel any better?"

"Excuse me for not gushing with sympathy," he said facetiously. "We saw the croc, but that is a nature preserve. It's a sanctuary for wild animals and uncontaminated water. Hypothetically, let's just say you were throwing a plain old sandwich bag through the air, with nothing more than a few crumbs in it. Guess what? You'd still be sitting in front of me."

Wanting to sleep, she closed her eyes.

Vega's powerful voice took on an air of authority. "Am I keeping you awake, Miss Mulligan?"

"What? I don't know what you want from me." The florescent lights reflected off his black shiny hair. She blinked, but her lids were heavy. *I'm tired, can't you leave me alone?*

"Namely the truth, I've heard the truth has been known to set people free."

A photo of Mark Shegg flashed on the television. Displaying bleached white teeth, he grinned like an evil troll. When she saw her assailant, the sight of him jolted her wide awake.

Linda looked at the screen and pointed. "You want truth? That man is sick and depraved. I can't believe he's running for office. What types of people elect candidates that attack women?"

Vega glanced at the television and back at Linda. "You've met him?"

"Unfortunately, yes. He's the one who should be behind bars, not me." She cursed herself for saying anything, realizing she may have opened up a can of squiggly worms.

"Sounds like a story you need to share with us. Maybe, your anger toward a political candidate, is the motive you needed to plant explosives."

*Change the subject, she yelled, inside her mind.* She had to get off the topic of Mark Shegg. "Detective Vega, I don't know what that object is on the video. Seriously, do I look like a bomb expert?" Yawning like a hippo stuck in a quagmire of thick mud, she felt trapped. First, Mark, then a bear, now this annoying detective had her cornered. *It would help if she weren't exhausted. Think Linda, think.*

"We have teams combing the area. These professionals, take measurements, bring in drug enforcement canines that can sniff out anything, while scuba divers and an army of volunteers make sure the protected, historic region remains safe. Mark my words Miss Mulligan, they will find out if you're lying. They will find your plastic bag, and let me reiterate, these are experts who will find the contents. After which, you may have to spend years in prison. Wouldn't it be easier to tell me what really happened?

Raising his voice, he continued his monologue. Linda stared at her hands and didn't say anything.

"Why are you trying to distract me with some story about politics? It seems like a ruse. In fact, you seem devious and clever. I'm not suggesting a hearing until we find something." He stood, pushing the chair against the table with a violent shove. "Nancy Mulligan you are pissing me off."

Good, he didn't believe her comments about Mark Shegg. Based on all the news reports, that douchebag would get what he deserved anyway. At the moment, she had to worry about her own butt. One thing she knew for certain: they could burrow all the way to China, and they still wouldn't find any plastic bag, or any of the secret contents, in that cesspool of unblemished and protected mud.

# CHAPTER FORTY-TWO

There's a feeling of comfort that takes place seconds after stepping off an airplane. An invisible weight, lifts off the shoulders, you inhale fresh air, and there's the anticipation of sleeping in your own bed. *Now I understand why homeowners put up little plaques that say, 'Home Sweet Home', thought Eric. Travel is great, but there's nothing like home.*

The minute he stepped into the airport; his phone went off. "Hey Milo thanks for calling, buddy." Eric continued without listening. "Are you going to meet us tomorrow morning? Linda should be there by now. If not, the neighbor has my key."

Humbled by heroic teammates, Milo couldn't begin to understand, or explain, how glad he felt knowing Eric had returned. The last two weeks had been heavy duty, more than he could imagine, plus a lot of responsibility. Milo sighed, waiting to see if Eric wanted to keep talking. *Please keep talking. Go on, don't stop. Eric should talk all day. Even the sound of his voice felt like a salve upon a wound.*

*Up to this point, the burdens had landed on him. The bizarre calls, the waiting and pressure, the uncomfortable situations, not to mention the sad decisions no one should have to make alone.* Finally, Eric stopped babbling and took a breath.

"Glad you made it back safe," Milo said. But he had to end the small talk, and get to the point. "Linda's still in Florida. Seems she had trouble in Wakulla Springs. They kept her for questioning. It's all over the news."

"Shit. Are you serious?" It felt like an obstruction had landed in his throat; so much for home sweet home. At least I'm at the airport." He didn't hesitate for a second. "Guess I'm going to Florida."

"You must be kidding. I can't imagine how tired you are from all the traveling."

"How tired am I?" Eric tried to make a joke. "I'm so tired, I feel like a rug. And not a bright colored Persian rug, but a faded-out piece of trash you find rolled up behind a dumpster. It's so gross even the poorest of the poor wouldn't want it. Most dogs wouldn't sleep on it. Well, a chihuahua might poop on it."

"Okay, okay, I get it." But Milo didn't laugh. He knew Eric had to sugarcoat his weakness. *The guy had to be beyond exhausted.*

"Hope we're back soon. Doubt they can hold her for more than a few days. What's the scoop?"

"There's video of her screaming and running from the edge of the water, after seeing a croc. They filmed her tossing something over her shoulder. The worst part is, these idiots are convinced its plastic explosives. They have bomb sniffing dogs and a research team searching the entire park."

"Man, you're full of good news, anything else?" He searched for a place to sit down.

"Well kind of, but nothing worse than losing Juan. I still can't believe that happened."

Eric sat on the edge of a concrete planter. He watched the fast-moving, grim-faced, crowds shuffle past him. *How many days, he wondered, until something would change? This giant experiment in saving the world might not even work. Brace yourself, he thought, but keep thinking positive.* "Spill it Milo, I'm catching a flight to Tallahassee."

"Jack's staying on the Peace boat, like forever. He's retiring on it. Told me to tell you, he's happiest preaching and sailing down the Nile."

"I get that. What else?"

"Let's see, Etienne bashed his knee on a rock. He slipped on ice in Russia and might need surgery. Anyway, he had to go home a few days early."

"Oh, poor guy, that must have hurt. Going home makes sense. What about our man Sparky?"

"He's doing fine. On his way to see his mom--probably won't come by for a few days-- said he wants to sleep for a week."

Eric nodded. Like a group of zombies, people rolled their baggage past him in a daze, as if he belonged with the plants in the enclosure. Mothers held tiny fingers and scolded bigger kids, while balancing awkward packages. Babies cried. Men in elegant plaid suits gripped silver attaché cases, taking long steps towards their gate. No one looked happy. Everyone looked miserable.

"Did you zone out, or can you hear me?"

"I heard everything."

"I'm not coming down until you get back, besides, I like Canada. The people are super nice."

Eric laughed, "So I've heard. And that's without medicine."

"Oh Eric, there's one more thing. I'm putting together a small memorial for Juan in your old Long Beach neighborhood.

I called his family, and his dad told me there are a few soldiers who want to attend."

"That's awesome. Too bad his fashion industry co-workers live so far away. What about Giulia, do you think we should invite her?"

"No way," Milo replied, sounding adamant.

# CHAPTER FORTY-THREE

While flying across the country, Eric had time to devise a plan, to spring his beloved. The only problem, he envisioned, centered on the fact, that she might hate his idea. Either way, they didn't have much of a choice. She'd have to go with the flow, or leave them all exposed and vulnerable. He mumbled a prayer, and hoped the good Lord heard his plea.

Once the plane landed, he called Milo back. "Okay, I'm in Florida. Where are they hiding my partner in crime?"

"The television news said, she's being transferred to the Florida Women's Reception Center, sometime today."

"A reception center, huh? Has a nice ring to it."

"Place is off Highway 75."

"Guess I'm off to find my wayward woman."

"What are you going to do?"

Eric sighed. "It's complicated, watch the news."

Milo laughed, "Got it boss. Go save her. Talk to you soon. I'll be at your place in a few days."

Good thing he slept on the flight, because after renting a car, it took ages to reach the facility. Eric turned onto a private road. A beige sign in front of the center said, "We Never Walk Alone." Small white clouds dotted the horizon and decorative palm trees flanked the front door. Soft music flowed from speakers.

The lobby consisted of a white laminate counter, and a few plastic chairs. There were brochures for understanding various mental health issues, and a large stack of flyers listing locations for AA meetings. When his arm brushed against the counter, he accidentally knocked a pink pamphlet to the floor. He shuffled after it, his tennis shoes squeaking on the tile, but none of the noises bothered the receptionist. She stared at her computer. "Excuse me?" Eric asked. "I thought I saw my girlfriend, Linda Simpson on the television." He pulled out Linda's old driver's license. The one with the picture Linda didn't like. "This is Linda, have you seen her?"

The lady behind the desk put on her spectacles. Like a garden snail, she stood and shuffled to the front counter. She took the picture from his hands. "No, we don't have anyone who looks like that." The woman shook her head, and said she was sorry.

"Did you get any new inmates, today?"

"We did, but none of them look like your lady friend." She turned toward her desk and mumbled a goodbye.

Eric didn't come thousands of miles to be turned away. "Ma'am, I'm sorry, but is there any chance I can see some of the recent arrivals? This is an old picture, and I'm almost positive, she's here. Did anyone come in from the Wakulla Sheriff's department?"

"Well, there are a few from Wakulla County." Each word seemed stretched out to Eric, as if she enjoyed torturing him by drawing out the conversation, for no reason at all. "We have orientation the first day. Right now, there's one young woman walking around with a counselor, learning about our wonderful facilities. We like to make our girls feel as comfortable as possible, considering most have extended stays. Isn't this a lovely day to be in Florida?" She grinned, as if he had asked her to pose for a photo.

"Yes, it is—er—I agree," answered Eric. "This is a first-rate place, and today's a wonderful day. Of course, it'd be even better if I could see my girlfriend."

"Sir, I'm sorry," she said, with her southern drawl. "She's not one of our guests. Maybe she's at the facility in Jacksonville."

"Would you mind looking in your computer?"

"Why don't you believe me? In case you can't hear very well, I'll repeat myself. There is no one in our facility by the name of Linda Simpson. Anything else?"

Eric felt defeated, but not completely. He still had a few options. He could stay, maybe speak to someone else, or blow her entire cover in a giant messy heap. All he would have to do is ask for Nancy Mulligan, but deep in his heart he felt torn. He had to wait, especially because he loved her and wanted everything to work out. "Fine, I'll come back, maybe she'll be here later."

The woman looked annoyed, and sat down with a huff. Red circles appeared on her cheeks, when the chair-cushion made a squeak. Eric waved goodbye.

He yanked open the heavy door and noticed Linda strolling, alongside an attendant. She wore blue pants, white socks and gray sneakers. The small clouds had grown larger and the air felt humid. Only thirty-feet, of warm, moist air, separated them. He had to talk to her. Linda saw him coming and her eyes grew enormous. "Linda, it's me, he shouted."

*Linda wanted to run to his arms, but, right now anyway, that wasn't happening. Never in her life had she felt happier to see another human being. A person she loved with every molecule in her body. She admired Eric's large, perfect nose and decided that despite the piercing; it looked mighty, and his face belonged on a coin. She couldn't stop staring at his protective arms, his long eyelashes and his lovable, reindeer eyes. While away, during his travels, he had a haircut, which made him look like a fresher, almost lovelier version of the previous Eric. Two weeks of work had kept her busy, and her mind occupied. At that moment, it felt as if they had been apart for years.*

When he called her by her real name it took her by surprise. Eric locked eyes with the athletic, middle-aged attendant who dragged Linda in the opposite direction. "Who are you?" the woman asked with a snappy tone. Eric moved closer.

"My name is Eric, and that's Linda, my girlfriend." He grabbed Linda's hand and tried to pull her from the muscular woman.

"Have you lost your mind?" This is Nancy Mulligan. Please go away immediately or I will contact security."

He held up the license, but the woman tried to push him away. "Look, she left this driver's license with me. Her apartment collapsed during a flood. She must have bumped her head. Her name is Linda Simpson. Ask her if she has a sister called Becca."

The attendant took a phone from her pocket and dialed a number. "There's a man here—could be dangerous--says this inmate isn't Nancy Mulligan. Yes, I'll ask her." She paused to listen to the person on the other end. "Okay, we'll go to the office." Returning the phone to her pocket, she said, "Nancy, why don't you tell this clown to bugger off before he's arrested and thrown into jail too?"

Linda looked down at her clean prison scrubs. When she spoke, it was a soft whisper and the woman didn't hear her. Eric's clammy fingers held on tight and didn't let go. *Voices were muffled by the sound of her heart pumping blood. Blood that coursed through her body, on its way to Eric, where it turned around, returning in an endless loop. They were connected. He had come to rescue her, and it felt like bliss.*

"I can't hear you," the woman shouted, much like a commanding officer. "Let go of his hand so we can continue your orientation."

Linda mumbled again but wouldn't let go of Eric's hand. "He's telling the truth. My name is Linda and I work in advertising. My sister's name is Becca."

"This is ridiculous," the woman said. "First off, I can hardly hear you. Did you say you're in advertising? What does that have to do with anything? Secondly, strange men are not supposed to be holding hands with our prisoners. Lastly, we need to get this resolved. Advertising specialist or not, you committed a crime and are guilty anyway. And, that's whether you know this guy or not, or whether you're Nancy, or George fricking Washington."

Adding fuel to the fire, Eric squeezed Linda's hand, and spoke up in her defense. "She didn't commit a crime."

"We'll see about that. Come with me before I call for backup," she yelled at Linda. "You too," she said, pointing at Eric.

# CHAPTER FORTY-FOUR

Calls that came into the sheriff's station in Wakulla, rang ten times, before being routed to voicemail. From behind a glass door, a barrage of curse words bounced off the walls and slid under the door.

The Chief Deputy swung open his office, shouting across the room. "Kocsma, why aren't you answering the phone?" Big and bald, the six and a half-foot Chief couldn't help being an imposing figure, and realized he should calm down before scaring away the more sensitive members of his staff. The employees pretended to work and stared at their computers. The Chief took a few long steps and stood by the front desk, where he consciously inhaled and took several deep breaths. His wife had suckered him into yoga classes to help reduce his blood pressure, but he wasn't sure all the hype and namaste was working. He'd have to admit, that the breathing exercises kept him from wanting to pull his weapon on a few idiot deputies.

Ever since the bloody debacle at the Liquor store on 9th, Officer Kocsma had been placed on desk duty, and the moron didn't like it. "Awe boss, I'm working on the best way to answer.

Listen to this: 'Thank you for calling Wakulla Springs Sheriff's Department where we shoot the bad guys.'"

The Deputy Sheriff had a lot to do. Kocsma, more than anyone else in his department, got on his nerves. He sat down on the edge of a desk and listened. "I don't think so. Have you lost your mind?"

"How about this: "Wakulla Springs, where evil drowns?"

"You're kidding, right?" The sheriff wasn't sure what to think. With Kocsma it could go either way, and, if this was the numbskull's idea of humor, he didn't like it.

Kocsma pouted. "Any hope of a transfer back to patrol?"

"Save it Kocsma. Not anytime soon. Good whiskey ages in ten years. Maybe we'll start there. You need work boy, especially, if you insist on answering the phone like a wacked out teenager running from a Levy County meth lab. Take it from me boy, you're lucky you weren't suspended, permanently." The Chief inhaled and pointed at the phone. "Now answer the phone like an officer of the law."

"But Chi...chief, I don't think you understand...."

"I understand everything, and the answer is a resounding, no."

The phone rang. Kocsma smiled and answered on the second ring. "Thank you for calling the internationally acclaimed Wakulla Springs Sheriff's department, where everyone is in a great mood."

The Chief turned beet red and marched back to his office to take the call. "I'll deal with you later Kocsma," he said, through clenched teeth. The door slammed and the glass on the door wanted to shatter into a million pieces. But it didn't. A few staff members snickered before returning their gaze to computer screens.

The call came from the Warden of the women's jail, regarding Nancy Mulligan. The Warden explained that the woman in question had a male companion who came to pick her up. According to the boyfriend, her real name is Linda Simpson. After checking with the officials in her hometown, it checked out. Nancy Mulligan is Linda Simpson. The Chief needed to follow up.

"I'll get back to you...don't release her yet. Having an alias makes her even more suspicious. Does she have next of kin?"

"One sister," the Warden replied.

"Thanks." He hung up and returned to the front of the building. As he passed by, several pair of eyes rose above the monitors. "Kocsma, get me Vega. I need to talk to him about that terrorist woman he transferred out of here. If you reach him, tell him I want to see him right away. Hurry up." The Chief walked out the front door. He needed fresh air and a strong cup of coffee from the donut shop. "Back in fifteen."

## CHAPTER FORTY-FIVE

Linda and Eric sat in the Warden's office on a new leather couch. A large window looked out onto a grassy yard, where a group of women sat on concrete picnic tables, taking part in a craft class.

The Warden shuffled some papers and put on reading glasses. "Young lady, I don't know what to do with you. According to your record, as Nancy Mulligan, you were throwing plastic explosives into Wakulla Springs. According your friend here, your name is Linda Simpson, and, you almost drowned back home. If you are Linda, and we have good reason to believe you are Linda, then, what are you doing way over here in Florida?"

Linda shrugged. "I'm not sure."

The tall, athletic woman sat like a queen at her expansive desk. The pastel pink suit didn't hide the fact that she seemed stronger than the attendant who gave the orientation. Veins and muscles were exposed on her thick neck, because she wore her blondish hair in a loose bun. Linda thought she looked like an

Olympic shot putter, trying to hide under a pretty silk blouse. Eric would probably say she needed estrogen supplements.

"You might want to figure it out, because the Sheriff's department is sending a detective over, right now. I spoke with the Chief, and also the detective. Neither one sounded happy."

"Can I take her home?" Eric had repeated this question about a hundred times. "If you spoke to anyone in her hometown, they can verify the flood, her apartment complex washing away, and, they even found her car in a ditch."

"Eric, when we get to that point, we'll discuss alternatives for getting her back to California. I'm sure you don't want to hear this, but I can only release her to immediate family. That's if she's getting released. Don't count your chickens. She might have to spend ten years here. That's if she's not transferred to a regular prison." The Warden pointed and wagged her index finger at Linda. "This woman is accused of a serious crime."

The phone on her desk made a small beep, and she picked up the receiver. "Yes, ask him to come in."

Linda admired the walnut paneling on the desk. When she saw detective Vega, she wanted to figure out a way to crawl under it. The last time they spoke, he had shouted, acting like he wanted to throw a chair at her.

Detective Vega waved, and even made a small deferential bow in the direction of the Warden. He came over to the couch, shaking hands with Eric. When he shook her hand, he squeezed hard and said, "Hello Nancy, nice to see you again."

Linda yawned and turned to look outside at the happy artists.

Vega moved to a chair by the desk, sat down and crossed a leg over his knee. He didn't wear socks, which seemed normal in Florida. "So, what's this I hear about you having an alias?"

Linda continued to gaze at the people outside. Eric

answered, "It's not an alias. She forgot her name. She forgot everything."

The Warden stretched out a hand to halt the conversation. "Let me call our nurse from the infirmary." She punched in some numbers, and a lanky woman wearing a white, zip-front dress and white sneakers appeared in front of them. Linda noticed she had large pockets filled with pens, a stethoscope and what appeared to be a bottle of imported water. The nurse stood by the Warden's desk.

Vega looked exasperated. The foot he balanced on his knee shook nervously, as if music played in his head. Linda thought maybe he needed to replenish his blood sugar. Dark, calculating and impatient eyes darted all over the room, creating tension, while seemingly searching for hidden clues. Today, he wore a gray suit with a peach colored shirt, even sporting a peach colored pocket square. The medallion sparkled from his neck. The guy wanted to pounce.

"So, let's try this again. Why am I here, Miss Nancy Mulligan or Linda whatever?" Vega looked around again but locked his gaze on the Warden.

"We want to know whether you found the evidence you were looking for to keep this woman detained. It seems she has family in California."

"The Army Corps of Engineers is still on it. They are scouring every foot of that lush, tropical area, until they find what they need, and so I can throw the book at this phony perpetrator. I'm fed up with her lies. Far as I can tell, she's guilty as a fox in a henhouse." He uncrossed his legs and brushed a hand through thick, shiny hair. "I'm just glad nothing blew up and no lives were lost due to her insanity."

"You won't find anything," Linda interjected.

"Look, if you really are that missing woman from California, then why don't you explain to me, and everyone present, why you went to New York, Connecticut and Orlando before stopping at Wakulla Springs? Come on, hurt me with the truth."

Eric piped up in her defense. "She wanted to remember things. Her name, where she came from, and all the things she forgot,"

The nurse spoke up. "May I say something?"

"Of course," the Warden replied. "That's why you're here."

"I examined this resident and I have concluded that she suffers from what's called global amnesia, which was brought on by sudden trauma to her head. I believe it happened during the flood. Hitting her frontal lobe while being trapped in a vehicle, and the shock of trying to escape, may have caused the loss of memories. The good news is that her recollection of things seems to have improved, since the gentleman arrived."

The Warden shook her head. "I remember seeing an APB on this woman and even a short news clip from her hometown. I wondered at the time why they couldn't find a body. That's because her body is here in front of us, sitting on that couch. And, before that, she spent two weeks wandering around aimlessly, trying to figure things out. Detective Vega, this woman is no criminal. Let's send her home."

"Tell me why she was running around Wakulla in the middle of the night, throwing things over her shoulder?"

The Warden looked at Linda. "Well?"

"Remember, I arrived late? I don't recall throwing anything, but if I did, it might have been a small plastic bag of crumbs, from my dinner. Guess I could be guilty of littering. Sorry. Once I saw that crocodile, nothing mattered but running away. I may not have remembered everything, but even with a limited memory, I knew that reptiles with big teeth are dangerous."

Vega shook his head in disagreement. "I don't believe you, and I think the nurse is wrong."

The Warden opened a drawer, took out a bottle of water and took a sip. "Hasn't this woman been through enough?" The Warden asked. "She lost her home and her car before being chased by a crocodile, and now you want to send her to prison, even though she has amnesia?"

Vega didn't answer but Linda could tell he looked angry.

A few delicate tendrils fell from the Warden's bun, and she pushed them behind her ear. She opened up another file, with detailed information about Linda's ex-boyfriend. In a mugshot, a grinning, pierced and tattooed man stared wildly at the camera. Folsom State resident, Wayne Harrison was facing a life sentence in a maximum-security prison. No relations, no children, no parents. The one name that jumped out from the paperwork showed Linda Simpson as the person picking him up, upon release. Thank god for computers. The Warden smiled.

"Detective, it's warm outside, would you like a bottle of water?"

"No, I've had about all I can around here. Send me a report." Before leaving in a huff, he turned to Linda. "You're getting away with something, and if I find out you're lying; I'm coming after you."

# CHAPTER FORTY-SIX

The Warden dialed a number and put the call on speaker phone. "Is this Becca Wood?"

"Yes, it is."

"I'm calling from a women's prison in Florida. Don't worry, everything is fine. I just wanted to know if you can come get your sister. We can only release her to immediate family members."

Becca sighed. "Oh no, what did she do?"

"Not anything serious. It seems, she hit her head during that big storm and also forgot where she lives. Losing her home didn't help. Meanwhile, her lapse of memory is returning. We're pretty sure, she'll be back to her former self, in a couple of days."

Linda spoke up. "Can you come or not?"

"Oh Linda, is that you? Of course, pumpkin, I'll come get you, it's just that.... Well, we just got back from Hawaii, and I'm unpacking and doing laundry. Will you have to stay in prison if I don't come right away?"

The Warden answered. "Yes, she'll have to stay until you arrive. We think it's like a country club, but it's still prison."

The nurse clasped a hand over her mouth to stifle a giggle.

"Oh, for goodness sakes, I'm coming. Gary had to rush off to some giant cockroach convention in Omaha, and I don't have to go back to work for a few days. I'll leave for the airport right now."

"Thank you, Mrs. Wood," the Warden said. "You sound like a wonderful sister."

Linda knew this was a lot to ask from any sibling, even one as caring and nurturing as Becca. "Thanks Becca, I love you."

The Warden disconnected the call and squeezed her eyes shut for about ten seconds. Once open, she pointed at Eric. "I was trying to imagine the two of you as an old married couple. You know, maybe ten or twenty years from now. Funny, all I could see were red and pink hearts floating in front of my eyes."

"Oh no," said Eric taking a hold of Linda's hand. "Nurse, did you hear that? The Warden is confused and having hallucinations." Everyone laughed, but he worried there might be some truth to her delusions. These women loved drinking fancy bottled water, and Etienne might have done a great job spreading drops of liquid happiness. Eric stood. "Can we wait in the lobby, or outside?"

"Of course, anywhere you like." the Warden replied, sounding sweet and chipper as ever. "You're welcome to dine in the employee cafeteria, and, after that, you can lounge around in my office, or take a nap outside, in the sunshine." She glanced out the large windows, where the concrete tables were now empty. "It's such a beautiful day," she said with a sigh. "I'm so glad this is going to work out for Linda. Don't worry about that Detective. My report will be rock solid and he won't be able to say a thing." Pausing, she motioned for Linda to come to her desk. "You wanted to change your name because of

Wayne?" The Warden whispered, hoping Eric didn't hear what she said.

Shocked that she knew, Linda nodded. "Yes, he threatened to kill me because I called the police about animal cruelty. Oh my god, that poor dog." Linda tried not to cry but her lips were quivering. "When the cops came, they checked our apartment and took the computer. They found weird images of underage children on his hard drive." Linda glanced at Eric. The Warden took her by the hand. A tear slipped down her cheek.

"I understand. I'd change my name too," The Warden whispered, and then she sighed again, but this sigh sounded heavier and filled with deep emotion. "Don't worry, he's in for life without any possibility of parole. Now, go be free. Looks like this time, you found a good man."

"Thank you for your help," Linda said squeezing the Warden's fingers. "I won't forget your kindness."

"And I won't forget this love, you two batty young kids obviously have for each other. It radiates all over, like a campfire. Keep it up."

Once outside, Linda jumped into Eric's arms. "Oh. My. God."

"I know, right?"

"It's working Eric." She hopped up and down in one place, like a rabbit in an Easter parade. "I can feel it spreading all over the world."

"Shh, settle down." He put a finger to his mouth. "We can't talk about that here. But I feel it too, baby, I feel it too," he kissed her on the lips, silencing her for a few seconds, tasting and dreaming of all the sugar he had missed. "I can't wait to get home."

"Me too," she whispered. "I like your haircut. It makes it easier to nibble on your earlobes."

The time of separation was over. "I missed you so much."

"Well, I missed you too. Especially when I needed a knight in shining armor, which was like most of the time. Please don't leave me anymore."

"I'd have to be certifiably insane to abandon the girl of my dreams." He thought of the country song they had danced to, on their second date. "And, I love everything about you," he said, pulling her lips back onto his.

The Warden pointed out the window and turned to the nurse. "Look at those two. That's true love."

# CHAPTER FORTY-SEVEN

After a bland meal in the cafeteria, Eric and Linda settled into soft, upholstered chairs in the prison library. Groups of hard-luck women, and pimply teens, wandered past them to check out books.

"Glad I'm wearing my own clothes again. A uniform makes you lose your identity."

"I think you're right, as far as this place is concerned. But, wearing a uniform in the service made me feel like part of something bigger. I was no longer just one man, but a soldier who was part of a corps. A small crumb in a large pie, but still important, because without every crumb, the pie falls apart."

She smiled at his analogy. "So, you didn't mind giving up your identity?"

"No, it's not like prison. That's why it's called serving your country. When you're a member of troops sent to different parts of the world, you represent the United States. It's a cool feeling that makes you proud, and sort of invincible. Going by myself, like I did this time, made me feel like I'm acting alone, and of course, I felt vulnerable. My clothes reflected my own shabby taste. Though my goals were big, we stood united as a small, seven-man team. And that's it." He leaned close and spoke in hush tones when discussing the team. "It was different, you know?"

She whispered back, "Don't forget Giulia makes eight."

"Yeah, about that," he kept his voice down. "Giulia left Juan for some dude, and believe it not, she moved to Scotland."

"Are you serious?"

"It gets worse. Juan didn't know anything about it. Milo didn't want to give him any bad news." Eric inhaled and leaned closer. When he shut his eyes, small droplets leaked out the sides.

"Baby?" Linda could tell this wasn't good.

"His plane crashed. Into the Amazon." Eric wiped his face and kept a hand over his eyes. Tears dripped from his fingers.

"What?" Linda gasped.

"Juan," he said with a small sob, his eyes still cloaked by his hand. "Juan isn't with us anymore."

Shock made her gulp and almost choke on her own breath. While coughing, a group of young women walked by and said, "Shh," at the same time. Linda waved and attempted a fake smile. Eric dried his hands on his jeans.

*She couldn't believe the dreadful news. Stunned into silence, she thought about Juan, a man of character and various contrasts. Most of all, he was Eric's best friend. Though she didn't know Juan, she knew he worked in the fashion business in Rome, but could also pass as a brawny weightlifter. A funny guy, who detonated bombs in the service, bought the best burgers, knew how to open metal canisters, and how to drive a big truck. That Juan? Their Juan?*

She continued to cough but didn't say anything for a few minutes, Eric took her hand.

"You okay?"

Linda cleared her throat. "Yes, sorry, I'm surprised, that's all."

"Look, it's not like you didn't have trouble too. This arrest and everything could have been worse."

*Yup, could have been much worse. I could have been eaten by a bear.*

## CHAPTER FORTY-EIGHT

Becca went to the front desk and asked for Linda Simpson. The same woman, who had greeted Eric, stood up and shuffled to the counter. "Someone else asked about her earlier. I told the young man the same thing. We don't have any current, or past residents, at this location, with that name. Believe me lady, that guy was so adamant, he made me check twice."

Becca pointed at the woman's computer. "Would you mind taking another look in your database? I've come a long way to pick up my sister."

"Ma'am, I'm sorry to disappoint you, but we don't have your sister in our files. Maybe she committed a felony? They take the uncontrollable, whacked out ones to Jacksonville. What did she do?"

She clenched her teeth and firmly replied, "Nothing, my sister is innocent, and shouldn't be here."

The woman laughed. "They all say they're innocent. Look, I'll give you a list of the other facilities and you can call them while you're here. Do you have a phone, or do you need to use our counter phone? If I were you, I'd suggest using your own phone. This line is recorded."

"What happens if I use your counter phone to call this place? Who answers if I call here?"

"I will, of course. We don't get too many calls after business hours."

"Can you please look at your papers, or call the warden? I think it was the warden who called me this morning."

The woman looked annoyed, as she dawdled back to her desk. "The warden is gone for the evening." She put on her spectacles and dialed a number. "Sam, there's a lady here looking for someone. I told her, real nice, that the person she's looking for isn't one of our inmates. Would you mind escorting her to the parking lot?"

There's a fight or flight feeling that, under the right circumstances, makes a person who feels boxed into a corner, by unfair behavior, want to run away or attack. Being a nurse and a gentle soul, Becca's interpretation of attack meant she wasn't going anywhere, and had no intention of leaving without her sister.

"I'll wait," the woman said into the receiver. "This person in front of me said she's looking for someone by the name of Linda."

Becca crossed her fingers.

"I'm here 'til nine," she said, with a loud audible sigh. "Yeah, I know what it's like. My kid works the night shift at the burger place. We pull the shades and don't know if it's day or night." Five minutes passed and she giggled. "You crack me up. You're getting your prison inmates mixed up. She didn't steal fifty clams. It's a slangy way of saying money. She stole cash, and she'd be here, even if she stole shellfish. You're the expert. Stealing is stealing, right? You like them? No Honey, steamed or fried. There's a bunch of great places. I'll send you a link.

Really? Well that's news to me. Uh-huh. Hmm, guess I'm out of the loop on that one." Her facial features calmed down, becoming serious. "Okay. Thanks, don't work too hard."

The woman hung up. "Doesn't everyone know that clams are dollars?" she asked under her breath. "Anyhow, there's a young woman called Linda in our library. She is ***not*** an inmate. I told you we didn't have a resident by that name. I believe she's on her way over."

"Becca," Linda screamed, embracing her sister in a strong hug. "Thank goodness you're here."

Eric followed and waved, "Hey, Becca."

"Oh wow, Eric is here too." Confused, she shook her head. "Wait, if Eric is here, why do I need to be here?"

"Oh that," Linda rolled her eyes. "I'm only allowed to leave this place with immediate family. So, you have to sign some papers."

Becca turned to the woman sitting at her desk. "I'm supposed to sign some release papers?"

The woman produced a file folder and waddled to the counter. "Are you a member of Nancy Mulligan's immediate family?"

## CHAPTER FORTY-NINE

Becca sat next to the window, and Eric slept in the aisle seat. Linda felt safe, sitting between two people she loved the most, in the entire world. Her sister held her left hand, and she clenched Eric with her right.

Becca tried to whisper but to Linda, her voice sounded loud and cutting. "What in god's name were you doing down in Florida? Come on, you can tell me. I'm your sister and, in case you're forgetting, I'm also a nurse. From what I can tell, there are no bumps on your head."

Linda pouted, and rubbed her head. "Maybe it healed up."

"Stop it. You've never lied in your life, and you're not good at it now." She leaned in closer, "If this guy, that I introduced you to, got you into trouble or gave you drugs, then I should know about it. Maybe I made a mistake and the two of you aren't a good match. I want to help you."

"Becca, shut up. Isn't it nice we're together? Settle down, please. Do I look like a drug addict? I think you should be glad I'm not locked up in some Florida prison. Besides, you've already helped. Just relax."

"I'm just wondering how you got locked up in the first place? And, why did someone mention bombs?"

"Hush. Would you shut up?" Linda looked around to make sure no had heard anything. Eric continued to sleep. "We're on a plane. If you keep blabbering, they will land this plane in a state filled with cornfields, and throw us off. I am trying to get home. My sister should be on my side, no matter what. It's not like I killed anyone." Exasperated, she took a deep breath. "That's all you need to know. Now go to sleep or read your book. Leave me alone."

"You used to tell me everything. Is Eric making you say these things?"

"No, Eric is wonderful. I'm happy you set us up."

"Something's not right. If you had amnesia, then I'm the Queen of Siam."

Linda grabbed her pillow and buried her face into the soft folds. "I'm not listening anymore." *She imagined yanking on a ten-inch piece of duct tape and slapping it over her sister's Grand Canyon sized mouth.* "Shut up," she mumbled into the pillow.

The flight attendant came by reminding them to put on their seat belts. Linda's ears perked up when asked a sensible question. "Would any of you like soda, wine, or bottled water?"

Linda moved the pillow and asked for red wine. Then, pointing to her sister, said, "I think the Queen of Siam wants bottled water. Do you have that fancy, sparkling spring stuff from France?"

"See, how thoughtful you are? We should never fight. You're the sweetest sister in the world."

*Linda snuggled closer to Eric. If she only knew, thought Linda, if she only knew.*

# CHAPTER FIFTY

By the time they landed, Becca had stopped all of her pestering. They hugged and said goodbye at the airport. "I'll call you soon, Sis," Linda promised.

Relief, like a gentle rain, washed over every particle in her body, when she stepped into Eric's condo. It felt like home; all she wanted to do was eat, maybe curl up on the couch and watch television. Eric prepared a snack tray of olives and crackers, while she took a shower. Wrapped into Eric's big fluffy robe, she plopped down in front of the wide screen television.

"I'm zoned out," he said, flipping through channels. "This sounds horrible, but I'm too tired to...you know. But, don't think, for even one nanosecond, that every molecule, nerve ending and neglected hormone, doesn't want to jump those lovely bones. I've missed you so much."

Linda kissed his cheek and smiled. "Me too," she yawned, suddenly feeling like an old, married woman. "Once our batteries are charged, we'll catch up big time."

"Hmm, I like the way you think," he nuzzled closer but

continued to surf channels with the remote. "You smell like my favorite soap."

"So, Milo and Sparky are coming tomorrow?"

"Yes, we'll celebrate."

"It won't feel right without Juan, Etienne and Jack."

"I know, but it's over. The mission is done. Don't you think that alone deserves a party?"

When Eric stopped on a news channel, Linda put her hand on his arm. "Look at that," she pointed at the T.V. "I don't want to rain on anyone's parade, but maybe we should wait with our celebrations."

The screen showed a massive protest in front of L.A. City Hall. Seconds later, the camera moved to a freeway chase on the 405fwy. 'This is Sandra Beck with local news. We want to update you about the shooting that took place in downtown. The protestor threatened police, jumped into a vehicle and is now being pursued. As you can see, our news helicopters are tracking the perpetrator, as he evades authorities.

After a short break, we'll be interviewing Donna Wheatland-Jones; the wife of death row inmate Dickerson Jones. You might recall our channel's in-depth coverage that shocked the world. Remember, Jones had wounded his own children with kitchen implements, before he buried them alive. After months of crime scene drama, DNA analysis and testimony regarding a shaky alibi, Donna Wheatland-Jones can finally share her frightening story. Stay tuned for more--I'm Sandra Beck with local coverage of all the things that matter--on your best channel for news.' Sandra Beck smiled and the station went to a commercial.

"Same old crap," said Eric, pushing the remote's off button. "Did they ever find out what kitchen implements that SOB used?"

"Poor kids, I don't want to know the details. Hurts my brain just thinking about what happened."

"You're right. Let's not think about any of that trash."

Silence opened like a cavern between the two of them. Seconds turned into minutes and Linda could tell Eric was lost in thought. "What if it doesn't work?"

"Don't go there, either." Too tired to argue for, or against anything, she kept quiet. Maybe she could disregard the horrid news and placate Eric with a few words of inspiration. Except at that moment she had no words, and inspirational contained too many syllables. A pool of darkness, the size of the Grand Canyon enveloped her weary body, surrounding her in melancholy. If, it turned out to be an exercise in futility, at least she had juicy stories to tell about fishing for trout, manic bears and sailing past the Statue of Liberty.

His phone buzzed. "Hey Milo, you stopping by tomorrow?" Eric spoke about details they needed to work out for Juan's memorial. "Sure, sure, I understand. Not much we can do about that, but let's talk tomorrow. Oh, by the way, we're having burgers. Juan loved burgers."

When he disconnected the call, she asked, "Not much you can do about what?"

"The Los Angeles River and the L.A. reservoir--seems Juan planned to do those two places on his way home. We have no product left, and I can't risk producing anymore. It's too bad."

"Too bad is an understatement, especially because we live here."

'Look at me," he put the remote down and reached for both of her hands. "Baby, what if none of it works? What if it's all a pipe dream and the Happy War is a bust? Understand, that no matter what happens, I'm on your side. Don't forget we broke all sorts of laws. Heck, we're guilty of a myriad of felonies, misdemeanors and who knows what else. In some countries we would be executed for less. I hope you know, you're my partner and soul mate in everything. The team did their best. You did your best. Let's not be sorry we took some chances.

Imagine for one second how hard it was for me to go back to a war zone, where I almost didn't survive, and, where I lost patriotic, God-fearing friends, on the front lines? Linda, I didn't look afraid, but I'll be honest, it wasn't easy. We did what we could, because it felt like the right thing to do, here, in our hearts." He brought her hands to his chest. "If, for some reason our plan doesn't work, I don't want you to give up on your dreams of peace and hope. We'll think of other ways."

"Like what?"

"Your hopeful attitude is one of the things I love about you. Maybe it's too early to think about this, but," he paused, "I want to marry you and have kids with you." He clenched her wrists in a passionate grip. "It breaks my heart thinking about bringing kids into a rotten world, where evildoers use guns to massacre each other, even kitchen implements...shit...and trucks to run innocent folks down. Linda, there are no guarantees. Once the winter icepacks melt, diluting all the water, there might be the thunderous roll of nothing. Crickets.

Let's not be fools, thinking we can play God by hiking up and down rivers, sprinkling pixie dust along the way. You know He has the final say about everything." Eric pointed at the ceiling. "It's all up to Him." Filled with emotion, he raised his voice and his eyes were rimmed with tears. "He helped us get everywhere. The Almighty helped me, you, even... Juan."

"Do you really think God helped Juan?"

"Yes, of course, but it's not something I understand, so I'll leave it at that. We'll know more about His reasons, later. Like when we meet our friends and family in Heaven. Knowing Juan, he's making sure everything will be perfect, for when we get there, someday."

# CHAPTER FIFTY-ONE

A time of renewal, spring pirouetted into California, with warm breezes, and hillsides filled with poppies. Eric strung up white lights, and Linda decorated the outside table. Small red containers held succulents, on top of a blue and yellow tablecloth. From a distance, it almost looked like the scene of a party.

Eric held his beer bottle firmly, with both hands. Quietly, Milo tore the label off his beer, and after he finished tearing off several labels, he concentrated on folding his napkin into various designs. Linda noted some of his creations looked like birds or pyramids. As the night progressed, he shredded his napkins, and rolled them into a ball.

Normally the life of the party, even Sparky looked serious. He tapped his feet and hummed to the tunes coming from the speakers. An occasional crunch of a corn chip, added to the beat, filling the awkward silences between friends who had a lot to say but didn't feel like talking. Linda kept asking everyone whether they wanted more to eat or drink. *They were tired,* she reasoned. The tray she carried around overflowed with refills of chips, heaps of guacamole and giant bowls of salsa. *Feed them, she thought, and they'll be happy. Feed them more and they'll be happier*. Sadly, her theory didn't seem to be working.

"Linda," Milo asked, "do you have another napkin?"

Glad to be of service, she rushed to the kitchen and produced a stack of napkins. Milo created more origami.

Eric's cell phone rang. "Hey," he yelled into the phone in a bright, carefree tone. "Are you all right?" Beaming like he hadn't smiled in days, he announced to the table that it was Etienne. Milo, Sparky and Linda all shouted, "Hi Etienne." Eric laughed and looked glad for the call. "Chocolate souffle? You're choosing fancy desserts over us, huh? How's the family?" They chatted a few minutes, before Eric said goodbye. "Guess they're all going on some sort of gourmet, French cooking cruise. Milo, he told me he won't be able to attend the memorial, and said he's super sorry."

Sparky shrugged, "I figured that, but can he overnight some soufflé?"

"It's a long way to come for something so..." Linda didn't want to say 'sad' but couldn't think of another way to phrase her thoughts. The memorial was intended to be a celebration of a remarkable man's life. It wasn't meant to be sad. And yet, the only word on the tip of her tongue, was one she didn't want to use.

"Far, it's far," she blurted, after a short pause. I mean the poor guy hurt himself and flew all over Europe. Bet it's just what the doctor ordered."

Milo placed his napkin artwork down. "Jack's not coming either. He has decided to suffer the heat of the Nile but sends condolences and prayers. Must be his idea of penance, kind of like nuns who beat themselves. Said he'd say a special rosary for... Juan." Milos's hands shook when he picked up his folded napkin.

"Milo, I doubt it's self-flagellation, but there's no denying that man is a saint." Eric lifted his bottle in the air and toasted his friends, "To a hardworking team and amazing friends. Thank you for going out of your way, and completing this unusual task. You were asked to participate in something dangerous--alone. You took giant risks without knowing the outcome, because you wanted to make a difference." He looked at Linda and winked, "Balls, all of you have gold-plated, titanium balls. Cheers."

Linda laughed and held up her beer.

"To world peace—to world peace—world peace," the bottles clinked, but the smiles were weary, and their collective hearts expected a miracle.

# CHAPTER FIFTY-TWO

"Welcome," said Eric at the podium. "Thank you for coming to remember my friend Juan." Eric almost choked when he mentioned his friend. Linda couldn't get over the dashing Eric in the dark suit, with his short new hairstyle. *She felt that her black, lace dress and pearls might look washed out next to his elegant, commanding presence.*

The community church held nearly fifty people who knew Juan from the military, or from his old neighborhood. Two posters stood on the altar. In one of the photos, a serious Juan wore military dress blues, and in the other, a casual Juan grinned from ear to ear with an ice cream cone. Juan's father spoke, two other friends got up to speak, and a reverend delivered a touching eulogy. Milo had organized everything, perfectly. Juan's favorite songs filled the sanctuary. Eric's voice reverberated throughout the sanctuary.

"There are men who come and go in our lives, such as teachers, managers, bosses, sergeants, captains, classmates and colleagues. The lucky ones have brothers and fathers. Juan came into my life, when I was a kid. We roughhoused as kids and did all kinds of boy-type things. Before we liked girls, we chased cats up trees, built little soap-box derby vehicles, and made the coolest looking forts out of appliance boxes. We played baseball until sunset. Through the years we became brothers. We signed up for the military and served our country with pride."

"After that, we needed careers. So---we gave up our adventures and studied in the library. This guy, the one with the infectious smile, understood geometry, physics and excelled in chemistry. No one thought he looked, or acted, like a geek. Especially with biceps like Adonis. Women swooned, especially one curvaceous beauty in Italy."

"Juan went to Rome and became a buyer for a large department store. His vacations took him hiking in Yellowstone, windsurfing in the Mediterranean, or down to the Amazon jungle. There's nothing this guy couldn't do." Eric paused. "That's why, all of it makes sense." Eric began to tear up, but delivered his last line. "Angels, like my friend... are Juan in a million."

Afterward, Sparky came over and shook Eric's hands. He hugged Linda. "See you guys."

Milo said he'd take care of putting things away. They were going to pay the reverend's fee and donate to the community church. Milo put his arms around Eric and pounded twice on his back.

The mourners clapped; others cried. Groups of people brought flowers and put them by the pictures. Linda knew in her heart that Eric felt guilty at this outpouring of love. Juan's family cried buckets of tears. The uncontrollable sobs made him feel responsible. Linda watched Eric move towards the altar. When he dropped onto his knees, begging for forgiveness, she felt awful. He was innocent. It was her fault. All because, they saw an outlandish movie on their first date, which led to her twisted idea, that ended up taking a life. Even though she

***almost*** lost her own life, she knew that ***almost*** doesn't count. Juan sacrificed his life for her selfish dreams. *It has to work, she said to herself, for everyone, and especially, for Juan.*

Linda knelt beside Eric. "You're a great speaker," she said through her sniffles.

"Thanks, I have to speak to doctors all the time," he whispered back. "Did I tell you how gorgeous you are today?"

She forced a smile, thinking about the rivulets of mascara flowing down her cheeks. "Thanks, I need a tissue, but thanks. Want some good news?"

"I could use some good news right now."

"Becca and Gary are pregnant. She had an ultrasound. They think it's a boy."

They were still whispering, but the place had cleared out. They stared ahead at the two large photos of Juan, a nice medley of potted plants and flowers, under a large wooden cross. Red-rimmed eyes turned to her and smiled, "That is magnificent news. I bet you're stoked."

Linda nodded. "Listen, here's the best part," she said, quietly. Eric pulled her fingers under his chin, closed his eyes and continued to pray. "I asked her to call the baby Juan. Becca said she loves that name, so she called Gary, and he loves the idea."

Returning his gaze to the altar, Linda could tell, maybe from the way his shoulders relaxed, Eric's heart had flooded with lifted burdens, love and forgiveness. "Thank you, God," he mumbled, squeezing her fingers and kissing the top of her hand. "Thank you for everything."

# CHAPTER FIFTY-THREE

When they left the chapel, and crossed the street to the car, Linda felt certain she recognized a homeless woman sitting on the ground. At least an hour from where they had originally met, Linda couldn't believe it. Yet, on further inspection there was no doubt it was the woman from the gym. The same frazzled woman she had met the night of the brutal rainstorm.

"Eric, I know that woman. I have to do something. She lived in my apartment building."

Pulling a ten from his wallet, his cheeks grew pink. "I'll wait in the car." "It's not much," he said with a shrug. "But all the cash I have, right now."

"Oh, you're so sweet, don't be embarrassed. That's better than nothing. Of course, she needs more, but I still have a few bills in my waterproof wallet." Linda put the ten into her purse. "Maybe I can call her daughter in Connecticut."

Linda went over to the woman. "Hello, do you remember meeting me, the night of the storm? We talked a long time."

"Oh, sure, that was a night to remember." The woman

nodded, clutching a large plastic bag filled with what looked like blankets and clothes, with one hand. Uncovered, the shiny brass urn sat at her feet. "You're all dressed up, and look different."

"How did you get all the way over here, from Riverside County?"

"I took a bus," she replied. The setting sun made her squint.

"Have you called your daughter, lately?"

"She's no help. Jennifer's full of herself, living the high life in that big house. My daughter sent me more photos of her house, than her own kids. Shows you what's important to her, huh?"

Linda laid down her sweater, kicked off her heels, and sat on the ground next to the homeless woman. "Can you tell me her number?"

"But why? Lately, she hangs up on me anyway; thinks I call too much. Last time, she didn't even bother to speak; the phone went to a dial tone. Click. Some sort of caller I.D. Even threatened to change her phone number if I kept calling. I don't have much, but I always loved my baby. Wish I understood...."

Linda held up her phone, "Okay, well let's give this a try, anyway." The woman gave her the number, and Jennifer answered.

"Hello, this is Linda Simpson from California. I met your wonderful mother during a storm. We had to spend the night in a gym, after our apartment washed away. Did you hear about it?" Linda used her official business voice and hoped for the best.

Jennifer seemed surprised. "What?"

"The storm in California. Did you hear about it?"

"No, we get rainstorms here too."

"Is there any way you, or your husband, can come get her? It looks like she's been sleeping on the street." Linda heard some mumbling in the background. When Jennifer spoke, Linda smiled and gave the older woman a thumb's up.

"That's wonderful. She'll be waiting at the Long Beach Airport coffee shop." Linda thought she better reiterate. "Just want to make sure you understand that she needs to be picked up here, in California. This is crucial. Do you understand? Okay then, Long Beach Airport coffee shop. I think it's called The Little Bronze Café. Got it?" Linda waited for an affirmative answer and hung up.

"Your daughter's coming to get you. They should be here in about eight hours." Linda looked at her watch. "That's around midnight. Until then, we'll take you to get something to eat, and we can buy a clean outfit for you to wear on the plane. Your daughter sounds sweet."

"Maybe you had the wrong number. My daughter is about as sweet as a saltine cracker."

"People change," Linda answered with a confident smile. "Now let's go shopping." She stood up, slipped into her shoes and pointed at the urn. "Don't forget Rick."

# CHAPTER FIFTY-FOUR

A few weeks later, Milo stopped by Eric's luxurious office, located at the pharmaceutical company headquarters. "Hey, how's Linda?"

"Good, she's back at work. I guess her boss got the surprise of his life when she showed up, wearing a suit, saying she's ready for work. They already planted a tree in the parking lot, in her honor."

Milo covered his mouth so he wouldn't spew spittle onto his friend. "Whoops." Milo laughed. "I hope it becomes a massive tree."

"What's with the box?" Eric noticed Milo held a sizeable box under his arm.

"Oh, oh, didn't you hear? Pendalon was bought out. Happened yesterday, before the stock market closed."

Eric knew that another company had bought the firm, but he didn't think it would jeopardize anything in his department. It happened all the time in the pharmaceutical industry. "Heard some rumors. So now you're bailing, huh?"

"Actually, I'm going back to Canada. You and Linda will have to visit us."

"I've heard it's nice and green."

"Not just that, but everything's clean and the people are considerate. They even use their turn signals."

Eric laughed. "I think it's supposed to be like that here. Someday," he said, with a wink.

Milo shook his white mane. "I doubt it, Juan skipped L.A. remember?"

"It doesn't matter. He got the Colorado River, which has water going into the L.A. River. Plus, don't forget rain. All the water that evaporates and comes down on us will have traces. I sure as heck hope the city of angels will benefit. Same with Chicago, they get tons of rain."

"Hope you're right. It's good to stay positive."

"Keep the faith, bro. You'll have to give me your new address." Eric picked up a pen and his brows came together in a quizzical fashion. Something didn't sound right. "Wait, go back one minute. Sit down and tell me what's going on. You said, 'us." He pointed to the chairs across from his desk. "You gonna hold a good story from your pal?"

Milo set the box on the desk and sat down. "You'll think I'm weird. Maybe I shouldn't tell you."

"Spill it, we've all been through different versions of hell lately, and now you're leaving. What's going on?" Concern showed on Eric's face, but Milo smiled like a dog begging for bacon. "There's no way you are being laid off. You're this company's award-winning, and irreplaceable IT guy. One more plaque and you'll need to hire a contractor to build a reinforced beam to hold them in place."

"I told you Pendalon is going to be another company."

"That part's true, but don't lie. That's not the reason you're leaving. There's something else. I can smell coyote scat a mile away."

Milo's face turned red. He bent over, put his head between his legs as if wanting to throw up. He wore loose, gray jeans, and a handmade sweater.

Eric came around the desk, sat in the chair next to him and placed a hand on Milo's back. "Buddy, I'm sorry, I didn't mean to snoop. Forget it."

Milo sat up, and waited until the blood drained from his head, before taking a deep breath. "No, you my friend, deserve the truth. I'm glad I know you. You're a good man and I was proud to be part of the team."

Eric wondered what caused Milo to be so emotional. "Thanks" replied Eric. "The feelings mutual; you kept all of us rolling."

"Anyway, the first week up there in Victoria, there wasn't much communication with the team. All I had to do was make sure everyone made it to each destination. But, every single night, I received calls from a sobbing Giulia. She'd cry and holler about reaching Juan, who was up in the Northwest part of the U.S."

"Every night?"

Milo ran a hand through his hair and nodded. Nerves made him speak faster than usual. "Actually, early morning, because she didn't think too much about the time difference. Anyway, she sounded like an angry bitch. I hated those calls. If a door jamb needed fixing, she'd yell and scream about needing to talk to Juan. There was a broken espresso machine, some inoperable faucet, and a sad story about how she lost a heel on the banks of the Arno. When I told her, I couldn't reach Juan she'd shout at me in Italian. In hindsight, I can't blame her."

Eric leaned back, realizing he had almost solved the mystery. "But wait a second, I thought she took off with the plumber and they moved to Scotland?" In his mind, he flipped through the evidence, wishing he had read some romantic fiction to balance out his linear thinking.

"She did, but the guy hated the place, couldn't find a job, and didn't understand the local brogue. Meanwhile, I made sure I threw away all the communication I had with her. Man Eric, I was mad; I even deleted her phone number. Everything. How could she do that to Juan? She would have caused him unbearable pain. After he died, I never wanted to talk to her again. Your friend loved her so much."

"So, then what happened?"

"Out of the blue, she tracks me down on social media; tells me she's looking for Juan."

Carefully, Eric clamped his lips, and perked up his ears, in anticipation of what might be an interesting story. He turned off his phone and placed it into a drawer. *Was it the cowl neck sweater making Milo look like he couldn't breathe?*

Grimacing, Milo sputtered, "To me, her request sounded like a legitimate reason to have a discussion." His hands shook, and he kept putting strands of hair behind his ears. "I mean he was dead; he died in a horrific accident. This conversation took place after we had the memorial. She carried on about how the whole thing is impossible and she didn't want to believe it. At this point, she's in denial, wants to meet in person, and is crying into my phone, like a baby wearing a wet diaper.

Eric, you have to understand—she had trouble grasping the truth--and wanted to hear it directly from me. Maybe she thought Juan was faking his death, I don't know. Anyway, I felt I owed her a face to face explanation, because she wasn't buying it. You know, out of respect for the deceased?"

The desk phone began to ring. Eric spoke to the receptionist in a pleasant, professional voice. "I'll call him back but I'm not sure I have the number," Quickly, he disconnected the call, and looked back at his friend. "Sorry Milo, keep going. I'm hanging on every word."

Milo inhaled, acting like he might keel over. Eric didn't feel like calling the paramedics. "Breathe buddy, are you okay? Can I get you some water?"

Milo began to sob. With trembling hands, he reached into his cardboard box and pulled out a wrinkled, color-copy of a stunning woman. "Eric, I met Giulia at that garden restaurant on Rodeo. Every phony, plastic head turned. Every jealous, Botox-lipped woman gawked, men went gaga and I was in shock."

Eric pulled open a drawer for tissues. "Hey, relax, I'm fine. You're my friend. I'm not going to judge you." A shiver ran up his spine when he glanced at the picture of Giulia. Not because she was undeniably gorgeous, but because of Juan, the whole sordid saga involving the plumber, Scotland and Italy. When he looked at her, he wondered whether Milo was just stepping into a pile of luxurious, European cow patties. "A real looker, huh?"

"Eric, never have I seen anything like her in my life. Beyond movie star quality, she is beyond anything I could ever imagine. This must be part of God's plan. There's no way, Juan would have let her go. And, that stupid plumber, didn't have a chance. I think it's meant to be."

Dumbfounded, Eric didn't know what to say. He wanted to roll his eyes and tell his friend to take a cold shower, maybe take up sheepherding in New Zealand. Anything--maybe he could sign up for goat yoga classes or learn to make petit fours and bonbons. Or that complicated looking pastry called baklava—that had to be a challenge. There are people who knit sweaters for chickens, and scuba divers who remove golf balls from water hazards. The list of distressing options filled Eric's mind. Maybe Milo could audition for a musical play, or try one of those shark cages. If he needed a challenge, Eric had some ideas. But Giulia?

Milo's heartbreaking story made him think of water torture. The man was tiptoeing over dangerous land mines. There was no denying the Italian woman's beauty. But, in his opinion, Linda was better looking than Giulia. Though polar-opposites, and both sexy, they could have dropped from different galaxies. Linda's wholesome freshness brought out her eyes, giving her that girl next door look. A look you could trust with anything, especially your heart. Based on everything he had heard, Linda was kinder, smarter and better in every way. Couldn't Milo find someone, other than Giulia? There are good choices and lethal ones; and his friend Milo had never gone to war. His friend's weakness was, not knowing real pain. He had to learn it for himself.

Milo wiped tears off his face with a tissue. "Are you mad?"

Eric shook his head but didn't smile. He felt sorry for Milo. "Are you kidding, why would I be mad?"

"Juan was your friend and I've moved on his girl."

"It's fine. You're the best. Like you said, 'he's dead'. I hope she appreciates you."

"Sorry for my outburst. I thought you'd hate me."

Eric stood. "I've got to get back to work, Bud. I'll never hate you. Good luck with everything." He reached for his cell phone and turned it on. There were many things he wanted to say, but he kept silent and shook Milo's clammy hand.

Milo picked up the box filled with pens, papers and the color copy of Giulia. "Thanks for being my friend."

"Always."

# CHAPTER FIFTY-FIVE

That evening, when Eric returned home, Linda had made dinner and set the table. "I felt domesticated today. After all my wild adventures, it felt good to be in a kitchen."

"I thought you went to work today."

"I did, but they were so shocked about everything, that the manager sent me home early. Seems they gave my accounts to someone else. I figured something like that would happen." She shrugged. "No worries, it's only natural. Judging by the all-around hug-fest, they were happy to see me. Said they'll think of something for me to do. I mean if it doesn't work out, there are other places, right?"

He wrapped his arms around her waist. "Whatever you're making smells good."

"Oh, it won't be ready for another hour." She took off his glasses and gave him a kiss."

"That means we have time?"

"Yes, come with me." She pulled him towards the bedroom and shut the door. The lights were off. Eric's glasses were still on the granite counter.

"I can't see a thing."

"This way, I'm in charge of things."

"You have power issues."

"Maybe," she answered, removing his shirt. "And, in case you didn't know, I also have excellent night vision."

He kicked off his shoes and she slipped out of her skirt. "Fine, I'm willing and able as long as you can manage."

"Manage? Oh, I can manage all right," her tone assertive and her fingers aggressive. She reached for his belt, unbuckled, unzipped and yanked off his pants. He sat on the edge of the bed. "What kind of management do you like?"

"I'm partial to laissez-faire, but right now I'm open to anything." This woman, a vision from his dreams, stood above him in sexy lingerie.

"Turn around and move to the center." She slapped his bottom, "How about authoritative?"

"I don't mind if you dominate, but please don't tie me to the bed. Let me remind you, there are at least six, basic managerial styles." Nestling his head into the center, between the two pillows, he asked, "Should I be scared?"

"Depends, you're almost up for your six-month review," she giggled. "As luck would have it, this is a sleigh bed, and, since it doesn't have bedposts, I can't tie you up." She took off her shirt, unhinged her bra, allowing her breasts to fall onto his mouth. They kissed for several seconds and she sat up again, acting like she might move off the mattress. "Don't forget Eric, there's managing by walking around, and democratic management. Let me remove my new panties. Aren't they cute?"

Linda looked desirable, with, or without, lace underwear, and Eric nodded like a shipwrecked sailor. With flailing, desperate arms, he pulled her back to his lips. He wasn't going to let her tease him anymore. "Maybe you're not ready for modern styles of management", she whispered into his ear.

"You and I both want results. We'll concentrate on achieving results, but you better like my cooking."

"Will you shut up?"

"I'll use results-oriented techniques, mixed with a touch of the collaborative managerial style. After all, it's good to get feedback."

He muttered, "be quiet".

When she positioned her body on top of his, and returned her lips to his awaiting mouth, he gasped for air and groaned. Thirsty for love, she noticed his face becoming red. *Perhaps she had tormented him too much.*

Strong arms held her derriere. Eyes closed; he pulled her near. "You take my breath away. Is that good feedback?"

*I love it Eric. I love what you do to me.* Releasing weeks of pent-up tension, loud moans filled the entire condo.

Watching him sleep, she counted the scars on his back. This was it. She wanted to stay in that bed for the rest of her life. The thought of ***forever***, a double-edged sword, spliced her thoughts into fearsome fragments. *Could this fantasy last forever?* Chills ran up her spine causing goosebumps on her arms. *Can love last*?

When Eric grunted and turned around, she said, "Sorry, but management wants you to hold your questions and complaints until the end."

"Trust me, I'm not complaining."

# CHAPTER FIFTY-SIX

They sat on the couch and Eric held her hand. "You almost burned the lasagna."

"Me? I think it takes two, besides it was worth it." Linda brushed her hand over his crotch and laughed. "Maybe we should have waited with the shower."

"Oh baby, that was a nice shower. I've fantasized about you in the shower."

"When? In the desert?"

"No, all the time. You, naked under a giant spout, water pouring over your delicate shoulders, waiting for my arms, my loins, my love to embrace you. Your love is a gift from above, quenching a lifelong thirst, and filling my soul."

"Whoa, a poet and doesn't know it. No wonder the lasagna turned out crispy. When you're hot you're hot."

He laughed. "It was delicious, and I liked the crunchy corners. Guess we have enough for tomorrow."

"Maybe tomorrow, I'll make salad and garlic bread to go with it. What do you think?"

"Wow, you're too good to me. I'm so glad you agreed to go on a blind date. I love you."

"I love you too," she replied, handing him the remote. "I would have dug out mom's cookbook earlier, had I known it took cheesy lasagna, to win your heart. Why don't you find us a romantic movie?"

"Hold on, I'll be right back." He disappeared for a few minutes, returning with a small velvet box. "Linda," he said, bending down, onto one knee. "Will you marry me?"

Startled, she stared at the box, and imagined bubbles escaping, rising from her lips as if she were at the bottom of a river. When she inhaled, it felt thick, and different than air. Her ears heard the gentle murmur of the dishwasher, and a car horn in the distance, but otherwise they were together in a quiet place, surrounded by the ebb and flow of love. When she moved to speak, it felt like being covered in sweet, warm molasses. Filled with anticipation, his eyes continued to be locked onto her eyes. "Yes, of course." Though words came from her mouth, she couldn't hear her voice, and noticed Eric's smile. *I gave the right answer,* she shouted inside her head. They were floating together in a magic river, a river filled with the elixir of happiness.

Dashing, mysterious and spicy, like the overpaid leading man in a box-office smash, Eric opened the little box and produced a gleaming ring, with several diamonds in a row, set in white gold. A stunning work of jewelry, each princess-cut diamond had been set next to each other, seemingly flowing around the band, soon to flow around her finger and never to be removed. When he slipped it on her finger, she knew, they were sealed, in an unending bond; connected, like tears, drops of rainwater, dew drops on rose petals, splashing pools, mist, and rivers.

Splashing to the surface, she gasped, "Eric, where did you get this?"

"On my way home, I stopped at Fashion Valley mall, in San Diego. I hope you like it." Embarrassed, that he had purchased the ring, weeks ago, he avoided her eyes. It had felt strange keeping a secret from her. "You do like it?"

"Are you kidding? This represents us so well. I can't imagine anything prettier, or better." She held her hand out to admire the twinkling eternity band. "Wow, you're incredible."

"I'm not that incredible without you. It's like, you can take whatever stupid thing I'm talking about, and turn it into something meaningful. You turned my solitary life into a constant spring of joy. I mean, think about it, you took our first date, and turned it into a world-wide adventure."

"Awe baby, that's so sweet." She clasped her fingers over his, but looked serious. "Don't forget, my big ideas caused you pain too. You lost your friend." *Did he thrive on danger? It would be fun thinking of ways to keep him on his toes.*

"Linda, you can't blame yourself for an accident."

"I guess there's a reason for everything."

"Yes, yes, my dear, I believe that's true. We have an extra guardian angel looking down, making sure we're safe. Juan knows you had good intentions, and more importantly, the Lord above, knows our team had good intentions. In case you are wondering, God forgives us."

# CHAPTER FIFTY-SEVEN

The next morning, Linda called her sister to tell her the exciting news. "Hey, you matchmaker, you," she laughed into the phone. "Guess who is wearing an engagement ring?"

Becca shrieked. "Oh, my goodness, don't get me too excited, or I'll have to pee."

"Sorry, Sis, I thought you should be the first to know. You fixed me up with a real person. He's solid as a rock."

"Don't mean to rain on your parade, but did you know his company was just purchased by the biggest pharmaceutical company in the world?"

"He hasn't mentioned anything about a buyout. Anything else I should know?"

"No, just that tidbit, about how Pendalon is no more. I'm sorry, but Eric might need to find another job. So, have you two lovebirds set a date?"

"No, of course not, this just happened last night. What about you? When's the baby due?"

"January, which sounds like a wonderful way to begin a brand-new year, doesn't it?"

"It does. You know what? We'll hold off on the wedding, until baby Juan is born. I want him at our wedding."

Becca laughed. "Oh, that's so sweet. Reminds me of something I just saw on the computer."

"Tell me."

"There's a little boy in Juarez, Mexico, who has MS. His parents are too poor for the medicine. So, a whole bunch of folks in El Paso, got together and started a computer fund. They raised enough for his medicine, and now they plan on having a huge fiesta with hundreds of people. So, here's the best part: they want to have the fiesta at this little boy's house. The house is like five hundred square feet. Anyway, Linda, you won't believe this, some contractor, and his crew, are donating their time, and are going to add several rooms to the original house, a big patio, an inground pool with landscaping, piñatas and decorations."

Becca continued, "During the fiesta, they'll have mariachis, donated food, and a Texas bakery wants to deliver cakes and desserts. Not only is it amazing, but these people want to stay home in Juarez. Even though a wall is separating them from the United States, they only want to be good neighbors."

"Of course, there's nothing like home. I love that story."

"But wait, you haven't heard the punch line."

"I'm listening."

"The little boy, his name is Juan."

# CHAPTER FIFTY-EIGHT

Dr. Jackie Bloomfield stared at her computer screen, and blinked several times at what appeared to be unusual numbers. She pulled charts from a file and began comparing ideal ranges of certain elements. The figures marked in red indicated the molecular, chemical bonds between atoms, and how they reacted to hydrolytic, catabolic enzymes. Researchers from the various states, had sent her memos over the last few days, with readings above normal gauges.

At that moment however, everything seemed to be leveling off, and the changes looked stable, almost acceptable. Still, there were microscopic elevations of phosphates and amino acids, on all the recent reports. She opened files from neighboring states to compare the fluctuations. Though minimal, the drinking water had changed considerably.

Tom had left six, dramatic and somewhat emotional voicemails and four text messages, written in all upper-case letters. *The man had to have anal* tendencies. *If every pen didn't fit into the correct pocket protector, he'd doubtless keel over from a coronary. Relax Tom,* she thought. *There's probably a logical explanation for all of it. Why was she worrying about that research nerd and his high blood pressure, anyway? Maybe someday he'd understand* ***he*** *worked for her, not the other way around.*

Her immediate concern had to be, how this water, and the consumption of it, affected humans. Based on what she saw, with a little help from Mother Nature, this would blow over soon. Tom had a low tolerance for anything out of the ordinary. His poor wife and kids, ugh! Aside from waiting for a rainstorm to dilute everything, she didn't have any options, or answers anyway. Deep in thought, when her cellphone rang, she jumped, thinking it was Tom, but recognizing the number, felt relieved.

"Mom it's me."

That voice. She hadn't heard her son's voice in weeks. "Where are you?"

"I'm coming home. Our platoon gets to go home. Haven't you heard?"

"No, what should I have heard?"

"That we're coming home."

Jackie never cried at work, but a tear rolled down her cheek.

"Mom? Mom?"

"I'm here. I'll go get you at the base. What time should I be there?"

"I'm home. They brought me all the way home."

Jackie closed her laptop and grabbed her purse. This would have to wait. Her little boy was home.

# CHAPTER FIFTY-NINE

Eric and Linda held hands on the couch, while watching television.

"I heard about Pendalon. Guess you didn't want to tell me the bad news?" She squeezed his fingers and he muted the sound with the remote.

He shook his head. "No bad news, Hon. Really. Today, some suits came and had a meeting. They asked me into their office and looked at my production. Remember, I mentioned early retirement?"

She nodded, hesitantly.

"Well another company buying Pendalon had bothered me for a long time, making me nervous. I thought, the minute they'd mess with me; I'd quit, learn to golf or whatever. Then, I met you," he paused, and kissed the top of her hand, before continuing his story. "So, listen to this. These men that came today, promoted me to regional vice-president. On top of that, I'm getting a raise."

"Are you serious? Were you worried?"

"Maybe a little, when they asked me into the conference

room. Let's watch the news. He turned up the sound and Sandra Beck came on the screen with news about a hang-gliding accident in Switzerland, and a woman who turned one-hundred and twenty years old.

The next story had to do with the passing of a famous cartoonist, 'Finally, it's a sad day for fans of the Balloon Man animated character series'....'Eric changed the channel.

"Wait, I like Weekend Recap, it's on the same channel. Can we watch that?"

"I don't care. I'll watch anything. It's been a nerve-wracking few weeks."

'Hello and good evening. I'm Adrienne Brae and that handsome fellow is Conner Names. Thanks for joining us. Here at Weekend Recap, we bring you important news highlights, from the past week. By broadcasting the essential bulletins, we keep you, our viewer, updated and well informed. Our first story involves a politician in Colorado. Conner, give us the latest scoop on that developing story.'

'Thanks Adrienne, I think this story has reached a dead-end. And, I mean dead and buried. It seems Mark Shegg not only lost the election, but, is on his way to psychiatric counseling as we speak. I'd like to spell out loser, but that wouldn't be politically correct, so I'll let you decide'.

'After his plea-bargain with the Denver judge, he opted for therapy, rather than jail. Sounds like a smart move Mr. Shegg, considering several women came forward with accusations of sexual assault throughout your campaign. The Colorado politician lost to Melodie Sweet in her first bid for governor; in a landslide victory. The race wasn't even close. Huge upset. Congratulations Miss Sweet—the Rocky Mountains are looking sweeter already.'

'That's good news, Conner. Glad Mark Shegg will get some help. It will make the world a safer place to live.'

'Have you heard the latest? Famous illustrator and creator of Balloon Man, passed away today, at sixty-nine. Flags in Hollywood will be flying at half-mast.'

'I don't know about you Adrienne, but I grew up wanting to be Balloon Man.'

Adrienne laughed. 'Tell me Conner, does Balloon Man have hot air inside, or was he born that way?'

'Very funny, you're obviously not a fan.'

'Sorry Conner, he was before my time.' Adrienne winked and picked up a sheet of paper. 'Listen to this adorable story from the San Diego Zoo. Seems a male lion escaped his enclosure and they couldn't find him anywhere.'

'What happened? That sounds wild and scary, rather than adorable.'

'Well hold on, give me a chance. Concerned about the public's safety, the staff combed the neighborhoods around Balboa Park, and found nothing. The employees didn't want to open the zoo this morning, but when park officials arrived, they went ahead and opened the ticket booth and the gates anyway. You wouldn't believe what a guest filmed with her camera phone?'

'Oh right, I heard something on social media, but didn't have time to watch the video. Adrienne, do we have a clip?'

The now viral video showed the lion licking a small lamb. Moments later, a sheep walks up to her lamb and acts like the lion is simply another one of her rams. After that, the lion goes to sleep next to the lamb.

Conner's face shows shock.

'Too cute,' said a giggling Adrienne. 'That's all I have for Weekend Re-cap, join us next time and goodnight.'

Linda pried the remote from Eric's hand. "Something is happening."

"What do you mean?"

"Weekend Recap never has stuff like that, and the news stories weren't about guns, shootings and violence." She put the regular, local news station on where Sandra Beck stood in front of a film backdrop that showed troops marching, firing and landing helicopters in Afghanistan.

'In an unprecedented move, the White House has recalled all combat troops from Afghanistan. In fact, all one hundred-and fifty-thousand active duty personnel, stationed all around the world, are being recalled to their home base, in the United States, for the Easter holidays. The Department of Defense has provided our channel detailed information, regarding all military deployments. The men and women of the Army, Navy, Marines, Air Force and Coast Guard are coming home. Contact this station, or go online, for more information.'

'In Sports, Los Angeles Laker, Bernie Holbrook is helping the hungry in various parts of Africa. We'll be showing you a clip from his charitable tour around Ethiopia.'

'Speaking of hunger, in other news, we'll take you to Venezuela, where the government has decided to feed the homeless, and build sustainable housing as shelter for thousands. After many peaceful protests around the country, the government has admitted they have money to feed and house everyone, if, they cut back on military spending.'

'Last but not least, there's word that the North Korean government has shelved all future nuclear research, testing and development. In recent talks, between the North and South, the two countries have decided to pool resources, hoping to create an understanding of peace and harmony. One goal they have in mind, is to build a giant theme park on the border, uniting the two countries. All of this, and more, after our break.'

"Close your mouth Eric."

"Me? Look at you. You're drooling." She wiped her lips on

her sleeve and sat back in disbelief. "Are you thinking what I'm thinking?"

His words sounded like slow-motion, an unreality in a real world. "Unless it's a giant coincidence, it looks like...the Happy War worked."

Linda didn't know what to say. What felt like her fluttering heart, did little dives into a crystal-clear spring. "I love you."

His cell phone rang, "Etienne? What's going on? Yes, we're watching the news right now." Linda couldn't help but notice Eric's joy, and the sparkling eyes that complemented the dimples on his cheeks. "I did, I did, and, she said yes," he laughed. "Thanks, we'll let you know. Yes, thanks again. Yeah, adieu." He put the phone away.

"It's happening all over the world, Linda. People are putting away guns, shaking hands, hugging, forgiving. I'm floored." Tears formed in the corner of his eyes.

"What were you thanking Etienne for?"

"Oh, he wants to come to our wedding and hopes we live happily ever after."

Dear reader,

We hope you enjoyed reading *The Happy War*. Please take a moment to leave a review, even if it's a short one. Your opinion is important to us.

Discover more books by Eve Gaal at

https://www.nextchapter.pub/authors/romance-from-the-inland-empire-author-eve-gaal

Want to know when one of our books is free or discounted? Join the newsletter at

http://eepurl.com/bqqB3H

Best regards,

Eve Gaal and the Next Chapter Team

# ABOUT THE AUTHOR

**Eve Gaal, M.A.** is the author of **Penniless Hearts** and a standalone sequel titled, **Penniless Souls.** Also, available is her short novella, titled, **The Fifth Commandment.** After a long career in advertising, she has written countless stories, poems and articles. Her work has appeared in ***The Los Angeles Times*** and *Datebook, a weekend edition of The* ***Daily Pilot***, several anthologies, and online. Born in Boston, but a longtime Californian, she lives with her husband and a rescued Chihuahua. Find out more at www.evegaal.com

The Happy War
ISBN: 978-4-86751-616-4

Published by
Next Chapter
2-5-6 SANNO
SANNO BRIDGE
143-0023 Ota-Ku, Tokyo

1st April 2022

Lightning Source UK Ltd.
Milton Keynes UK
UKHW041930270123
416101UK00004B/63